ANN BENNETT

The Forgotten Children

Published by Bookouture in 2023

An imprint of Storyfire Ltd.
Carmelite House
50 Victoria Embankment
London EC4Y 0DZ

www.bookouture.com

ISBN: 978-1-80314-717-8
eBook ISBN: 978-1-80314-716-1

In memory of my dear sister, Kathy.

PROLOGUE
HELGA

Paris, 1941

As the driver accelerated towards Place de la Concorde, Helga clutched her suitcase to stop it falling off the back seat. She'd only had time to throw in a few clothes at the last minute and her one precious photograph. They'd been driving through the city at breakneck speed for half an hour now, swerving round corners, overtaking other vehicles, the tyres squealing on the road. Every so often the woman in the passenger seat would turn round and give Helga a reassuring smile from under her wide-brimmed hat.

'It will be all right, little one, you'll see,' she'd said, holding out her manicured hand and squeezing Helga's reassuringly.

At first Helga hadn't been so sure she wanted to leave the city but every time she looked out of the car window, what she saw sent chills right through her. Red banners bearing swastikas fluttering from the façade of every building. On the pavements, Nazi troops goose-stepping in formation, their jackboots pounding the stones. Armoured cars crawling amongst the traffic, alongside open-backed lorries loaded with German troops. She'd seen this before and had thought she'd left it far behind. This could be Berlin all over again.

The car paused at a junction, stuck behind a slow-moving lorry. Glancing over at the pavement, Helga noticed a group of officers in grey uniforms and long leather boots, guns slung over their shoulders, talking and laughing together.

'Get down, Helga, before they see you.'

She ducked beneath the window, her heart thumping, just as one of the officers glanced over at the car. The driver accelerated away from the junction, leaving the officers far behind, and Helga sank back against the leather seat, breathing heavily, letting her heartbeat slow down.

The tyres of the vehicle were now rumbling over the cobbles of Place de la Concorde. The car flashed past the majestic Hôtel de Crillon. Helga cowered on the back seat, staring up at the once-beautiful building. Red banners with their swastikas covered every surface here too. Tanks and armoured cars were parked up outside the hotel and a group of guards were saluting a dignitary emerging from the building. They held their arms aloft in the Nazi salute, triggering terrifying memories. Helga turned away in fear.

'We'll soon be at the Gare de Lyon and then you'll be on the train, getting away from all this. You'll be safe then,' the woman said.

Helga closed her eyes, hardly believing this could be happening again. And all the time tears were streaming down her face at what she'd left behind.

ONE
NAOMI

Paris, 1990

Naomi almost missed the entrance to the apartment building as she trundled her suitcase along the pavement on Avenue Carnot past the little shops and outdoor cafés. There it was, nestled between a boulangerie and a tabac.

Relieved, she propped her luggage up beside the door and tapped the number she'd been given into the keypad. There was a reassuring buzz and the door clicked open. She stepped inside the entrance hall and paused, taking in the gloomy brown tiles and the smells of cooking from the various apartments in the building. She fumbled in her bag for the key to box marked No 3, unlocked it and felt inside for the apartment key.

The old-fashioned lift beside the stone staircase looked frighteningly small, so she began to heave her suitcase up the steps to the first floor. When she had got up the first flight of steps, she heard the click of a door opening on the ground floor. A woman in an apron and a headscarf emerged, shuffled on her slippered feet to the bottom of the stairs and stared up at Naomi.

'Are you the young Englishwoman?' the woman asked in French in a gravelly voice, her face without expression.

'Oui, madame. I've come to stay in apartment number three.'

The woman, whom Naomi guessed must be the resident concierge, nodded briefly, turned around and shuffled back to her door. Naomi continued on up to the second floor, gratified that her first encounter with a Parisian had passed without language difficulty. There, she stood in front of the panelled door to apartment number three and put the key in the lock. Here it was, the end of her long journey; the place she would be calling home for the next six months.

With a mixture of excitement and trepidation, she turned the key in the lock and went inside. The air was stuffy and the apartment was shrouded in darkness. Dumping her suitcase and backpack by the door, she flicked on a light and looked around her. She was in a small, square, high-ceilinged living room, with low, pale furniture and oak floorboards.

Taking it all in, Naomi crossed the floor to the two tall, narrow windows opposite, threw them wide open and pushed the shutters back. Light flooded in. The windows had elaborate wrought-iron railings along the bottom and overlooked the cherry trees that lined the cobbled avenue. The trees were in full blossom, pale pink petals fluttering in the faint breeze of the spring afternoon. She leaned out gratefully and took a breath of the warm, fragrant air. She hadn't expected this fabulous view over the avenue. Craning her neck to look to the left, she could just about see the towering pillars of the Arc de Triomphe at the top of the hill.

Tearing herself away from the gorgeous view, she turned back inside to inspect the rest of the small apartment. In one corner of the living room was a tiny galley kitchen with a sink and a fridge and a small hob. The kitchen window overlooked a small courtyard where more cherry trees were in bloom. Through another door was a large bedroom with a double bed and windows overlooking the avenue. There was a door to an en suite bathroom on one side.

Naomi sat down on the bed. She wasn't sure what she'd expected, but the place was even nicer than she'd imagined. It was a little unlived-in, perhaps, but she could easily brighten it up with some flowers and colourful cushions. Easing off her jacket, she laid it on the bed and noticed a spot of food on her jeans from the sandwich she'd eaten on the boat train from Dieppe early that morning. That already felt an age ago, although it was only a few hours. She felt sweaty and dirty after her journey – sitting upright all night in a reclining seat on the cross-Channel ferry from Folkestone, trying to concentrate on not feeling nauseous.

She checked her face in the bathroom mirror. Her skin was even paler than usual and her dark eyes looked tired. The make-up she'd applied before setting off from home was smudged now. Her long, dark hair, usually luxuriant and hard to tame, hung lankly about her shoulders.

It felt strange, being here in Paris at last. She'd expected to be ecstatic when she arrived, but for some reason she felt deflated. That was odd. After all, she'd fought for this. Fought off all the competition at work for a sought-after six-month placement to the Paris office; she'd even fought with Liam. Poor Liam. She sighed, feeling bad about him now. He'd looked so downcast when they'd kissed goodbye the evening before at Victoria station. If only he hadn't tried to stop her making this move that meant so much to her. His opposition had made her more determined than ever to do this.

Thinking of Liam reminded her that she'd promised to let him know as soon as she arrived. There was a telephone on the bedside table. She lifted the receiver and to her relief a ringtone buzzed. She dialled the number of the flat in Islington. Liam answered straight away.

'Are you in Paris already?' he asked, his voice distorted by the long-distance line.

She laughed. 'I've just arrived. I wasn't sure if you'd be up yet.'

'I couldn't sleep, to tell you the truth. What's the flat like?'

'It's very nice. Well... the only thing is, it doesn't feel very lived-in.'

It was his turn to laugh. 'Not like our place, eh? The kitchen looked like a bomb had hit it after yesterday's curry.'

'Oh, I'm sorry to have left you with that.'

'Don't worry, it gave me something to do when I got back from the station.'

She felt another wave of guilt mingled with sadness, picturing him there alone.

'Have you got any plans for today?' Her voice was unnaturally bright.

'I thought I might go up to Kilburn to see Dad. Haven't seen him for a while.'

'That's a great idea.'

There was a short silence. There was so much up in the air between them, so much to say, but now didn't feel the right time.

'Well, I expect you need to get on and unpack,' Liam said after a while.

'I suppose so. I'll call you later on, shall I?'

'Did you think about me coming out to see you next weekend?'

She paused, wishing he'd not raised that quite so soon. 'I'm not sure, Liam... It might be best to wait a day or two before making any decisions about that. I don't know what they might have planned for me at work. Why don't we talk about it again tomorrow?'

'All right.' She could hear the disappointment in his voice.

After they'd said goodbye, she went to investigate the kitchen. Speaking to Liam had sent her emotions into turmoil. Knowing he was lonely and missing her tugged at her heartstrings, but she couldn't help remembering the things he'd said before she left, the way he'd tried to stop her going to Paris. She wasn't ready to let that go yet.

The letting agent, or perhaps someone from her law firm, had thoughtfully stocked the fridge with milk and other essentials. She made herself a cup of tea and wandered into the bedroom. Perhaps, if she were to take a shower and freshen up, change out of these travel-stained clothes, she might feel a bit better about being here. At least it felt good to be alone at last, to have some space from Liam.

It was early afternoon when Naomi left the apartment, refreshed and changed. Stepping out of the gloomy hallway, everything was bathed in sunshine and she lifted her face to feel its warmth. She walked to the top of Avenue Carnot and shaded her eyes to take in the majestic stone pillars of the Arc de Triomphe. Then she turned left and started to wander down the Champs-Élysées. The cafés and shops that lined the wide pavements were buzzing with life. She squared her shoulders and let out a grateful sigh. It felt better to be strolling here, mingling with the Sunday afternoon crowds, than alone in the unfamiliar apartment.

She found a patisserie, sat down at a table under the shade of a horse chestnut tree overlooking the street and ordered a café crème and a baguette. As she ate, she watched the people strolling past. Chic Parisians in dark glasses and designer clothing enjoying the sunshine, groups of tourists snapping pictures of each other, young lovers, arms entwined. Again, she thought of Liam and another stab of guilt pierced her conscience. She imagined him setting off alone to cycle to Kilburn to visit his ageing father. He would be lonely without her. She would miss him too, of course, but she needed to do this, for herself and for her career, and once again, she wished he hadn't tried to stop her.

Watching a young couple heading down the Champs-Élysées arm in arm, gazing into each other's eyes, she thought back to a weekend she and Liam had spent in Paris when they were first together more than three years ago. They'd been backpacking across Europe and had stayed in a cheap hotel in Montmartre. That was on their year out, before they'd got sucked into the heavy demands of their careers.

Or at least before she had. Liam had seemed to sail through his years as a trainee teacher with ease and good humour. He was a natural, seemingly born to teach, whereas Naomi had had to work hard to complete her training as a lawyer in the City: long, gruelling hours, dealing with difficult clients and difficult colleagues. She'd often wanted to quit but sheer stubbornness had prevented her from doing so. That, and her mother Helga, who had always been an inspiration and a role model to her. Helga and Harry, Naomi's father, had built a successful property development business from nothing when they'd met in London after the war.

'Don't give up at the first hurdle,' Helga had advised as Naomi sat miserably in her mother's kitchen in her house in Primrose Hill one Saturday morning after describing an exhausting week. 'You young people, you don't really understand what true hardship is,' Helga went on. 'Not your fault, of course. Your generation has been lucky. But it does mean you need to develop some grit and sticking power.'

Naomi looked at her mother, smartly dressed even at home, her greying hair carefully tinted, her make-up subtly but expertly applied. She never let her guard drop, Naomi realised.

She was always so self-disciplined and expected that in others too.

She couldn't deny the truth of her mother's words. Although Helga never spoke of it, Naomi knew that she'd been evacuated from Germany to America at the beginning of the war, before somehow finally ending up in London, and that her father too had come to England, on the Kindertransport, fleeing the Nazi regime. Neither of them had ever seen or heard of their own parents again once they'd left their homeland. They'd had to make their own way in the world. She'd often thought that was what must have drawn them together. So, part of her reason for wanting to succeed in her quest to gain this placement to Paris was to please her mother. It was strange therefore that when Naomi had told her the news, Helga had seemed far from pleased.

'Paris?' She'd even looked shocked; in fact, her face had gone quite pale. 'I knew you'd applied for a secondment to one of the overseas offices but you never told me you might go *there*.'

'Don't worry, Mum, it won't be for long. I'll come back at weekends sometimes. And you could always come and visit me if you like? I should have plenty of room for guests.' Then she'd paused and frowned, wondering. 'Have you ever actually been to France?'

Her parents had travelled extensively, both for business and for pleasure, but to Naomi's knowledge her mother had never been to France. It was strange, now she thought about it.

'No, I have not,' Helga had said with a shiver, drawing herself up. She'd clammed up and gone silent and prickly after that, as she sometimes did when something was troubling her.

After that the subject was closed and Naomi didn't dare broach it again. And Helga had still been stiff and distant when Naomi had gone to say goodbye to her the day before she'd set out. Naomi knew that something was bothering her but try as she might, Helga wouldn't be drawn on what it was.

Naomi felt a wave of loneliness now as she sipped her coffee and watched the family groups walk past, laughing and joking together along the wide boulevard, underneath the yew trees. The partings with both Liam and her mother had left her feeling sad and deflated. She'd been so looking forward to this move, but leaving the two of them like that had soured the experience. Why did it have to be like this?

Her mind returned to Liam and their previous stay in Paris. They had both fallen in love with the city, with the beauty of the buildings, the elegant boulevards, the romance of the River Seine. She recalled it as a time of carefree happiness. In those days everything had been so much simpler. They didn't have much money, but they seemed to have more fun, to take pleasure in small things – a meal in a simple bistro, a walk beside the Seine, drinking beer in a pavement café and watching the world go by for hours on end. She recalled how they'd wandered around a flea market in Montmartre and bought some cheap trinkets to take home with them as gifts. Recalling the simple pleasure of that innocent afternoon, she suddenly had a strong desire to revisit it.

Why not go there now? She had the rest of the day to herself. She could unpack and get food for the apartment from the local shops when she got back. There was bound to be a late convenience store somewhere in the neighbourhood. She quickly took out her guidebook and flicked through the pages to the section on Montmartre. There it was: The Brocante des Abbesses, a Sunday flea market.

She paid the bill and walked quickly back to the Charles de Gaulle–Étoile station at the top of the Champs-Élysées and took the metro across the city to Abbesses.

Walking up the steps from the stuffy gloom of the metro station, she could already hear the hubbub of the market, which was set up around the entrance on the wide pavement. Her heart lifted as she emerged between the stalls and began to wander round examining the antiques and bric-a-brac on display. It was exactly as she remembered. Stalls with canvas awnings filled the pavements of the cobbled streets. A genteel crowd of Sunday afternoon browsers were wandering around the little tents that sold everything from antique furniture to statues and ornaments, garden pots, paintings, dusty bric-a-brac and jewellery, china and glassware, tapestries and carpets, even second-hand clothes.

Soon she was completely absorbed, poking around amongst the artefacts, and her cares were gradually lifting. She loved flea markets and would often spend her Saturday mornings in London at Camden Passage in Islington, just browsing the antique stalls. Now, she examined some intricate paintings of exotic birds, a silver tea set, some nineteenth-century book-shelves. She knew that none of these things would look right in the apartment on Avenue Carnot, but it gave her pleasure just to look at these quirky pieces and imagine where they might have come from.

On the corner of the first street was a stall selling old post-cards and she stood for a long time, examining seaside scenes from the Côte d'Azur in the nineteenth century, pictures of the Alps and châteaux of the Loire, postcards of hotels sent from the French colonies – Indochina and the French West Indies. Then her eyes alighted on a framed postcard that seemed strangely familiar. She picked it up and stared at it.

It was a black and white photo of a large, white-painted villa, with elaborate balconies and a grand porticoed entrance. The postcard was inside a wooden frame that itself looked decades old. As she stared at it, Naomi realised with surprise that it was the exact replica of a photograph that her mother had on her bedroom windowsill. She'd never really considered it before; it had just always been there, part of the fabric of her childhood home, and she'd never even thought to ask what it was. But now she looked closely, she realised that the villa

appeared unmistakeably French. She peered at it, searching for
a name or some clue as to the identity of the building. She
turned it over and looked at the back. But there was nothing
written there either.

'You want to buy that, mademoiselle? That postcard is a
collector's item, but it is yours for only ten francs. A real
bargain.'

She tore her eyes from the postcard and looked up at the
stallholder, who hovered over her with an expectant look. He
was a thin, elderly man with wiry grey hair and gold-rimmed
glasses. Her curiosity was piqued now.

'Do you know where this villa is, monsieur?' she asked the
stallholder. He shrugged and shook his head.

She would have to buy it, just so she could take the back off
the frame and see if there was an inscription on the postcard
revealing the name of the villa and where it might be.

'I'll buy it,' she said eagerly, producing a ten-franc note from
her bag, and the old man's eyes lit up. Perhaps she should have
bargained, she wondered, but what was the point of that? She
would gladly have paid twice that price for the chance of
unlocking this mystery that had suddenly captured her interest.

Once the old man had wrapped the frame in an old copy of
Le Monde, she slipped it into her bag and made straight for the
metro station. She wanted to get back to the apartment and
investigate the postcard as quickly as possible and she'd already
browsed most of the stalls in the market. As the metro train
swayed to and fro in the tunnels, rattling back towards Charles
de Gaulle–Étoile, Naomi considered unwrapping the frame
and seeing if she could get the back off, such was her impatience
to find out more about the villa. But she managed to restrain
herself. The train was too crowded to do that and there was far
too much going on – an old couple, busking with an accordion,
singing haunting folk tunes from Eastern Europe, paraded up
and down the carriage, rattling a tin for spare change.

Back at the apartment, Naomi found a sharp knife in the kitchen drawer and loosened the clips that held the picture frame to its wooden backing. It was stiffer than she'd imagined and it took some effort to prise the clips off the frame. And once she'd done that, the wooden back itself was wedged tightly into the frame and it needed some more work with the knife to remove it. But once it was out, the back of the postcard was exposed and she could see that there was some tiny typewritten lettering along the bottom. She picked it up carefully and carried it over to the window, where the afternoon sunlight streamed in.

Villa Helvetia, she read, *Montmorency, Paris, Maison de Convalescence.* She frowned, puzzled. Why did her mother have a photograph of a Parisian convalescent home in pride of place on her bedroom windowsill? She could see it from the dressing table where she sat every morning to comb her hair and put on her make-up. Had a friend of Helga's once stayed at the villa? There was no date on the postcard but it looked as though the photograph was taken before the war.

Naomi burned with curiosity. There was one quick way to find out and that was to call her mother and simply ask her about it, but somehow the idea of doing that made her feel anxious. If it had anything to do with the war, it would need sensitive handling and she wouldn't be able to ask such a thing casually in a phone call. Helga never spoke of the war and Naomi had learned as she grew up that it was a subject she must be very careful about bringing up in her mother's presence for fear of upsetting her. Once again, she recalled Helga's strange reaction to her going to Paris.

She had no idea what Helga had been through exactly, she'd never said, but Naomi sensed that she must have suffered terribly. Her father had told her that, like him, Helga had had to leave her home for ever.

'We've both come to terms with what happened in our

different ways,' Naomi's father had explained when she was about eleven and getting curious about her family history. 'I don't mind telling people about how I came to be here, but your mother doesn't like to talk about it, so probably best not to upset her by bringing it up.'

So, Naomi had agreed to tread carefully on the subject of the war. Even after her beloved father died, less than two years after that conversation, she'd kept that promise. She wondered, though, if there was another way of finding out more about the villa in the photograph. Perhaps if she called later on she would be able to casually mention the flea market to her mother and the fact that she'd seen the picture of the villa there. If Helga showed any signs of sounding distressed she could move the subject on without probing further. Either way, she decided that the following weekend she would go out to Montmorency and try to find the building.

She needed to find out more about it and why her mother might have a photograph of a French villa on her windowsill when she'd recently professed never to have visited the country.

TWO

HELGA

London, 1990

Helga stood at her bedroom window aimlessly watching the empty street. A couple of cats slinked across the road and disappeared under parked cars. She had no energy that morning. It was Sunday and the empty day stretched ahead of her. Normally Naomi would have come round for a few hours in the afternoon and they would have gone for a stroll on Hampstead Heath or wandered down to Camden High Street together to have tea in a café or do some window-shopping. Now that Naomi was in Paris, that wouldn't happen again for several months.

Since dear Harry had died, when Naomi was twelve, Helga had relied on her daughter more than she'd realised. But now that Naomi had gone too, Helga felt even more alone.

She pulled herself up straight and frowned at her weakness. It was something she never allowed in herself. She'd been through worse. Far, far worse. What was a little loneliness in

comparison to what she'd endured as a child? And she'd got
through it. She'd never been one to give in to self-pity and she
wasn't about to start now. It troubled her, though, that Naomi
had gone off to Paris of all places. If it had been almost
anywhere else, Helga would have gladly hopped on a plane or a
train to be with her for a weekend or even for an extended stay.
But not Paris. She'd vowed never to go back there. The memory
of that city and everything that had happened to her there
would be etched on her mind for ever, but she only let those
memories surface in her deepest, darkest hours.

Her eyes wandered to the picture of the Villa Helvetia on
the windowsill and she sometimes wondered why she kept it
when it was so painful to look at, but it was the one reminder
she had from those years and she couldn't let go of it completely.
She picked it up and traced her finger around the outline of the
building and recalled her first sight of it on that fateful day back
in 1939. It had looked so beautiful, so welcoming, then, with its
gracious lines and with the flowering jasmine climbing over the
railings of the balconies, that she'd put her little battered suitcase down and wept with relief. She could even recall the sweet
smell of those delicate white flowers, wafting towards her on the
warm evening air. You smelled it every time you went in and
out of the front door. Even now, if she passed flowering jasmine
in a garden or in a public park and caught a breath of that delicious, perfumed scent, she was instantly transported back there.

She set the photograph down with shaking hands. Best not
to dwell on the past. Villa Helvetia was a wonderful, bright
memory, but it was an oasis in a desert. It was surrounded by
dark ones, so black and terrible that she had banished them
from her mind for decades. Now, she sat down on the bed and
pressed her forehead with both hands, trying to stop the memories from flooding back.

A car hooted outside, breaking into her thoughts, and she
took a deep breath. This wouldn't do. She must act quickly to

stop herself sliding down into the abyss that was her past. She squared her shoulders, went downstairs, found her walking shoes and a coat, and left the house. A stroll round the crescent and up Primrose Hill would do her good and perhaps she would drop in to see her friend Kitty, who lived round the corner.

She set off at a fast walk. How lucky she was that at the age of sixty-two, apart from a few occasional aches and pains, she was still fit and strong and as healthy as someone twenty years younger. She put it down to her daily stroll to the top of Primrose Hill, where she would stand at the top, marvelling at the view.

After several minutes of steady walking, she reached the crest of the hill and stopped to survey that view now. It still amazed her after all these years that from here she could see the whole city stretching out beneath her. It was a clear spring day and the bright blue sky was almost cloudless. How she loved this city! It was where she'd found love, built her business and raised her daughter. And it was where she'd lost the man she'd loved and who had been her life for over thirty years. It had welcomed her when she was vulnerable and given her a new start in life. She sighed deeply, brushing away a tear.

What was wrong with her today? She must be missing Naomi. It was good that her daughter was ambitious, she reflected. Hadn't she herself encouraged her to work hard, make the most of her gifts? So, it was natural that she would want to branch out and seek out opportunities abroad. But it would still leave a hole where she had been that it would be difficult to fill.

Helga turned away from the view and headed back down the hill, stepping aside for the groups of people trudging upwards: families with children, couples arm in arm. Another pang of loneliness struck. It was mid-morning now. Perhaps, later on, she would be able to persuade Kitty out to one of the cafés in Regent's Park Road for lunch. It would probably do them both good to get out. Kitty spent far too much time in her basement flat with her four cats and her Afghan hound Millie, poring over old photos of the West End shows from the 1950s and '60s she'd once starred in.

As Helga made her way across the lower slopes of Primrose Hill towards the road, she thought about her friendship with Kitty and why it had blossomed over the decades they'd known each other. They were so different; opposites in every way. Kitty was decidedly English; the most English person Helga had ever met, in fact. Many of the other people she knew, either through the business, or through the Jewish community that dear Harry had so enthusiastically embraced, had arrived in London from other parts of Europe. Like Helga and Harry, they were first-generation immigrants; the war had ruptured their lives and washed them up here. And while there was comfort in being amongst people who implicitly understood her story without even knowing the details, sometimes she just wanted to forget, to be somebody different, try to put aside the trauma of her past at least for a few hours. Perhaps it was the fact that she and Kitty were so different that had drawn them to each other.

She reached Kitty's house and went carefully down the spiral metal staircase towards the front door. Two of Kitty's cats, a huge ginger tom and a pretty tabby, were sitting patiently on the mat. Kitty looked as glamorous as ever when she opened the door in a cream cashmere sweater, her blonde hair carefully coiffed, her face made up. When she saw Helga standing there she broke into a broad smile.

'Darling!' she said, putting her arms round Helga and drawing her to her as the two cats streaked through their legs and inside. Helga got a waft of her friend's expensive perfume. 'I don't normally see you on a Sunday, Helga sweetie. Come on inside. Would you like a martini? It's nearly time for a pre-lunch sharpener.'

'It's a bit early for me yet, Kitty,' Helga said with a smile, stepping into the cluttered interior where potted palms and aspidistras vied for space with a chaise longue, pink velvet armchairs, polished occasional tables and various sculptures. The dog stood up and stretched, wagging her tail.

'I suppose you're right,' Kitty admitted, glancing at the carriage clock on the mantlepiece. 'Perhaps it is a tad early. Coffee then? Why don't you sit down? I was just thinking about pottering along to the shop to get the Sunday paper.'

'Coffee would be nice,' Helga said, sinking down onto the chaise longue. 'Maybe we could go along to Mustoe's later for lunch?'

Kitty raised her plucked eyebrows. 'Now I *am* honoured. Doesn't Naomi normally take you out for lunch on Sundays?'

'She did, yes, but she's in... in Paris now,' Helga said stiffly, trying to keep her voice neutral. 'She starts work there tomorrow.'

'Paris? Oh yes, you mentioned she was going abroad, but I'm sure you didn't say Paris.'

'I didn't know myself until recently,' Helga said evasively. 'This opportunity only came up in the last few weeks.'

'Well, what a *fabulous* opportunity that will be for her. A young woman in Paris! I can't imagine anything more romantic, can you, darling? Cappuccino, is it?' Kitty bustled past Helga to her kitchen. Helga could hear her fiddling with her complicated Italian coffee machine.

'Yes please,' Helga replied. She didn't want to get into discussing Paris with Kitty, but knowing her friend now the subject had been introduced it would be unavoidable.

'I remember motoring over to Paris with another girl from the cast of one of my shows – can't remember which one now – and a couple of young guys. Filthy rich they were, no expense spared.' Kitty's eyes were dreamy as she came back with two large cups of cappuccino rattling in their saucers. 'We stayed in the Hôtel de Crillon on Place de la Concorde. What a beautiful hotel! I'd never been anywhere so grand...'

She set Helga's cup down on the little table beside the chaise longue and sat down opposite her.

'Oh, listen to me, reminiscing! That was yonks ago. Only a few years after the war... the place was a bit run-down, only just recovering from the occupation.'

Helga sipped her coffee, her eyes still far away.

'Are you quite all right, sweetie?' Kitty leaned forward and peered at Helga with her piercing, cornflower-blue eyes.

Helga dropped her gaze. She couldn't meet Kitty's. She was sure she remembered the name of that hotel, although she hadn't heard it spoken for decades. Wasn't the Hôtel de Crillon where the Nazi High Command had their Paris headquarters? She had a sudden memory of being driven through the city at breakneck speed, the tyres of the vehicle rumbling over the cobbles of Place de la Concorde, staring up at the forbidding buildings as they flashed past, the red banners bearing swastikas, German soldiers goose-stepping along the pavements.

'Are you quite all right?' Kitty repeated. 'You look as if you've seen a ghost. You've gone quite pale.'

Helga surfaced into the present. 'I'm fine, Kitty,' she muttered.

'Are you sure?' There was genuine concern in Kitty's eyes. 'Are you having a funny turn?'

'No! I'm *not* having a funny turn,' Helga insisted, but she knew that the colour had drained from her face and that her hands were shaking so much she didn't trust herself to pick up her coffee cup again.

'You don't look well at all. I think it *is* time for that aperitif.' Kitty got up nimbly and crossed to the ornate sideboard in the bay window and poured two brandies from a decanter. She handed one to her. Helga took it with her trembling hand, took a sip and felt the liquid instantly warm her insides.

'There! You look better already.' Kitty retreated to her

armchair. 'I'm sorry, darling, was it something I said?' Her voice was gentle.

To Helga's horror, she felt hot tears welling in her eyes. How could she be so weak? She tried to blink them away. She didn't want to draw attention to them by lifting her hand to brush them away, but Kitty missed nothing. She sprang forward and slipped her arms round Helga's shoulders.

'What is it, darling? Is it Naomi going away?'

Helga shook her head slowly, working her mouth to stop the tears, doing her level best to control herself, but it was as if a dam had burst. All the barriers she'd so carefully constructed over the years, all the layers of protection, had suddenly peeled away and left her exposed, vulnerable.

'I wish you'd tell me what's wrong. You can talk to me, you know, about absolutely anything,' Kitty persisted.

Helga looked at her mournfully. This was precisely what she'd wanted to avoid. She'd wanted to be able to enjoy Kitty's company without the past encroaching but perhaps she'd been living a lie all these years, not telling her closest friend about the events that had shaped her life.

She drew a deep breath. 'When you were talking about Paris... It brought back a few memories, that's all.'

'Oh... I see. I'm so sorry, Helga. I had no idea.'

Kitty was still holding her tight and they sat like that together for a few moments, as the tick of the carriage clock and the distant hum of the city filled the room.

'Would it help to talk about it, darling? You don't have to, you know. I've never asked, and I never would, but I'm always here and ready to listen if you'd like to.'

Helga felt in her pocket for her handkerchief and blew her nose.

'That's kind of you, Kitty, but I don't think so. Best to put these things behind us, I always think.'

'If you're quite sure, darling,' Kitty said gently, sounding unconvinced.

Later though, after they'd finished lunch and their stroll around the block with Millie, and Helga was walking home alone, her thoughts returned to Paris. What would Naomi be doing now? It was about the time that, on previous Sundays, her daughter would have left to go back to her flat in Islington and Liam.

Helga had never been sure about Liam. She'd always thought he was a brooding, intense sort of young man. He clearly doted on Naomi, it was true, but was he right for her? On the other hand, Naomi seemed happy enough and had never hinted that anything was less than perfect between the two of them. Helga wondered how Liam would be feeling about Naomi's departure for an extended stay across the Channel. He must be feeling as bereft as she herself was. More so, probably.

Helga reached her front door and let herself into the empty house. She shivered. All of a sudden it felt chilly and she turned the thermostat in the hall up a couple of notches. It might be springtime but there was a definite nip in the air. She took her coat off. As she was hanging it up, the telephone in the living room started to ring. She crossed the room quickly to pick it up.

'Mum, how are you?' The line was crackly. Helga sat down heavily, pleasure rushing through her.

'I'm fine, thanks. How are you? I've been thinking about you. How's— how was your journey?'

'Good, thanks. A bit tiring, but I got here in one piece. I just wanted to make sure you were OK. What did you do today?'

'Oh, Kitty and I had lunch at Mustoe's then we went for a walk with the dog. I've just got back.'

Helga could sense Naomi hesitating at the other end. Even from the bristling silence she could tell that her daughter was building up to asking her something, but was struggling for the right words.

'Was there something you wanted to say to me?' Helga asked finally.

'Oh, nothing very important. I went to a flea market this afternoon. Liam and I went there when we came here years ago and I just fancied seeing it again.'

'Oh, that must have been nice, darling. You do like your bric-a-brac, don't you?'

Naomi laughed. 'I do. And it was well worth the trip. When I was there, I stumbled across a photograph. A photograph of a villa...'

'And?' Helga's hands were beginning to shake.

'Well, it's exactly the same as the one you have on your bedroom windowsill. It says on the back it's called the Villa Helvetia. It's in one of the suburbs, just north of Paris. It was a convalescent home at the time. I just wondered... I was curious, that's all...'

'Wondered what?' Helga asked, playing for time, trying to keep her voice steady.

'I just wondered if you knew anything about the place. If there was any connection... it's just that I thought you said you hadn't been to France.'

Helga swallowed hard. She wasn't going to succumb to tears now. Not for the second time that day. Her iron will came to the fore. She needed to be strong.

'It's just an old photograph, Naomi. No significance at all. Just for decoration. I didn't even know that it was French.'

'Oh.' Naomi sounded deflated. 'All right, I just thought I would ask.'

'What's the apartment like?' Helga put in quickly and listened to Naomi's description of her new home with only half her attention. In her mind she was back there, in the Villa Helvetia's garden, sitting under the cherry trees with a group of other children, picnicking in the dappled sunlight of an early summer afternoon.

'Mum?' Naomi was saying. 'Are you still there?'

'Of course, dear.' The cherry trees faded, the laughter of the children too.

'That's good. I thought we'd been cut off. Look, I'd better go now. I've got to get things ready for tomorrow. I'll call again. It would be lovely if you could come and see me while I'm here. There's a sofa bed in the living room, or if you prefer there are some lovely hotels close by.'

'Perhaps... But surely you'll be popping back to London at some point, won't you? To see Liam?'

'In a couple of weeks maybe.'

'Well, we can get together then.'

After she'd put the phone down, Helga walked slowly up the stairs to her bedroom and over to the windowsill. She picked up the photograph of the Villa Helvetia for the second time that day. Voices floated to her down the years again and she stared at the photograph until the lines blurred before her eyes. Then she replaced it carefully and crossed the room to the old leather trunk that stood at the end of her bed, folded the lace cloth that covered it and lifted the creaking lid. Kneeling down in front of the trunk, she rummaged through layers of eiderdowns and blankets before pulling out a wooden box, which she placed on the floor.

The photograph she wanted was hidden at the bottom of the box, under all the others. She quickly shuffled through the pictures that marked out her later life: several of her as a young woman in New York; one of her standing smiling beside Harry on their wedding day in London; and many snaps of Naomi as a baby and young child. Her fingers closed around the one at the bottom and she drew the battered black and white photograph out and held it in her shaking hands. There she was: a carefree twelve-year-old, sitting next to another girl. This girl was her double in every way, from the sparkling dark eyes to the curly black hair. Their heads were tilted together, touching at the crown, and they were both smiling into the camera. Helga ran a finger lovingly over the picture.

'I'm so sorry, Ruthie,' she murmured.

THREE

NAOMI

Paris, 1990

As the train ran through the grey outer suburbs, Naomi thought back over her first week in Paris. It had felt strange on Monday morning, entering the white-carpeted offices of her law firm in a graceful Haussmann building on rue du Président Wilson. The atmosphere was quiet, studious and sophisticated and the smells of freshly brewed coffee, cigarette smoke and expensive aftershave mingled on the air. How different from the bustling, modern London office, which was all glass and chrome and modern works of art. All the partners had their own rooms with sweeping views over the Trocadéro gardens and down towards the Eiffel Tower.

Naomi shook hands with four middle-aged men, who each greeted her politely if distantly before turning back to their work. By the time she'd met the rest of the staff, she'd started to forget everyone's names and had a fixed smile on her face that made her jaw ache.

Once introductions were over though, she'd spent much of the first morning alone, reading through a fat file for the case she'd been assigned to and feeling a little deflated. The case was instantly fascinating: one remote African state accusing its neighbour of acts of armed aggression, breaches of human rights and acts of genocide before the International Court. She was desperate to make a difference, to help in the case, but to her surprise and shame she'd been overwhelmed by feelings of homesickness. She had begun to wonder if she'd done the right thing in making the move from London.

Things picked up as soon as Naomi's new boss arrived and introduced himself.

'Oliver Charles,' he'd said, striding into the room, holding out his hand to give her a firm handshake. He was short with fluffy grey hair and rather flamboyantly dressed in a billowing white shirt, a yellow silk waistcoat and a floral bow tie. And he was British, too. Not at all what she'd expected.

'So sorry not to have been around when you arrived,' he said with a smile. 'Wonderful to have you here, Naomi. We've had excellent reports of your work from the London office. Look,' he glanced at his watch, 'it's almost twelve o'clock. My partners and I normally potter over to one of the restaurants a few minutes' walk away. Would you like to come along, as it's your first day?'

Walking beside Oliver towards the Place du Trocadéro, her loneliness evaporated. The lunch wasn't an entirely relaxing experience, though. The five men took it in turns to quiz Naomi, gently and politely, but quiz her all the same, on her background, the work she'd been doing in the London office and her knowledge of international law. She was able to hold her own and eventually they gave up and moved on to discuss something else.

When they all arrived back in the office around two thirty, Oliver had taken her to meet the only female lawyer in the firm,

Martine Clément, a neat and elegant middle-aged French-woman with short, dark hair, who had taken her to a bar-brasserie in Avenue Kléber after work. They shared a carafe of wine and Martine gave Naomi an affectionate sketch and potted history of each member of staff: their families, their personal traits, their likes and dislikes. Martine was amusing company and Naomi sensed that she was delighted to no longer be the only female lawyer in the office. The conversation flowed easily between them, but after an hour Martine glanced at her watch and her face became serious.

'I have to go, I'm afraid. My grandmother will be fretting by now. She lives with me, you see. She's in good health but she gets lonely in the evenings...'

'Of course. I understand,' Naomi said, thinking that Martine's grandmother must be very old. 'It's very nice of you to invite me out.'

'Not at all. It's so nice that you're here. There are so few of us women, we have to stick together.'

They parted outside the brasserie to go in opposite directions. Naomi walked back to the apartment along Avenue Kléber under the darkening skies, enjoying the fresh evening air and the scent of the Parisian night. It felt full of promise. And by the time she arrived back on Avenue Carnot, any traces of regret and homesickness she'd felt that morning had evaporated.

She'd buried herself in the work that Oliver gave her, but the week had been marred by a couple of difficult conversations with Liam. When she'd called him each evening, his voice had sounded echoey and very far away. She'd felt guilty each time they spoke and she heard the loneliness in his voice. One evening he'd told her that he felt shut out from her life. That was Wednesday, when he'd suggested that he should come over to Paris on the night train on Friday evening and she'd gently put him off.

'I'll probably have to work, Liam. There's so much on. Why don't we wait a couple of weeks until things settle down?'

It was a white lie – although there was a lot of work to do and court deadlines were looming, Oliver had already told her there would be no need for her to work over the weekend. The truth was, she was longing to get out to Montmorency and see if the Villa Helvetia was still there. She was certain, just from the tone of her voice, that her mother had not been telling her the truth about the significance of the postcard.

She was definitely holding something back and Naomi wondered why. Helga was normally such a stickler for the truth, for being open and clear with people. If she was keeping the truth to herself, it must be important. And that fact intrigued Naomi. If it was so important to her mother, she wanted to find out what it was. If Liam had come to visit, she would have had to put off the trip to Montmorency. She needed to do this alone and as soon as she could. The curiosity was burning right through her.

The train from Gare du Nord slid out through Saint-Denis and the northern suburbs of Paris. Naomi stared out of the window, watching the houses and apartment blocks flash past as the train gathered speed, marvelling at the colourful graffiti decorating every bridge and wall they passed. It was Saturday morning and she was on her first leg of the journey to Montmorency. There was no train station in the town and she had worked out that the spa suburb of Enghien-les-Bains was the closest she could get by train. This was her first opportunity to get out of the city and search for the villa on the postcard.

At Enghien-les-Bains station, she got down from the train and walked out through the ticket office. A couple of taxis stood on the forecourt. She got into the first in line and asked the driver to take her to Montmorency.

'Centre ville?' he asked, glancing over his shoulder.

It sounded as good a place to start as any. There was no address on the postcard, but from her guidebook and map of Parisian suburbs she knew that Montmorency was only a small place. If the old villa was still standing, she would surely find it. The taxi driver drove her the short distance through the pristine streets of the town, along the side of a lake to the pretty little town of Montmorency, where he dropped her in a square in the centre. She paid him and, as the taxi roared off, she looked around the quiet square, wondering where to begin.

Noticing a small café on the other side of the square where a waitress was cleaning tables in front of the building, she crossed the cobbles and sat down at one of the tables. She ordered a café crème and a croissant. She was hungry – she'd been so eager to start her journey that she'd forgotten to eat breakfast that morning.

When the waitress returned with her coffee and pastry, Naomi took the postcard from her bag and showed it to her. 'I'm wondering if you can help me? I'm looking for this building,' she said in her faltering French. 'I'm not sure if it's still here.'

The waitress peered at the postcard, looking puzzled. She shrugged. 'I'm not sure, but I don't think there is a convalescent home here nowadays. There are many big old buildings on rue des Carrières, though. It's only a short walk away. You might want to look there.'

The waitress gave Naomi brief directions. When she'd finished her coffee, Naomi thanked her and, leaving some silver coins on the table, left the café and set off down Avenue Foch. She walked along beside the railings of a well-tended park, past imposing old houses and more modern ones hidden behind high, lush hedges. She instantly understood that this was a wealthy suburb. People must have built villas and townhouses here to be near the lake and the spas at Enghien-les-Bains.

She reached rue des Carrières and slowly walked the whole

length of it, scrutinising every building she passed. As the wait-ress had said, there were many large, historic villas set back from the road but none of them appeared to bear any resemblance to the villa in her photograph. At last she came to one that was boarded up, weeds growing through the gravel on the drive. She paused and stood in front of the wrought-iron gates looking through, trying to compare the lines of Villa Helvetia on the postcard with the neglected building in front of her. But this building was square and had no balconies and the pitch of the roof was wrong. Disappointed, she turned away and continued her search.

She'd almost given up hope when she reached the end of the road and turned the corner into a smaller road, rue de Valmy. A large white building stood in a big plot at the intersec-tion of the two roads. It looked to be some sort of municipal building or an office; rows of cars were parked in front of it. She saw a sign on the gate that said COMMISSARIAT DE POLICE and was turning away from it to cross the road when she caught sight of the building from another angle. Her heart missed a beat.

The slightly down-at-heel police headquarters building had the same shape and structure as the Villa Helvetia. The balconies had been boarded over and painted white, and the lawn and trees in the postcard were no more, but there was no mistaking those three separate roofs – a square one in the middle flanked by two pitched gables either side. Chills coursed through her as she looked down at the fading postcard and back up at what that exact scene looked like today.

She stood behind the railings, staring. A couple of uniformed policemen emerged from the front door and strolled over to one of the cars. They glanced in her direction and, not wanting to appear suspicious, she stood back against the wall and pretended to be looking down at her map as the car swept out of the gate.

It was a satisfying feeling to be standing there in front of the building that had been burning in the back of her mind all week, but she felt a note of frustration too. She'd tracked the place down, but she was no closer to finding out its significance to her mother. Had Helga once been here? Had she known someone who'd lived here?

With a sigh, Naomi walked on, around the perimeter of the grounds, keeping close to the railings that bordered the car park. She walked until the fence was interrupted by another entrance with tall, wrought-iron gates that were firmly shut. This was grander than the gate the police car had gone through. It must be the main entrance. On one side was a sign that stated its opening hours, Monday to Friday, 9 a.m. to 5 p.m. There was also a telephone number. She vowed to come back on a weekday, if she could get the time off, or to try telephoning from work.

She scribbled down the number and, turning away, started back towards the square to find a taxi. Frustration washed over her. Although she'd found the building on the postcard, she was no nearer to finding out its significance to her mother; but now she was even more desperate to unravel the secrets within.

FOUR

NAOMI

Paris, 1990

On Monday morning the shrill buzz of the alarm clock woke Naomi at seven o'clock. Turning over to switch it off, she could hardly admit it to herself but she felt a hint of relief that the weekend was over.

When she'd returned empty-handed from her trip to Montmorency on Saturday afternoon, the evening and the whole of Sunday had stretched before her, empty and featureless. It was her own fault, she knew that. She'd put Liam off coming to stay, so what could she expect? She'd bought a takeaway pizza from a pizzeria on Avenue Carnot and spent the evening alone, watching an old French film starring Catherine Deneuve on the little TV in the corner of the living room.

On Sunday she'd once again ventured to the flea market at Montmartre and wandered between the stalls, sifting through the bric-a-brac on display, trying to recapture the carefree feeling she'd had there with Liam, but this time it had eluded her. At the stall where she'd bought the postcard of the Villa Helvetia, the old man looked at her blankly through his pebble glasses and, although she searched through the fading images on offer, not really knowing what she was looking for, she found nothing else of significance. The feeling of recognition and connection she'd felt the previous Sunday when she'd stumbled across the photograph of the villa had completely eluded her the second time.

Now, she showered and dressed quickly, downed a black coffee and left the apartment. Putting the loneliness of the weekend behind her, she struck out towards the Arc de Triomphe and Avenue Kléber with energy and purpose. When she reached the office building on rue du Président Wilson twenty minutes later, she felt refreshed, reinvigorated and ready to face her week at work. She was just getting into the lift on the ground floor when she spotted Martine rushing in through the outer door. Naomi held the lift door open.

'Bonjour, Naomi!' Martine squeezed in beside her.

Naomi closed the doors and the wobbly, antiquated lift inched its way up towards the second floor. Martine got a compact mirror out of her handbag and checked her startling red lipstick, puckering her lips.

'How was your weekend?' she asked, putting her compact away.

'Oh, good, thanks,' Naomi lied, smiling automatically.

'What did you do?' Martine dipped in her handbag again and took out a blue packet of Gitanes cigarettes. 'I hope you didn't spend it all alone? I'm really sorry, I've been feeling very guilty about you. I meant to catch you on Friday to suggest getting together, but you were discussing something with Oliver when I had to leave. I'm afraid I don't know the telephone number of the flat. You'll have to give it to me for next time.'

'That's very kind of you, Martine, but there's no need to worry about me. I had fun exploring.'

The lift creaked to a stop on the second floor. Martine pulled the bars aside and they both stepped out and walked across the marbled hallway to the double doors of the offices.

'Where did you go to explore?' Martine asked.

'Well, on Saturday I went to Montmorency.'

Martine laughed and pushed the doors open. Valérie, the receptionist, was at the reception desk and they all exchanged 'bonjours'. Then Martine turned back to Naomi.

'Montmorency, you say? Whyever there? Not the Eiffel Tower, the Louvre?' Her eyes were dancing with amusement.

Naomi hesitated, sensing colour creeping into her cheeks. Should she tell Martine her reason for going there? She wasn't sure, but what other explanation could she offer for visiting that particular outer suburb than the truth.

'It's a bit hard to explain,' she ventured, dropping her gaze to the white pile carpet. 'I was actually looking for a building. Family history, sort of.'

'Oh?'

At that moment Oliver emerged from his office and Naomi looked up at him. She was shocked to see that his eyes were bleary, his clothes dishevelled. He looked as if he'd already been at his desk for hours but his face lit up when he saw the two of them standing there. 'Ah, Naomi. I'm so glad you're here. There's something I need you to research quite urgently. Some new evidence has come to light on the Africa dispute.'

Martine raised an eyebrow, a teasing look in her eyes. 'We'd better get on. Tell me all about Montmorency later. Sounds fascinating. How about lunch? I don't need to go home today, my aunt looks in on Grand-maman on Mondays.'

Later, at a small café round the corner from the office, sipping Orangina and munching their way through croque-monsieurs oozing with butter and melted cheese, Naomi explained to Martine how she'd stumbled across the postcard of the Villa Helvetia and why the haunting black and white photo-graph had triggered such curiosity in her.

'I nearly missed it, it's changed so much from the photo-graph on the postcard. But I found it eventually. It's now the local police commissariat. I've got the phone number written down. When I have five minutes this afternoon, I'm going to call and see if there's any way of finding out about the history of the building.'

'I could phone them for you if you like,' Martine offered, delicately dabbing the grease on her chin with a napkin. 'It might be easier that way. But I don't hold out much hope that anyone there will know anything about that. I mean, do *we* know anything about the history of the building we work in?'

'I suppose not, but the police commissariat is a public build-ing. There must be some records somewhere.'

'Hmm, true. I was just wondering, though – have you considered that your mother might be telling the truth? That she might just have the photograph on her windowsill because she likes it?'

Naomi thought back to Helga's reaction when she'd intro-duced the subject and shook her head. 'I'm quite sure there is something she wasn't saying. I can always tell when she's hiding something from me. She clams up.'

'It sounds as though you two are very close.'

Naomi nodded. 'My father passed away when I was twelve and after that it was just the two of us.'

'I'm so sorry to hear about your father.' Martine's eyes were full of compassion. 'My father died when I was young too. That's why I ended up living with Grand-maman. So I know exactly how you feel. It must have been a very sad time.'

Naomi swallowed and nodded, thinking of the grief-filled days following her father's death, standing beside her mother at the synagogue as the Hebrew prayers were intoned, travelling in the big black funeral car to the cemetery in Finchley and standing at the graveside, watching the casket being lowered gently into the pit and the sound of dirt on the wood as the mourners sprinkled earth onto it.

'It was,' she said, 'a terribly sad time. But I have wonderful memories of him that I treasure. I feel that he's with me all the time, every day.'

'And your mother? It must have been so sad for her too?'

'It was, of course. But she's very tough. Once he'd gone, my mother picked herself up and went back to work within a couple of weeks. She had a business to run and she just got on with it.'

'She sounds a remarkable lady.'

'She is. She's incredible.' Naomi smiled, thinking warmly of her mother. 'And we *are* close, as you say, but I really wish I knew more about her childhood and what happened to her when she was younger. As I'm getting older it's becoming more and more important to me to find out.'

They had finished their food now and a waiter whisked their plates away. They ordered coffee.

'If you give me the phone number, I will call the police commissariat for you this afternoon,' Martine said, lighting a cigarette, taking a long drag and blowing the smoke out sideways.

'That's so kind of you.' Naomi took out her notebook, copied the number to a fresh page, tore it out and handed it to Martine.

'Perhaps we'd better get back to the office now.' Naomi started to pull on her jacket.

'Not just yet. I haven't finished my cigarette.' Martine glanced at her watch. 'It's only two o'clock, the partners won't be back from their lunch yet. There's no need to hurry. Sit down, relax, finish your coffee.'

'It's just that...' Naomi didn't want to offend her new friend, who was now looking at her again with that now-familiar amused, arched eyebrow. 'It's just that I've got to finish this case summary for Oliver.'

Martine sighed and stubbed out her lipstick-stained cigarette in the ashtray. 'I see he already has you at his beck and call,' she said with a smile, then her face became serious. 'It's good though, it's the first time in a long while he's had an assistant who's been useful to him. The last two weren't quite so able and in any case, they tended to work for the other partners. He's rather missed out because he had so much time off last year.'

'Oh?'

Martine nodded. 'I didn't say when we talked last week because it was your first day and I wanted to keep things light-hearted.' She paused. 'But poor Oliver... His dear wife died last year. It was tragic and he was devastated, the poor man. He took a few months off work.'

Naomi felt the colour drain from her face. 'That's terrible. I had no idea.'

'People in the office tend to avoid the subject, they don't want to upset him. But we're all a bit worried about him at the moment, to tell you the truth. He's been working all hours, burying himself in his work, burning himself out. The other partners made a decision that you should work exclusively for him, partly to relieve the strain he's putting on himself.'

Naomi thought about how unkempt and exhausted Oliver had looked as they went into the office that morning and her heart went out to him.

'How very sad,' she murmured. 'But if you don't mind my asking, what happened? How did she die?'

Martine shook her head slowly. 'Breast cancer, I'm afraid. It was so tragic. All very sudden. She didn't know about it until it was too late. And she was a lovely lady, Evelyn. A musician. They'd met at university and were devoted to each other.'

'Does he have any other family?' Naomi asked after a pause.

Martine shook her head. 'He and Evelyn would have made wonderful parents, but it didn't happen for them. They both had interesting careers, though, and loved living in Paris. I believe Oliver has some family in the UK, but he's lived over here so long he's more or less lost touch with them.'

Naomi was silent for a moment, digesting the news. Then Martine got to her feet, picked up her jacket and put some notes and coins in the saucer the waiter had brought with the bill.

'So, I suppose we'd better get back to the office. It's good that he's got some help on the case and the burden isn't wholly on him any more.'

An hour or so later, when Naomi was buried in law reports making notes, completely absorbed in the task, Oliver came into the office to speak to her about the research. His face was a little flushed from his lunchtime wine, but Naomi saw loneliness in his eyes and heard a sadness in his voice that she hadn't noticed before. She wondered if she should say something to let him know that she knew about his pain, but decided to wait until a more opportune moment arose.

In the middle of the afternoon, Martine popped her head round the door.

'Do you have a moment?'

Naomi looked up and Martine hurried forward and leaned on her desk. 'I've just come off the phone from the police commissariat at Montmorency.'

'Thank you so much, Martine. Were you able to find out anything useful?'

Martine shook her head. 'I'm so sorry, but I'm afraid the woman who answered had no idea where we might find any records for the building. She was a bit unhelpful actually, as I predicted. She suggested we should go to the Land Registry department.'

'What a shame.' Naomi put her pen down, disappointed. She'd been hoping Martine would have some joy with her phone call, but wasn't really surprised it had yielded nothing. 'Do you know where the Land Registry is?'

'It's at the Hôtel de Ville. I can take you there one day if we get a chance. But I have another idea.'

'Oh?' Naomi asked. Martine's eyes were brimming with excitement now.

'It's just occurred to me. Grand-maman might be able to help you. She's in her nineties now and although her memory is fading, she remembers the war quite well. Strangely enough, she can recall it more vividly than what happened yesterday or what she had for breakfast.'

'How confusing that must be for her,' Naomi said.

Martine nodded. 'Yes, it must be, poor old Grand-maman.' Then she lowered her voice and glanced round at the half-open office door. 'She often talks about what it was like here in Paris under Nazi rule. She has some incredible stories.'

'Really? Do you think she would know anything about Montmorency?' Her heart skipped a beat. Perhaps this was a route to finding answers.

Martine shrugged. 'I'm not sure, but there's a chance. Her family were living in the suburbs to the north of Paris. Not that far out, but you never know.'

'Well, if you don't think she'll mind...'

'I'm sure she won't. Are you free tomorrow evening?'

'I should think so.' Naomi smiled ruefully, glad to have something to look forward to. She'd already planned to work late that evening, so that by the time she got home there wouldn't be too long before bedtime and she would be able to fill the time with calls to Liam and her mother.

'Super!' Martine beamed. 'I'll talk to her this evening and let her know that I'm bringing a friend home tomorrow after work. She loves to meet new people. She gets confused some-times, but she loves visitors and she doesn't mind talking about the war. If you can bring your postcard along, it might jog her memory.'

As she walked across the reception area to the exit at the end of the day, Naomi glanced through Oliver's open door. He was still hard at work, the blinds pulled down and his desk lamp casting a pool of light on his papers. She knocked quietly and stood in the doorway. He looked up and, seeing her, a smile crinkled the lines at the corners of his eyes.

'I've finished the research you asked for and it will be typed up tomorrow,' she said. 'I found some quite useful stuff, actually.'

'That's great. Fantastically quick work, I must say. Let's discuss it in the morning. Are you off now?'

She nodded. 'If that's OK?'

'Of course, of course. I've already made it clear there should be no need for you to work long hours... unless you want to, that is. You're leaving quite late enough as it is.'

'I just got absorbed in the case law. It's so fascinating, I lost track of time.'

'I know the feeling! I'm glad you're enjoying the work. I must say, I'm finding it fascinating too.' There was an awkward pause as they both smiled, recognising the connection between them. She smiled at him, noting the light in his eyes, the way he smiled back at her. A feeling of warmth washed over her and she felt inexorably drawn to him.

'Well, I expect you'll be wanting to get out there and enjoy yourself,' Oliver said, 'Make the most of la belle Paris while you're here. Have a good evening, won't you?'

Naomi hesitated for a moment, then opened her mouth to say the same to him but closed it again.

'No need to worry about me.' He smiled. 'I'm perfectly happy to work on here for another couple of hours. See you tomorrow, Naomi. And thank you so much for all your great work. You've already made a very favourable impression amongst all the partners here.'

She felt the colour creep into her cheeks as she glowed with pride. 'Thank you,' she said. His words meant a lot to her. She'd heard rumours from previous assistants that Oliver Charles was a tough taskmaster, very hard to please. And he was so eminent in his field, such an acknowledged expert in international law, that she was genuinely flattered by his words. And there was something else too. It was more than just his professional eminence. She was deeply flattered on a personal level, feeling this connection between them, this link that she didn't yet understand and wasn't yet prepared to fully acknowledge.

As she walked back to the apartment along the now-familiar pavements, under the chestnut trees, she mulled over how Oliver had assumed she would be out on the town that evening, joining a couple of friends for a drink or a meal, heading off to a jazz club in the Latin Quarter perhaps. How wrong he was. She was planning to pick up another takeaway from the pizzeria in Avenue Carnot on her way home. She might perhaps chat for a few minutes to the kindly Italian woman who served at the bar before heading upstairs to eat her pizza alone, phone her mother and watch television for an hour or so before bed. She wouldn't call Liam that evening, she decided. She didn't want a difficult conversation with him to spoil the warm buzz she was feeling from her conversation with Oliver.

Her evening would be almost as lonely as his own, but perhaps not quite as sad. Her heart went out to her new boss as she thought about him sitting there still, burying himself in his work, the pain and grief he must still be suffering written all over his face. So plain to see to everyone but himself.

FIVE

HELGA

Berlin, 1938

Looking back, Helga found it hard to pinpoint the exact moment in time when she began to realise that things were changing in Germany for people like herself and her family.

As a child, for years she remained oblivious to the idea that there might be anything different about them. There seemed nothing to mark them out from the other families who lived in their tall apartment block in Leipziger Strasse, or even anyone else in their neighbourhood in downtown Berlin for that matter. But it was at some point during 1938, when she was eleven, that it began to dawn on her and her identical twin sister Ruth that the world they had been born into was becoming a hostile place for them and other people of their kind.

Until that point all they had known, from their earliest glimmerings of awareness and throughout their happy childhood, was the comfort and happiness that came from belonging to a warm, loving family. It was so natural to them that they were hardly even aware of their good fortune at belonging to such a loving environment. That security and love had cocooned and cushioned the two girls from anything unpleasant in the world since the day of their birth in that same apartment up on the fifth floor in Leipziger Strasse. That apartment, with its expansive views over the neighbourhood, was where they'd both learned everything they knew about the world: to walk and to talk and to read; and where they had spent those first blissful eleven years of their lives.

Their father, affectionately known as Tate, the Yiddish term for Papa, owned a tailor's shop a few buildings down and across the street from the apartment. Their mother, who they always called Mame, was a strong-willed, intelligent woman. She looked after the girls and cared for their home, fetched food from the local shops and markets, cooked and laundered for the family, and supported Tate in everything he did.

From the windows of the apartment, high above the street, so high in fact that they even looked down on the electric cables for the tramcars, they had a bird's-eye view of the whole area. The two of them would kneel together on the window seat and watch the tramcars moving in both directions up and down Leipziger Strasse towards Potsdamer Platz.

The pavements on either side of the street were always busy with well-heeled shoppers. They moved about like busy ants, in and out of the enormous Wertheim department store, the thriving shoe shops, the fur shops and tailors' businesses that had built up to serve the wealthy local community. There were cafés on Leipziger Strasse too, where in warm weather Berliners would sit outside and watch the world go by as they ate. Opposite the apartment was a dance hall, from which music floated across to them on warm evenings, and the girls would look out for a glimpse of couples swirling past its windows. A little way along from that, next to the shop selling Singer sewing machines, was Tate's tailor's shop. Helga always felt a little thrill of pride at the elaborate signboard, gold on black proclaiming the name – BEIDER – visible from the windows of the apartment.

But a few months before their eleventh birthday, at the beginning of 1938, things had started to change for Helga and Ruth. They began to notice that some of their friends had stopped inviting them home after school. The mothers no longer chatted amiably at the school gate either. Instead, they grabbed their children as they came out of school and hurried away, barely exchanging a word. Then one day after supper, Tate told the two girls he needed to speak to them. He sat them down on the settee in the living room and took a seat himself in the armchair opposite. This was very unusual and Helga immediately realised that what their father was about to say to them was both serious and important.

When he spoke, Tate's voice was grave and his forehead was pulled up in an anxious frown. 'I'm so sorry, my little darlings, but I have some sad news to tell you. I'm afraid you won't be able to go to St Elizabeth's any more.'

There was a stunned silence for a few seconds as the news hit them. They had loved their school.

'But Tate! Why?' the girls chorused as one, unbelieving, demanding explanations. Helga wondered if her father's business was in such trouble that he was no longer able to pay the school fees.

Tate cleared his throat. 'Your mother and I have decided to send you to another school, much nearer home. All the other Jewish girls from St Elizabeth's will be going there too.'

Helga and Ruth stared at him, bewildered.

'It's difficult to explain, little one.' Their father wrung his hands and Helga caught a look passing between him and Mame, who stood silently in the doorway, her eyes troubled.

'The government has passed a new law,' Tate said at last.

'Jewish children must go to their own school from now on. There can't be any mixing of children at schools any more.'

Suddenly all the snatches of worried conversations she'd heard between Mame and Tate over the past few weeks came back to Helga. Conversations that her parents probably didn't even realise she'd overheard. Through these, Helga had picked up that several of the Jewish businesses in the neighbourhood had been taken over by non-Jewish Germans.

'It's called Aryanisation,' she heard Tate say one evening as she passed the living room on her way to bed. She heard Mame's gasp in response and she wondered what the word meant.

But throughout all this, Tate had maintained his optimism. 'It will be all right in the end, Jessica, you'll see. This is just a passing phase. People will see how wrong they are and everything will go back to normal.'

But in Mame's reactions, as well as shock Helga heard caution and scepticism. 'The tide has turned, Yacob,' Mame kept saying. 'Ordinary Germans have been whipped up against us Jews. People are rude to us everywhere now. I get pushed on the street, elbowed aside. There are some shops I can't even go into any more.'

Now Helga stood in the doorway of Mame and Tate's bedroom, putting it all together in her mind, and chills of dread went through her as she began to understand some of what was happening around them.

On the bed, Mame had laid out two brand new school uniforms. Pinafore dresses, blouses and stylish woollen jackets. 'Here we are, girls. You will look so smart in these.'

Ruth rushed forward excitedly, but Helga hung back. In everything they did, Ruth was always first to take the plunge. She was by far the more outgoing: the better at sport, the more daring. Now, she held up the brown pinafore dress with the pleated skirt and cream blouse and turned to look at Helga, her eyes full of excitement.

'Look at these lovely skirts! Come on, Helga, let's try them on.'

Helga followed her sister's lead reluctantly. She wriggled out of the blue skirt and white blouse that were so familiar and pulled on the crisp cream-coloured blouse and stiff woollen pinafore dress that smelled of camphor. Finally, Mame held up the woollen jacket for her to slip on. On one of the sleeves she noticed a yellow star.

'What's that?' Helga asked, fingering the stiff material.

'You know what it is. It is the Star of David. I have sewn them on the arm of both jackets and onto your new school coats too.'

'But what for, Mame?' Helga asked.

'To show that you are proud Jewish children, my darling,' Mame said, her eyes glistening. She turned away, busying herself with the buttons on Helga's dress.

'Why do we need to show that?'

Before Mame could answer, Ruth chimed in with a touch of impatience, 'Don't ask so many questions, Helga. I don't mind wearing the star. What difference does it make anyway? Everyone knows we are Jewish. And why would we want to hide it?'

So, the next morning, for the first time Mame shepherded them to the Jewish school a few blocks away from the apartment, where they took up with some of the friends they had made at St Elizabeth's and others they knew from the synagogue. There were boys there as well as girls and, just as Mame had hinted, Helga and Ruth settled in quickly. They felt at home amongst these children and it was nice that the school was just round the corner from home.

And more had changed. Now, when they walked to school,

they would often see Gestapo officers on the pavement outside
buildings, guns on their shoulders, the swastika prominent on
their dark grey uniforms. Mame would gather the girls to her
and hurry past them, her head bowed. Once or twice, columns
of stormtroopers goose-stepped along Leipziger Strasse at a
frightening pace, overtaking them as they walked. On those
occasions, the fear of God would enter their mother's eyes and
she would pull the girls to her and hold them close, her fingers
digging into their arms. In those moments, they could both feel
the way Mame's body shook and her heart thumped, and sense
the fear she was trying to hide from them.

Sometimes angry people would block their way, stand in
front of them on the street and push them, or make them step
out into the road to pass. Once, a man spat in Mame's face.
'Juden,' he said, pure evil in his eyes. Outraged but powerless,
Helga knew then that even the power of a mother's love
couldn't protect them from the evil that had swept through the
city and infected the hearts of their gentile neighbours and
former friends.

Over the next few months, Tate returned home each day,
his shoulders drooping, his face haggard. Gradually, his
customers were abandoning him – all of them gentiles who,
through fear and prejudice, would no longer give him business.
Helga heard Mame remark that it was a miracle that Tate's shop
had survived until that point; so many Jewish shopkeepers in
the neighbourhood had had to sell up cheaply to non-Jewish
buyers. Many of them had left Berlin altogether. Added to that,
some of Tate's friends who worked at the university had lost
their jobs and had to take less well-paid work delivering news-
papers or working in factories. Even the family doctor, who
lived on the ground floor in their own apartment block, had lost
most of his patients because he was no longer allowed to treat
non-Jewish people.

Those Jews who had relatives abroad were leaving

Germany. Family after family left and several of Helga's new classmates had gone by the autumn of 1938. At school they spoke of waiting for affidavits from abroad to enable them to leave the country. But there would be no such wait for Helga and Ruth. Tate and Mame had no relatives abroad – their own parents and grandparents had all been native Berliners.

And then the worst happened. In the winter of 1938 Tate's health started fading. He was unable to struggle down the road to open the shop and Mame insisted on him resting at home; and when she collected the girls from school one afternoon, her face was a picture of anxiety.

'Hurry, girls.' She seized each of them by the hand. 'We need to get home quickly. Your father is worse. I didn't want to leave him, but I couldn't let you walk home alone.'

As soon as they got back up to the apartment, Mame rushed ahead to the bedroom, where Tate lay. Helga and Ruth followed and were shocked to see their beloved Tate still in bed, his face waxy and filmed with sweat.

'Girls, could one of you run downstairs and fetch Doctor Moshe?' Mame's voice was panicked. 'His fever seems to have got even worse.'

'I'll go,' Helga said, dumping her school bag in the hallway.

She flew down the five flights of stairs to the ground floor and banged on the doctor's door. The door was on a chain and when it opened, the lined and worried face of the doctor's wife appeared in the crack. Seeing Helga, she pulled it open wide and ushered her inside.

'Thank goodness it's you, my dear. We sometimes get ruffians in off the street banging on the door, so we keep it locked. Is something wrong?'

'It's Tate. His fever has got worse. Mame is very worried about him.'

'Aaron?' the old woman shouted and the doctor appeared in the hallway. 'You need to go up and see Yacob straight away.'

Doctor Moshe picked up a black bag from under the coat stand and followed Helga back up the stairs. She was desperate to run, but out of respect for the elderly doctor she held herself back. She could hear him wheezing and panting up the steps behind her.

Mame's face registered relief when Doctor Moshe appeared. She beckoned him into her and Tate's bedroom. Helga and Ruth stood outside in the passage and Helga felt Ruth's hand creep into hers. Automatically she gripped it and held it tight. It was something they did without even thinking if either of them was upset or afraid. And at that moment they were both upset and afraid for Tate.

They watched in silence as Doctor Moshe took his time listening to Tate's chest and taking his temperature.

'It is very high, Frau Beider.' The doctor looked anxiously at Mame. 'And there's a rattle on his chest... most worrying. I will write him a prescription.'

He paused, rummaging in his bag, and produced a ragged notebook on which he proceeded to scribble.

'I could go along to the Jewish hospital and get the medicine for you if you like, Frau. You have the girls to look after here.'

'That's very generous of you, Doctor, but I wouldn't dream of troubling you. I'm sure Frau Moshe wants you back home. Thank you very much for your kindness. How much do I owe you...?'

The doctor shook his head. 'No charge, Frau Beider. Yacob is a friend. We Jews all need to help each other in these difficult times.'

'You are too kind.'

Mame took the prescription from him and scrutinised it. The doctor shut up his bag and she saw him to the door. When he'd gone she turned back and looked at Helga and Ruth, who were still hanging about in the doorway of Tate's bedroom.

'I will go to the hospital, Mame,' Ruth said instantly.

'No. You girls stay here with Tate. I can walk there very easily. I know the way. I'll be as quick as I can. Please watch over Tate for me, will you? Sponge his face down with that flannel every few minutes to keep him cool. If I'm not back in an hour, the soup is simmering on the stove for supper. When you've had yours, make sure you dish some up for Tate, slice him some bread and try to get him to eat something.'

Then she kissed both the girls, caressed their faces briefly, smiling into their eyes, pulled on her gaberdine coat with the yellow star on the sleeve and left the apartment.

It must have been ten o'clock when they heard crashing and banging down in the street and the first roars of an angry crowd. Then came the sound of glass breaking, quickly followed by hysterical cheering. The girls' eyes locked together. Ruth slid off the bed and Helga rushed after her to the window, where they knelt together on the window seat and stared down at the scene below, their hearts pounding.

Down in Leipziger Strasse by the light of the streetlamps they saw a sea of people, men mostly but some women amongst them, surging forward down the middle of the carriageway with banners and placards, spilling round the trams, stopping the traffic. Shards of broken glass from the shattered shop window were strewn all over the pavement. A group of men broke away from the crowd and charged at another shop window, this one a shoe shop. They smashed at it with axes and hammers. Within seconds the whole of the plate-glass window had smashed to the ground and the attackers swarmed into the shop through the broken pieces. Items of furniture came crashing out, breaking into smithereens as they landed on the pavement; then followed the shoes, one by one, raining out onto the pavement to the ecstatic roars of the crowd.

'That's Herr Toucal's shop,' Helga breathed, thinking of the jovial shop-owner, a friend of Tate's who frequently dropped in to see their father.

Helga felt Ruth's arm creep around her shoulder and she moved closer to her sister. The two of them shivered there together, their faces pressed against the window, fear paralysing them to the spot, watching the horror unfold beneath them.

The crowd moved on, yelling and shouting. Shudders went through Helga as she heard the chants: 'Juden Raus!' – 'Jews out!' – and saw people waving their fists in the air triumphantly as they rampaged on along the street, smashing windows, storming into the buildings, looting and ransacking as they went.

'What about Mame?' Ruth muttered, giving voice to what they were both thinking. 'What will happen to her?'

'She might still be at the hospital. If not, she will hide somewhere,' Helga said, trying to convince herself that it could be possible.

'Look, Helga. Look what they're doing now.'

Ruth pointed with a shaking finger. Men at the fringes of the crowd were kicking down a door between two shopfronts that led up to the apartments above the shops.

'Professor Heinrich lives in there.'

They watched, transfixed with terror, as the door caved in and the crowd surged inside. Helga felt weak with dread. All she could think of was Mame. Where was she now? Had she been caught up in this angry, frenzied mob? What would they do to her? She closed her eyes and felt hot tears ooze between the lids. She knew what they would do to her darling Mame. And as if to answer her deepest terrors, the crowd gathering around the doorway of the apartment building opposite moved aside as others who'd entered the building came out, carrying a man at shoulder height. The crowd roared and Helga gripped Ruth's arm. They couldn't see his face, but the frail figure in a white shirt looked very much like Tate's old friend the professor. He was pushed to the ground and disappeared from view as the crowd set upon him, kicking him, beating him with weapons.

'What if they come here?' Ruth was the first to say it.

'I'll lock the door.'

It was all Helga could think of. She got down stiffly from the window seat and in a daze crossed the room to where Tate lay oblivious to everything. Forcing herself forward, she walked to the end of the passage to the front door. She went to pull the bolts across the door but stopped herself. What if Mame was coming up the stairs at that very moment? Helga pulled the door open and stepped out onto the landing. She peered down over the banister into the stairwell. She could hear the muffled shouting from the crowd in the street, even from deep inside the building. That second there was a sickening crash from the ground floor and the noise of the crowd erupted into their building.

'Juden! Juden!' they chanted, accompanied by more banging and thumping.

Helga threw herself back inside the apartment and slammed the door shut. With shaking hands, she pulled the bolts across and stood with her back to the door, her legs weak with terror, her heart hammering fit to burst.

SIX

NAOMI

Paris, 1990

Martine and her grandmother lived in a small apartment on the top floor of an old building in one of the backstreets behind Opéra. She and Naomi set off together after work the next day, this time at six o'clock sharp. It was several stops along on the metro, which at that time was crowded with office workers returning home. As they got into the carriage, they were separated by the press of bodies pouring in between them. Martine was washed up towards the middle of the carriage and ended up standing between the seats and Naomi was left in the lobby beside the doors, holding onto a plastic strap suspended from the ceiling.

It was a five-minute walk from the metro station to Martine's building. The lift in that building appeared even more antiquated than the apartment building on Avenue Carnot and Naomi eyed it sceptically. It looked as though it was only big enough for one person.

'I'll take the stairs,' she said hastily when the doors creaked open.

'Are you sure? It's a very long climb, we're right up on the top floor.'

'It's no problem, Martine, I need the exercise.'

She was out of breath when she reached the fifth floor. She had to wait on the landing for the lift to trundle to a stop and for Martine to emerge.

Martine unlocked the apartment door and, beckoning Naomi inside, called out, 'Grand-maman! Grand-maman, it's me. Are you all right?'

'Martine? Is that you, ma petite?' a thin voice came from the end of the narrow, dark hallway.

'Of course it's me, Grand-maman. Remember, I told you yesterday, I've brought a friend back from work. Our new *avocat stagiaire* from London?'

'Did you, dear?'

Martine led Naomi through a door at the end of the passage into a small, bright living room. The apartment was in the eaves of the building, under the steeply sloping roof, and there were two windows high up through which golden light flooded in from the setting sun. In one corner, a diminutive old lady with a shock of white hair reclined in a wingback armchair. She sat forward as they entered and looked at Naomi, her faded blue eyes vague. But gradually her confusion cleared and a smile lit up her wrinkled face.

'This is Naomi, Grand-maman. Naomi, meet my grand-mother, Madeleine Clément.'

Naomi stepped forward and took the old lady's trembling hand.

'My dear Naomi,' Madeleine looked straight up into her eyes, beaming, 'how wonderful to meet you. It is so nice when I get to meet Martine's colleagues. I hear so much about them.'

'It's lovely to meet you too.' Naomi wondered when the old

lady would release her hand, but she decided to wait there patiently, not to pull it away.

'Naomi, please sit down, make yourself comfortable.' Martine broke the spell and the old lady let go her grasp. 'Would you like tea? Wine? An aperitif? Grand-maman and I normally have a small pastis when I get home from work. Would you like one too?'

'I'd love one.' Naomi sank into the cushions of the settee, thinking how much more comfortable and homely this flat was than the apartment on Avenue Carnot. Although tiny, the room was bright and beautifully furnished, with bookcases filling every spare wall, soft armchairs and scatter cushions on the floorboards.

Martine disappeared briefly to the kitchen and returned with a bottle of pastis and three glasses on a tray. She poured a centimetre or so into the glasses and handed them round. Naomi took a tentative sip of hers and was instantly transported back in time to those weeks travelling round Europe with Liam over three years ago. She hadn't tasted the liquorice- and aniseed-flavoured spirit since then and it instantly evoked those heady summer days.

'Grand-maman, do you remember what we were talking about yesterday evening?' Martine was asking gently, taking a seat opposite her grandmother. The old lady took another tiny sip of her pastis and narrowed her eyes in deep thought.

'Remind me, ma petite,' she said.

'I told you a bit about Naomi's interest in the police commissariat building in Montmorency. Remember now?'

'Ah yes. Yes, I do remember you mentioning something about that but I don't know that I could possibly tell her anything about a police station. I'm an old, old lady who never goes anywhere.'

Martine gave Naomi a knowing look as if to reassure her to be patient.

'Well, as I said yesterday, Naomi was wondering if you knew anything about what might have happened to the building during the war.'

'Ah. The war.' Madeleine shook her head quickly and the light went out of her blue eyes. She fell silent again, sipping her drink absently, lost in thought. Finally, she spoke again. 'It was a terrible time. For everyone in Paris. Everyone in France, too. The whole world...'

'It must have been, Grand-maman. I know how tough things were for you then.' Martine's voice was soothing. 'We were wondering if you might remember something about the building in Montmorency from that time though? It was a convalescent home before the war. Naomi thinks her mother might have some connection to the building.'

'I have a photograph of it,' Naomi ventured on cue, dipping into her briefcase to take out the photo. 'It looks to have been taken in the 1930s.'

'Naomi's mother has the very same picture on her windowsill and Naomi is wondering why,' Martine added.

'Will your mother not tell you, dear?' the old woman asked, turning her vague eyes towards Naomi. 'If the postcard has significance, why is she hiding it from you?'

Naomi handed the postcard to Martine, who in turn approached her grandmother's chair and held it up for Madeleine to look at.

'I've tried talking to her about it,' Naomi answered, 'but she has put the war and everything that happened to her then behind her and refuses to talk about it. She had a terrible time, she was only a child.'

Madeleine peered at the postcard, then took it from Martine and laid it in her lap.

'Montmorency, you say? We were living in Saint-Denis, just to the north of Paris. Montmorency is a bit further out. We used to go there sometimes. And Enghien-les-Bains on Sundays in the summer to bathe in the lake when your father was young, Martine. That was before the war, of course...'

Pain flickered across her eyes then. 'I remember the Nazis marching into our town as clearly as if it were yesterday... goose-stepping through the streets. The stamp, stamp, stamp of their boots.'

Martine was kneeling beside her grandmother's chair now. She reached out and rubbed the old lady's arm soothingly. 'Look at the postcard again, Grand-maman. See if it jogs any memories.'

'The writing on the back says it was a convalescent home at the time the photograph was taken,' Naomi said. 'It is called Villa Helvetia.'

Madeleine frowned and went silent. She looked down at the photograph again, picked it up with both hands and held it up to her eyes. 'Villa Helvetia... Villa Helvetia. That does ring a tiny bell. Let me think for a moment.'

When she lowered the photograph to her lap a few moments later her face was drained of colour. She spoke slowly then, in a changed voice, a small voice full of shame and regret. 'I might be wrong, but I think I remember. I'm nearly sure it was that building. It's coming back to me now. I seem to recall walking past it once and seeing them all out in the garden. Orphans, they were. Jewish orphans.'

Shock washed through Naomi, although the revelation was half-expected. Orphans of Jewish heritage! There was surely a connection with her mother here. Her mouth dropped open and she stared at the old lady as she went on, staring at the floor in front of her as she spoke.

'Your father wasn't very old then, Martine, chérie, and he was curious about the children, naturally, but we had to hurry past. No one felt they could linger. The children were all out sitting under the trees, you see. It was a sunny day. Those trees in the picture here. There was a group of them. Girls and boys.

All ages they were, the tiniest only three or four. There was a young teacher there with them too and she was standing in front of them, giving them a lesson. They were all looking up at her, concentrating, listening carefully to her words. Everyone felt for them, those poor children, uprooted from their homes in Germany as they were...'

Naomi closed her mouth and tried to swallow. She wished she hadn't drunk the pastis quite so quickly. Nausea rose in her throat.

She knew it now. The reason her mother hadn't wanted to come to Paris. *She'd* been one of those orphans at the Villa Helvetia. Something had compelled her to keep the photograph of the building on her windowsill. But whatever had happened to her to make her deny any knowledge of the place, to even deny that she'd ever even been in France at all?

SEVEN

HELGA

London, 1990

Helga was in her bedroom listening to the radio that Thursday morning when the news came on. 'Today marks the first day of the official demolition of the Berlin Wall,' the newsreader announced.

Goosebumps rose all over her body. Tutting to herself, she automatically reached for the button to switch the radio off again, just as she had done every time since last autumn when Berlin and its infamous wall had burst into the headlines and there was no avoiding the newscasts and newspaper headlines. She recalled watching the television news, last November, half fascinated, half appalled, her finger hovering over the off-button, as impatient crowds had flocked to the wall and over-whelmed the checkpoints and the whole process of the unravelling of the communist regime in East Germany had begun.

She remembered the date – 9 November. It should have been a joyous time, but 9 November 1938 was a date etched on her memory with fear and horror, so she hadn't been able to celebrate. Now, she paused what she was doing and closed her eyes. She tried to imagine what it was like there now, with the wall cutting through the old familiar streets, but her imagination failed her. She switched off the radio and turned back to her task.

She'd spent a lot of time up in her room since that fateful telephone call the previous week when Naomi had revealed that she'd stumbled across an old postcard of the Villa Helvetia in a Parisian flea market. What a cruel quirk of fate that was. What Helga had dreaded since she'd found out where Naomi was going to spend the next six months had come to pass on her very first day in the city. And although they'd spoken on the phone almost every day since, and Naomi hadn't mentioned the postcard again, Helga wasn't fooled by her daughter's silence. She was quite sure that Naomi would not have been satisfied with her hollow explanation of why she'd kept that photograph on her windowsill for over forty years. She was well aware that the tone of her voice had given her secret away. She recalled how Naomi had asked her about the photograph once before, when she was about ten. All the other photographs she had on her windowsill had some sort of family significance – places they'd visited on holiday, family groups, Naomi's school photographs. Helga had simply replied that she'd found that picture in a junk shop and she thought it was interesting, and had left it at that.

And each evening since when Naomi had called her, a shudder had gone through Helga as she visualised Naomi there in that city, walking to work along those achingly beautiful boulevards. In Helga's mind they were still the places where Nazi Gestapo had once patrolled, where the swastika had festooned every public building and where hungry Parisians had queued outside boulangeries on the pavements for hours every day to buy necessities to feed their families. Where citi-

zens went about on foot or by cycle terrified of being appre-
hended, picked off the street and taken away for just not looking
right.

Knowing how tenacious her daughter could be, Helga was
sure that Naomi wouldn't be fobbed off with her lame explanation. It was the fact of her not mentioning it again that had
made Helga suspect that she could well be trying to find out
more about the place. And that led her to think about it again, to
wonder about the old building. Was the Villa Helvetia still
standing? Had it become a convalescent home again as it had
been before the war? She shivered, wondering exactly what
Naomi was uncovering, powerless to stop her unearthing the
past that Helga herself had done her best to bury.

On that first Sunday after Naomi had mentioned the postcard, Helga, rifling through the old photographs to get to the
one she was looking for, had in her shocked state taken a decision about them. She would take all the others out of that old
biscuit tin – all of them except that most precious one – sort
them by date and put them into an album. She would start from
the beginning: those photographs of herself in New York after
the war. That was the time at which her post-war life had begun
afresh. She didn't mind anyone seeing the photographs of her
from that point onwards. She'd even bought a new album with a
padded cream-coloured cover from WHSmith on Camden
High Street especially for the purpose.

Putting her pictures into an album was something she'd
been meaning to do for years but she'd always been far too busy
to even consider it, until she'd sold the business and retired the
previous year. Over the decades, the photographs had gradually
accumulated and been stored away.

So, over the past few days, she'd lain them out methodically
in date order on her bedroom floor. Now, she picked up the first
one and looked at it for a long time, her hands trembling. It was
the one of herself as a teenager in New York, sitting alone on a

bench in Central Park on a chilly winter's day. She was wearing an overcoat. It was a black and white photograph but she could remember the colour of that warm woollen coat. Chocolate brown. The trees behind the bench were bare against a pale sky. Where had the decades gone? She hardly recognised that slight young girl with bushy dark hair. Those sad eyes that stared back at her from a thin, white face betrayed the pain that her younger self had struggled so hard with. She carried the pain with her to this day, but over the years she'd learned to hide it; and now when she looked in the mirror, it was no longer so plainly written on her face.

Looking back at her younger self, separated from the present by the busy years since the war, it occurred to Helga that it was hardly surprising that she'd had no time to sort out her old photographs and reflect on the past. Her feet had barely touched the ground for decades. Almost from the day they'd met, she and Harry had led an industrious life. They would get up early every weekday and, even on Saturdays, catch the tube to Green Park and walk through the quiet streets of Mayfair to their company's headquarters in a red-brick Georgian house in Hill Street. There, they would work all day, returning home late in the evenings, well after the rush hour had died down. While Naomi was small, she was cared for by a succession of au pairs and nannies. They'd travelled abroad for business sometimes, to North America and to Europe, only occasionally able to snatch a brief sight-seeing trip in between meetings. And when Harry had passed away, Helga had carried on in just the same way, as if he were still beside her. The property development business they'd built up together employed dozens of people: architects, planners, surveyors, agents; and she owed it to them to keep going as Harry would have wanted her to. She'd also owed it to Naomi. There were school fees to pay and their home and life-style to maintain.

The shrill buzz of the doorbell startled her out of her

reverie. She quickly laid the photograph back on the floor with the others, closed the bedroom door firmly on the memories and hurried downstairs.

Kitty was standing on the step. Millie, her white Afghan hound, sat obediently by her side. Helga's heart sank when she saw her friend. She'd been carefully avoiding Kitty since that awkwardness about the subject of Paris the Sunday before last, when she'd let herself down and allowed the tears to fall.

'Hello, stranger.' Kitty's voice was bright. 'I haven't seen you for days. Are you all right?'

'Of course.' Helga opened the door wide, forcing a smile. 'Come on in. Let's go through to the kitchen, I'll make some coffee.'

'Whatever have you been up to?' Kitty asked as she followed Helga down the passage, the dog padding behind her. 'I thought you might have popped round on Sunday. I was going to call you, but in the end Jean phoned and I drove over to Hampstead to see her. You know Jean, darling, an old actress friend of mine.'

'Oh, that must have been nice,' Helga said vaguely, ignoring the question.

'It was. Jean is such good company. And so...?' Kitty asked. 'What *have* you been up to since we last met up?'

'Nothing much,' Helga said evasively, filling the electric kettle at the sink and plugging it in. Kitty plonked herself down at the kitchen table and the dog lay down elegantly at her feet, her head resting on her crossed front paws.

'I've been a bit worried about you, darling, to tell you the truth. I should have been over before. After... well, ever since that little chat we had. It's been playing on my mind.'

Helga kept her back turned, ladled three spoons of ground coffee into the cafetière. She didn't have an answer, but she felt her irritation rising. Why didn't Kitty just drop the subject? Helga had made it quite clear at the time that she didn't want to discuss Paris or the war. She'd taken a decision not to go round to Kitty's for a while after what had happened that Sunday, hoping the dust would settle and that Kitty would just forget about it. She filled the cafetière from the kettle, put in the plunger and left it to brew. Then she turned round to face her friend.

'There's no need to worry about me, Kitty,' she said coldly. 'I've just been a bit busy, that's all.'

'Busy?' Kitty frowned. 'You just said you weren't up to much and you were saying the other day how little you had to do and how you missed the office.'

'I've had a few things to sort out.'

She brought the cafetière to the table, set two mugs down beside it with the sugar bowl and fetched milk from the fridge.

'I see.' Kitty poured herself some coffee, spooned in some brown sugar and took a sip. 'I've been missing our chats.'

Helga sat down opposite her friend and poured herself some coffee. She kept her eyes averted from Kitty's. She'd been missing Kitty's company too, but the fear of being questioned about her wartime experiences and about Paris in particular had kept her from visiting; but she wasn't going to admit to that.

'Have you heard from Naomi?' Kitty asked when Helga didn't respond.

'Oh yes. Several times,' Helga knew her voice was defensive. 'We speak every evening, in fact. She's getting along very well. She's already extremely well thought of in the office. And she's made a friend at work. A female French lawyer.'

'That's nice. You must be very proud. She's such a bright girl.'

They both sipped their drinks in the awkward silence that followed. On the floor, the dog stirred and whimpered in her sleep.

'How's Liam coping without her?' Kitty ventured at last. 'Have you heard from him at all?'

Helga drew herself up and turned to look at her friend. 'Of course not, Kitty!' she snapped. 'Why should I have heard from Liam? The boy's very busy and besides, I'm sure he's not got the least bit of interest in seeing me.'

'I'm sorry, darling. I didn't mean to offend you. It's just that it occurred to me that he's probably missing Naomi as much as you are. I just wondered, that's all.'

There was another silence. Helga took a deep breath, holding on hard to her indignation. It was the one way she knew of defending herself. It was the only way of stopping her vulnerability from bubbling up and breaking out on the surface.

'About the other Sunday, Helga,' Kitty began again, this time in a conciliatory tone. 'Look, I've been thinking about what you said when you were upset. It must be very hard for you to know that Naomi is there in Paris, if you had a terrible experience there during the war. It must be bringing back all your dreadful memories. I expect you're missing her and would like to go and visit, but... Well, I just wanted to let you know that I'm here to help if you need to talk about it.'

Kitty extended her hand across the table. Helga stared at her, unblinking, pursing her lips, pushing back the tears that threatened. She sat there looking steadily at her friend, a mix of anger and other powerful emotions swirling around in her heart. In that moment she was aware that she could have melted, taken Kitty's hand and allowed the floodgates to open. She could have told her friend everything but the flint in her heart was too strong, she couldn't allow it to dissolve.

'I told you the other day,' she blurted, her dry eyes snapping. 'I don't want to talk about it, Kitty. Nothing good will come of it.'

'All right,' Kitty's tone was sceptical. 'I understand. In that case, why don't we finish our coffee and drive up to Kenwood? Milly could do with a run in the park and I could do with the company.'

Helga drained her mug and put it down firmly on the table.

'That's a kind offer, but I've got a few things to do here today. I wasn't planning on going out.'

'All right, darling. As you wish.'

Kitty stood up and the dog stirred herself and yawned, stood up and shook out her coat. 'Come along, Millie. We will have to go up there by ourselves.'

Helga followed them along the passage to the front door.

'Goodbye, darling,' Kitty said, opening the door and pecking Helga on the cheek. 'Take care and do give me a call, whenever you feel like it.'

Helga stood in the doorway, her throat aching with regret as Kitty loaded the dog into the back seat of her ageing Jaguar and got in the front seat herself with a flutter of her hand. She watched the car pull off erratically into the street and accelerate along Gloucester Avenue towards Regent's Park Road until it rounded the bend and disappeared out of sight. Then she went inside, slammed the front door and bolted it shut. She leaned against it with her forehead, her heart beating fast. She stayed like that for several seconds, paralysed with emotion. Then she turned and went as quickly as she could up the stairs to her bedroom. There, once again, she took out the last remaining photograph in the biscuit tin and stared at it, her whole being shaking with emotion.

'Ruthie, darling,' she breathed, letting the sobs rise in her chest and overwhelm her until, sinking to her knees on the carpet, she finally let the tears fall.

EIGHT

HELGA

Berlin, 1938

Helga opened her eyes and stared up at the unfamiliar ceiling. For a moment she wondered why she had been sleeping in her parents' bedroom. As she shifted her body she saw that Ruth was beside her, in her usual position, sleeping on her back with her mouth open. They were lying together at the foot of the bed and Tate was sleeping too, propped up on his pillows at the other end.

Like a thunderbolt it came back to Helga: Mame wasn't with them, she hadn't come home. Like an ugly, distorted kaleidoscope, fragments of memory from the previous evening came tumbling back into her mind.

Carefully, slowly, she pushed back the covers. Shivering in the chill of the unheated apartment, she slid down from the high bed, trying not to wake Ruth or her father. She tiptoed across the room, knelt up on the window seat and peered down into the street below. In the grey light of dawn, the devastation wreaked by the rampaging crowds was now visible in all its horror.

Many shop windows had been shattered. Piles of broken glass glistened on the pavements, shopfronts stood exposed and broken furniture and wrecked stock was strewn amongst the broken glass. On some of the remaining doors and on any blank wall-space, the words 'Juden Raus' had been daubed in red paint. Helga prickled at the sight of it – it looked so much like blood.

Peering along the street, she saw that not all the shops had been attacked. Some had been left untouched. Helga knew that they were the ones that were owned and run by non-Jewish Germans.

From behind the buildings opposite, she noticed columns of smoke curling into the sky. She frowned, wondering. Something was burning in the narrow streets behind Leipziger Strasse.

There was hardly anyone about on the wide street itself. Just a few brave shopkeepers trying vainly to clear up the wreckage with rakes, brooms and barrows. There was no sign of any of the violent marauders now. With a shiver, Helga peered down at the spot where Professor Heinrich had been set upon by the crowd, but there was no sign of him amongst the rubble. Where was he now? Had his attackers taken him away? And wherever was Mame? What had become of her?

Helga's heart ached with longing for her mother. She clung on to the hope that Mame could still be coming home. She warmed to the thought. Perhaps even now Mame was picking her way along the street, making for the front door of the apartment building. Helga slid down from the window seat and, checking that Ruth and Tate weren't stirring, heaved the upturned chair away from the door handle and slowly opened the bedroom door. Cautiously, she tiptoed along the passage to the front door of the apartment.

The bolts were still across the door. She pulled them back

slowly, afraid even now that there might be someone outside
waiting for her. The trauma of the previous night, when the
crowd had surged into the building, flashed through her mind.
When she'd heard their hate-filled shouts, she'd run back into
Tate's bedroom, slammed and locked the bedroom door. Ruth
had dragged Mame's chair over from her dressing table and
together they had wedged it under the handle of the door.
They'd talked in urgent whispers about moving the dressing
table itself over to barricade the door, but when they tried it
proved far too heavy. All the time, they were listening out for
the hammering of weapons on the front door, the shouts of
hatred from the mob.

She and Ruth had slipped into the end of Tate's bed and
had lain there shivering, clinging to each other, praying to God
that the angry crowd wouldn't make its way upstairs. They
stayed like that for hours, their ears straining for the sound of
boots on the steps, barely speaking, just holding each other
tight for comfort. Eventually, the banging and shouting from
down in the street subsided and the girls, exhausted by the
effort and the tension of the evening, had drifted off into a fitful
sleep.

Now, Helga leaned over the banister and peered down into
the stairwell. A strange noise floated up to her. It was the faint
sound of someone crying, several floors below. Whoever it was,
they were sobbing and wailing. It seemed a crazy thought, but it
flashed through Helga's mind that it could be Mame. Perhaps
she had actually made it home at last, shaken and exhausted.
Perhaps she couldn't manage the final climb up the steep stairs
to the apartment and was sitting there on the bottom step,
sobbing with frustration and exhaustion.

Helga needed to find out if it was her. In her bare feet she
started down the cold stone steps, hoping desperately that it was
Mame down there, but half afraid of what she might find. She
passed the fourth floor, then the third, where non-Jewish fami-

lies occupied the apartments. Their front doors were firmly shut but showed no signs of damage.

She moved on, past the second and first floors. As she made her way down, she paused. One of the doors on the first floor was hanging off its hinges. She stopped and stared, dread surging in her beating chest. She knew the Jewish family who occupied that apartment. The Abramsons were an elderly couple who lived there with their two grown-up daughters. Hovering in front of the door, splinters of wood and debris digging into her bare feet, Helga wondered what to do. Should she go inside the apartment and see what had happened? Should she check the Abramsons were all right? If they were injured, they would need help. It's what her mother would have done, she was sure.

But even as she moved towards the door, a prickle of fear stopped her in her tracks. What if some of the rioters were still in there? She moved quickly past the door, feeling guilt and shame wash through her as she did so, taking care not to look inside. She turned the bend in the staircase and looked down towards the ground floor. Someone sat hunched on the bottom step, shoulders heaving, and Helga knew in a heartbeat that person with the straggly grey hair and knitted shawl wasn't Mame. But she did recognise the huddled form.

'Frau Moshe!' She rushed down the last few steps, her feet pounding on the hard surface. 'What's wrong? What happened?'

She sat down beside the old doctor's wife, the chill of the cold concrete cutting through her thin nightdress. She didn't know what to do. Should she put her arm round Frau Moshe? She'd always been a little frightened of this fierce old woman, whom she'd assumed was unafraid of anything and who had always ruled her husband, the kindly doctor, with a rod of iron.

'It's my Aaron,' the old woman sobbed, rocking back and forth in inconsolable grief. Helga's heart went out to her and her shyness and reluctance dissipated. She slid her arm round Frau Moshe's shoulders and the woman collapsed against her.

'They have taken him. They have taken him,' she wailed.

As the words sank in, Helga looked around her and noticed the devastation in the lobby for the first time. The big double doors leading out onto Leipziger Strasse were hanging off their hinges, splintered and broken, and the front door to the Moshes' apartment stood wide open, the doorframe smashed to pieces around the lock. Helga shuddered and dropped her eyes to the floor but what she saw there sent more chills right through her. Filthy, muddy footprints covered the tiled entrance hall and smeared amongst them were the unmistakeable red-brown streaks of dried blood.

And then Frau Moshe looked at her as if she had only just realised who she was. 'I'm so sorry, little one,' she said, her voice breaking. 'But I know your mother left. I heard what happened to her. And I'm so sorry, but she won't be coming home.'

NINE

NAOMI

Dieppe, 1990

Naomi waited with the other foot passengers from the boat train on the quayside while the metal gangway was lowered on its rattling chains to make a bridge between the cross-Channel car ferry and the dockside. From her viewpoint on the quay, she could see the steady flow of traffic rumbling over the vehicle ramp to board the boat. Container lorries, vans, family cars, mobile homes, caravans all streamed on board. The huge car park at Dieppe docks had been full of vehicles before the ferry docked, all waiting for a passage across the Channel to England. The ship seemed to have infinite capacity, swallowing them all up in its voluminous interior.

Naomi shivered in the late-evening air. It was chilly for spring and she pulled her jacket more tightly around her and rubbed her hands together to keep warm. She was dreading the night to come, knowing that it would be spent trying to get comfortable enough to sleep on an unyielding, reclining seat in

the passenger deck. She hoped it wouldn't be stormy on the
Channel that night – she couldn't bear listening to people being
seasick into their little paper bags, it made her nauseous just
thinking about it.

She knew that if she'd told her mother she was coming
home, Helga would have offered to pay for a flight. But she'd
kept silent about her plans to come back to London that
weekend when they'd spoken during the week. Telling her
would have inevitably involved answering awkward questions
about the reason she had come back. Naomi wanted them to be
together, face to face, when she told her mother what she'd
found out about the orphanage at Montmorency. She wanted
to see her reaction, not give her time to think up more
subterfuge.

Liam had been delighted when she'd told him late the
previous evening that she was coming back to London that
weekend. But when he'd got over his initial surprise, he also
started to ask difficult questions.

'It will be brilliant to see you...' he said slowly, in a questioning tone, '...but wasn't the idea for *me* to come out to see
Paris to see *you*? I thought you wanted to show me your new
apartment? I thought we were going to spend some time in Paris
together?'

There was a pause. He was quite right. 'I know,' she stumbled over the words, 'and that would be lovely. I really want you
to come over soon. In the next couple of weeks, I promise. It's
just that there's something important I need to come home for.'

'Oh?' Liam's voice suddenly sounded deflated and suspicious all at the same time. 'What's that for, then? Something to
do with work, I take it?'

'No, actually,' she replied, irritation rising already. 'It's
something to do with Mum.'

'Ah... She's not ill, is she?' Now, his voice changed again,
registering concern immediately, and Naomi berated herself for

having been irritated at all. 'I could pop round and see if she's OK if you need me to?'

How like Liam to offer to help! A warm feeling of relief went through her at his reaction.

'It's OK, Liam. Mum's not ill. I'll explain when I get back.'

'Sounds mysterious.'

The queue was moving forward now and Naomi walked with the other travellers across the passenger ramp and onto the ferry, relieved to get on board and feel the heat of the interior. Once inside the ship, she followed the signs and the other passengers, along passages and up a metal stairway. She eventually found the seating deck and her allocated seat. Dumping her belongings there, she went out onto the deck to watch the ferry set sail into the gathering dusk. She leaned on the rail, enjoying the salty taste of the fresh sea air, and watched as the twinkling lights of the port of Dieppe gradually disappeared over the dark horizon.

She sighed deeply as the ship moved away from France and into the Channel. Was she doing the right thing going home? It had seemed important when she'd made the decision on her way back from her visit to Madeleine Clément. She had bought her ticket from the travel agents in the Champs-Élysées on her way to work the very next morning. But now she was beginning to experience a few pangs of guilt about it. She had so much work to do, preparing for the upcoming hearing at the International Court that she could easily have filled the whole weekend poring over documents at the office, but Oliver had been very understanding when she'd asked if she could leave early on Friday to catch the boat train from Gare du Nord.

She smiled now, thinking of the conversation they'd had on Thursday evening, when they'd both worked late in the office. Oliver had asked her into his room to discuss the deposition she had drafted for the case. Once again, the dark rings around his red-rimmed eyes betrayed his exhaustion, but he seemed

undaunted by his tiredness and his mind was as sharp as ever.
They had already built up an easy rapport and, as always when
she was talking about work with Oliver, the time flew by. But
her heart went out to him. She knew he was working hard to
forget his grief and she felt desperately sorry for him. She would
have loved to put her arms round him to ease his pain, but of
course that was unthinkable. When they'd finished discussing
Naomi's paper, Oliver leaned back in his chair, put his finger-
tips together and glanced at her appraisingly. It felt almost as if
he was looking at her for the first time. He smiled.

'I've said this before, I know, but I really *am* impressed with
your work, Naomi. Your research and drafting is of the highest
standard. You seem to have developed a real interest in this
area.'

He seemed to want to tell her something, so she waited, her
eyes on his face.

'I was lucky, actually,' he said after a pause, 'that the opportunity to come and set up an office in Paris came up when it did.
It happened at just the right moment for me. Serendipity,
really.'

'Oh?'

'Yes. It was just at the time that Evelyn – my wife, that is –
was lucky enough to be offered a position as first violinist with
the Paris Philharmonic. It all tied in very nicely. We moved over
from London together and were both able to do something we
loved in a city we loved. It couldn't have worked out better for
us at the time.'

'That sounds wonderful,' Naomi said, smiling. Was now the
time to let him know that she knew all about his wife's death?
She quickly decided that it was. But in the couple of seconds
she took to think of the right words, Oliver cleared his throat
and started speaking again.

'I expect people have already told you. Evelyn – my wife –
passed away last year.'

'Yes... yes, I did hear about it. Martine mentioned it to me. I'm so sorry, it must have been terrible for you.'

He looked down at his desk then. 'It has been. It was very hard for me to face at first, but my work keeps me occupied. It's been over a year now. The pain is lessening a little. I'm beginning to be able to look back on the good times we had together without feeling quite so sad.'

'That must be a comfort.' The words sounded hollow and trite, but Naomi was struggling to find the right things to say.

He looked at her and smiled briskly. 'And there were a lot of good times. We were very lucky.'

She smiled too. Then he went on, 'And what about you, Naomi? Do you have someone special?'

'Yes,' she answered automatically, slightly taken aback by the question. 'His name is Liam. He and I have been together since we were at university.'

'Is he a lawyer too?'

She shook her head. 'He's a teacher. An English teacher, actually.'

'Oh, interesting! It's good to have a companion who does something completely different from oneself!' Oliver said, his eyes suddenly reflective and dreamy. 'Things never get boring that way.'

Naomi laughed. He was right. Her relationship with Liam was certainly not boring.

'I expect you're missing each other if he's living in London...' Oliver said.

'We are... of course. But—'

She stopped herself. Why had she started down this track? She really didn't want to tell Oliver Charles, or even hint to him, about the arguments she and Liam had had about her taking up this position in Paris and spending time away from him. It was disloyal to Liam and to their relationship, and besides it would be highly unprofessional to speak about it to her boss. Aside from the fact that she and Oliver hardly knew each other. She wondered why he was asking her these questions, but quickly concluded that he was lonely, of course, grieving for his wife.

'But?' Oliver's eyes were steady on her face, an enquiring look in them. The way he was looking at her made her tingle all over.

By now she'd recovered her composure but was aware that her cheeks were hot. 'Well, I was just going to say, but we speak on the phone most evenings.'

'That must be very nice,' Oliver said wistfully. 'And it's good that you're going to be able to see each other this weekend. Is that why you're going back? When Evelyn and I were apart for any reason, we were hopeless if it was more than even a few days.'

Again, this felt like an odd question, but she realised that Oliver was assuming that her situation with Liam was parallel to his own with Evelyn.

'I'm actually going back to see my mother, although I will be seeing Liam too.'

'Your mother? Does she live in London too?'

'Yes, and I've been following up some family history since I've been in Paris. I wanted to tell her about it.'

'Fascinating. Are you able to tell me what that is about? History is one of my passions. I didn't realise you had family connections in Paris.'

'I don't, but I'm almost sure that my mother was evacuated to Paris from Germany during the war.'

'Really? Go on.'

And almost before she'd realised it, she'd poured out the whole story to Oliver. He'd listened, his eyes and his whole attention focused on her face. She told him how she'd come across the photograph of the old villa in the antiques market in Montmartre, how she'd made the trip out to Montmorency one weekend, how Madeleine Clément had remembered that the villa had been an orphanage for Jewish children in the late thirties.

'That's incredible,' he said when she'd finished. 'And it's incredible too how you've managed to get to the bottom of all that alongside all the brilliant work you've been doing for us here in the office.'

'That's very kind of you to say so, but I've just been doing my job and I've had quite a bit of spare time.'

'What do you think your mother will say when you tell her what you've discovered?'

Naomi had shrugged and bitten a fingernail. She'd been wondering this herself. 'I'm not sure. I may be completely wrong about it all, of course. She might try to deny it again, I suppose.'

'Why would she do that?'

'I've no idea but it's what I want to get to the bottom of. I want her to tell me about what happened to her when she was a child. She's so tough, she puts such a brave face on everything, but I know deep inside she's carrying some painful secrets. She's getting older now and I'd really like her to tell me about it. To bring us closer really. There's only her and me in the family now, you see.'

'I think that's an admirable aim. The scars that that generation have to bear are unimaginable. And what they suffered should never be forgotten.'

Then, after another pause, he said, 'Well, I had better let you get off now. I've kept you far too long already.'

Naomi got up to leave and picked up her files and papers from the table. As she crossed the room to the door, Oliver cleared his throat and said, 'Perhaps, one day next week, if we have to work late again, would you let me treat you to dinner? I don't get out much in the evenings and it would be lovely to have some congenial company.'

'Oh...' The suggestion had caught her by surprise and once again she felt her cheeks growing hot. She had muttered something non-committal in response before bidding him a hasty good evening and leaving his room rather abruptly.

But now, as she made her way across the darkness of the tilting deck and back inside the boat, found her seat again and settled down for the uncomfortable overnight journey, she thought about his request again and the rather odd conversation they'd had. She could forgive him for being curious about her life, she decided. After all, he was lonely and isolated, grieving the loss of his closest companion. And thinking about it more, she realised, to her surprise, that the idea of spending an evening in a restaurant, chatting easily with Oliver, was rather a pleasurable one.

TEN

HELGA

Berlin, 1938

Helga would never forget the days that followed that terrible evening when she was told that Mame was never coming back.

She remembered that time for the bleak feeling that weighed her whole body down, never letting up, not even for a moment. The thought that Mame might have suffered terrible humiliation and pain as she met her death was as hard to bear as the knowledge that Helga would never again feel her mother's comforting arms round her. She would never again experience the fierce, protective love that Mame had striven to put between her twins and everything terrible that was happening around them. Helga and Ruth didn't need to talk about it; Helga knew instinctively that her sister was having exactly the same thoughts as she was. The bond between the two of them had grown even stronger, if that was possible, since Mame's death. They relied on each other from moment to moment. So close had they grown that they could anticipate each other's thoughts.

Her mind twisted with agony as she went over and over what Mame might have gone through on the night that she died. Though she tried to stop it, her imagination ran riot all of its own accord. Images of how the angry crowd, whipped up with evil, had behaved towards Professor Heinrich flashed back through her mind again and again. She had recurring visions of how the murderous mob had set upon the frail old man like a pack of wolves on the scent of a weakened elk, but she kept reminding herself that wolves killed for a reason, not because they hated and despised their prey and wanted to drive them off the face of the Earth.

Tate had soon recovered from his sickness, but he was grief-stricken, of course. The loss of Mame had robbed him of any remnants of spirit he might have had left. He would sit in his bedroom for long hours, either on the window seat, looking down onto the ruins of Leipziger Strasse, his eyes ravaged with grief, or in Mame's chair in front of her dressing table, staring into her mirror, picking up her things one after the other and examining them closely. Watching him in his pain and grief was unbearable for Helga and Ruth, helpless as they were. It was as if Tate was trying to capture Mame's essence in the hairs left in her hairbrush, in the scent in her perfume bottle, or in the remnants of powder left in her little gold compact.

He had no answers for the questions his daughters asked him again and again.

'Can't we even just see Mame? Where is she? What happened to her, Tate? Please tell us!'

Tate would just shake his head helplessly and let big tears roll down his cheeks, unchecked. They knew he had heard more details from the neighbours, but was holding back.

But one day, Herr Hollis, from downstairs, came up to the apartment, his expression grave, and spent an hour or so shut away with Tate in his room. After he'd left, Tate called the girls in to speak to them. This time he didn't cry – he seemed to be beyond tears – but they could tell from his red-rimmed eyes that he must have been crying with their neighbour.

'Herr Hollis came to tell me that he's managed to find out what happened to Mame's... Mame's body,' he began, studying the floor in front of him. Helga and Ruth exchanged agonised looks.

'He told me some bad news, girls. He said that she'd been cremated at the hospital, along with several other... several other bodies that were taken there that night—' Tate's voice caught in his throat.

'Cremated?' Helga whispered, appalled. That meant burned, she knew that much.

'So, we won't be able to say goodbye to Mame after all, then?' Ruth's quivering voice was saying what Helga was about to say.

'No, I'm so sorry, my darlings,' Tate muttered, lifting his head to look into their eyes. 'But don't forget. Mame will always be with us. Always.'

The girls were stunned into silence. When neighbours and friends and members of the Jewish community they had known had died in years gone by, there had always been a funeral at the synagogue and then everyone in the congregation would walk behind the coffin to the Jewish cemetery. But poor Mame would have no funeral, no procession and no grave; no place they could go and visit her, talk to her and bring her flowers. There was nothing left of her to grieve over. It was too hard to bear.

'Can't we just go and see where... well, where Mame was found?' Helga asked after a long pause. She could hardly get the words out, her throat so constricted with grief. Tate looked into her eyes again.

'We don't know where she was found, my little one,' he said, his voice barely more than a whisper.

'The hospital, then. Can't we just go to the hospital where they took her?'

Again, Tate shook his head. 'You cannot go out on the streets. Not yet at least. It isn't safe. But one day... One day we will go to the City Hospital, if you would like to do that. One day soon, when things have settled down.'

It felt as if an age had passed before Tate judged it safe enough to leave the building. In the meantime, in practical terms they carried on as they had before that terrible news had torn their lives apart. Their routine kept them going. They still got up early, tidied and cleaned the apartment each morning and cooked the food that Tate managed to bring home. They still went down to Frau Moshe's place to keep the old lady's spirits up and to cook lunch with her for all four of them.

Even though they had each other and in some ways that incredible bond was all they needed, they still missed going out each morning and they missed the friends they had started making at the Jewish school. Helga wondered what had happened to all the children in their class since that night they heard from Frau Moshe people had started calling Kristall-nacht. Had all those children lost people they loved too? They asked Frau Moshe, who always seemed to know what was happening in the neighbourhood. She shook her head in dismay.

'Many menfolk were taken away by the Gestapo that night, just like my poor Aaron. So, plenty of children are missing their fathers, uncles and grandfathers. And many other people are simply missing or have passed away, just like your beloved Mame. Many more Jewish families have decided to leave Berlin since that night,' she said. 'Many more have received their papers from their relatives abroad and have left Germany for good. Everyone who can will leave. I've heard that some are sending their children out of the country, even if they can't go themselves.'

'What?' Ruth sounded aghast. 'Go on their own? Without their parents?'

Frau Moshe nodded. 'Yes, my child. There are people who are helping Jewish children go to live in safety abroad. There are special trains to take them. It is for the best. When all this evil is over, the families will be united again. It is a sacrifice worth making.'

Helga was unable to speak. She was digesting this information and she could tell Ruth was too. Where were these children being sent to? Who would look after them abroad? Which country would they be taken to? Then with dawning shock she realised what this might mean for herself and Ruth. Would they have to leave Berlin too? Would Tate put them on a special train with their luggage and wave them goodbye from the station platform?

Tate had never even hinted at anything like that. Surely he wouldn't be planning something without telling them? Later, when she and Ruth were alone, they talked about what Frau Moshe had told them.

'Perhaps Tate is thinking about that too,' Helga ventured. 'Perhaps that's what he's doing when he goes out in the mornings. Perhaps he's trying to find a way to send us out of the country?'

But Ruth shook her head. 'Tate would have told us if he was thinking about sending us away,' she said firmly. 'We both know what he does when he goes out.'

They knew that each morning when Tate left the apartment, he was going along to his shop to carry on clearing it of all the mess left by the raids and to try to visit each of those of his Jewish friends and neighbours who were left in the neighbourhood. He was trying to gather together enough money and help to get the building repaired sufficiently so that he could open up again and start working. The three tailors who had worked for him in the shop had gone already. One had been taken by the Gestapo a couple of days after Kristallnacht and the others had left suddenly to join family abroad. They hadn't even had time to let Tate know, but news of their departures had made its way to him on the Jewish grapevine.

But one day, in the morning he came into the girls' room as they were waking up. Helga propped herself up on her elbows and smiled at him, but her heart sank. He was about to tell them that he was going to send them away, she was sure of it.

He sat down slowly on the end of Ruth's bed.

'Girls, I have to tell you that I'm not going to go to the shop today. In fact, I won't be going there any more,' he said. 'I'm afraid the time has come for me to give it up.'

'Oh, Tate!'

'An official from the Gauleiter's office came yesterday and served me with some papers. They informed me that the government is confiscating the building and the business. They are taking it away from me and I have no choice but to comply. They will repair the place and put a non-Jewish business in there.'

'But the shop is yours, Tate!' Helga said, outrage rising inside her at the unfairness. 'What will you do?'

'I can salvage one of the sewing machines and bring it to the apartment. I will work at home, repairing clothes, if none of our Jewish friends want new ones. It's how I started when I was a young man, after all.'

'But how can the government do that to you?'

Tate shook his head slowly. 'They can do anything they want to us, my little one. I'm afraid that they want to make things so bad for us that they drive all of us Jews out of the country. So many have left already... it seems as though they are succeeding.'

'But why do they hate us? What have we done?' It was

Ruth's voice, but Helga was about to ask the same question.

'The government has done everything it can to convince people that we Jews are to blame for everything that has ever gone wrong in Germany. For losing the war, for people being poor.'

'But that's so unfair!' Helga burst out. 'It's not true.'

'You're right, it's not true. And one day, I hope people will see that. But it has made things very difficult for us to be here right now.'

Helga stared at him, aghast, anticipating and dreading his next words. He was going to send her and Ruth away from him, she was sure of it. He opened his mouth to say something. Helga screwed up the bedsheets in her fists, praying fervently that Tate wasn't about to send them away. God must have heard her prayers, because when he did speak it was to suggest something different altogether.

'We mustn't let what is happening around us stop us having faith in God and trying to carry on as best we can. Let us walk to the City Hospital today. I know you girls need to go and see the place where your mother was taken on that terrible night. So, if you still want to go, let us walk there this morning. The time is right.'

He paused, his eyes glistening with tears.

'I should have taken you before, but I haven't been able to face it myself. Herr Hollis is going to come with us. That kind man has given me hope. There must be so many like him throughout the country. And one day, the goodness and kindness he and others like him are showing will prevail again.'

So the girls got out of bed, shivering in the cold of that winter morning, and got dressed in their warmest clothes. Tate handed them their old coats that had no yellow star sewn on the sleeve, so that they wouldn't be noticed. He gave them woollen scarves to cover their hair.

Downstairs, he knocked on Herr Hollis's door and their

neighbour appeared and greeted them warmly. They all walked together down the stairs and out onto Leipziger Strasse for the first time in weeks. Helga looked around her, blinking in the cold, stark daylight. It struck her that everything in her world had changed beyond belief since she'd last been outside in the fresh air.

'Come, we should cross Leipziger Strasse and walk through the backstreets.' Herr Hollis hurried them on. 'We don't want to attract attention here.'

They hurried across the wide shopping street, where not so long ago, peaceful crowds would have been thronging the pavements, but that morning the sounds of hammers and saws of the workmen hard at work repairing the damaged shopfronts rang out across the empty street. They slipped into a side alley and on through the quieter streets of the quarter. Tate and Herr Hollis walked either side of the girls, shepherding them along. Helga was shocked to see that even in these backstreets, buildings had been destroyed, some with their windows and doors charred, their brick walls blackened with smoke, others burned to the ground. The street seemed deserted, but Helga knew that at any moment someone could step out from a side alley and stop them, demand papers, cross-examine them.

Helga felt Ruth's hand creep into her own and she gripped it tight.

'This is the way Mame used to walk us to school,' Ruth whispered.

'I know,' Helga replied, wondering if they would pass the Jewish Girls' School where they'd made such a promising start only a few months before. But her attention was soon taken by the conversation Herr Hollis and Tate were having.

'We have talked about this before, Herr Beider,' Herr Hollis was saying. 'You must give it some consideration. I have savings. I could help you with that and my wife knows a woman who does this all the time.'

Helga wondered what he meant and that feeling of fore-boding crept back into the pit of her stomach. Could this be what she and Ruth had been dreading? Was Herr Hollis talking about sending the two of them away to another country on a train? When she turned to look at Ruth, her sister was staring at her with wide, pleading eyes. There was a visceral under-standing between them that transcended conscious thought. In Ruth's expression, Helga saw a reflection of her own fear of what might happen to them and her own longing that every-thing could just go back to normal again.

They reached the river and crossed by the footbridge. Soon they were nearing the end of another road and crossing into Auguststrasse.

'There's our school,' Ruth burst out, pointing at the tall, red-brick building.

'Hush, Ruth,' Tate said under his breath. 'Remember, anyone could be watching us.'

They passed the school and Helga kept her head down obediently, but out of the corner of her eye she saw with relief that the building had survived Kristallnacht intact, but the big wooden doors were now locked and barred. Planks of wood were nailed over them, piles of leaves and rubbish had gathered in the porch. But the relief she felt was quickly dispelled when a little further on they passed something that sent tremors of fear coursing right through her again.

It had once been a synagogue. A huge, proud building. The front doors had been ripped off and windows blown out, and, as they hurried past, through the gaping, naked openings, they caught glimpses of what had happened inside. Everything had been destroyed or burned. There was debris all over the floor, the charred remains of chairs, picture frames and panelling lay strewn about and on the blackened wall was daubed the ubiqui-tous phrase, 'Juden Raus'.

Helga paused and stared into the wrecked building,

shocked to the core.

'Move on, don't look inside, girls.' Herr Hollis laid his hand on Helga's shoulder, propelling her forward.

A couple of blocks further on, two men stepped out of a doorway a few metres in front of them and stood on the pavement, staring at them as they approached. Helga was trembling now and Ruth's palm was sweating against her own.

'Just walk normally. I will handle this,' Herr Hollis muttered as they drew closer to the two men who straddled the pavement, arms folded, barring their way. They wore the brown uniforms and caps of the SA, or brownshirts, the red band with the Nazi insignia on their armbands, their legs clad in leather gaiters, batons dangling from their belts.

'Halt!'

They were both smoking cigarettes and the smell wafted towards Helga. It made nausea rise in her throat and the bitter taste of bile flooded her mouth. For a panicked moment she thought she would faint or vomit right there on the pavement. Keeping her eyes down, she fixed on the two pairs of brown boots in front of her. She grasped Ruth's slippery hand even tighter.

'Papers,' the man barked.

Herr Hollis stepped forward and spoke in a voice full of confidence and bonhomie. 'We do not have our papers with us, sir. My sincere apologies. I am Dieter Hollis, this is my brother, Fritz. His two little girls.'

'Everyone needs papers.'

'We left in a hurry this morning, I'm afraid. But we are all good German citizens here. My brother Fritz, here, sadly his wife is very sick in the City Hospital. These are her two daughters, anxious to see their mother. Have a care, officer, please. Wave us through. We won't forget again.'

There was an agonising pause. Helga kept her eyes fixed on the grimy pavement. One of the men threw his cigarette down and ground it into the concrete with the heel of his boot. Helga swallowed hard.

'Move on then, this time,' the officer said gruffly. 'Don't forget again. You won't get a second chance.'

'Thank you, sir. That is very kind of you.'

'We have to be vigilant, Herr Hollis. We often get filthy Jews wandering along this street, coming to wail about their damaged synagogue. Now on you go please. Heil Hitler!'

The officers both raised their right arms in the aggressive salute that sent chills down Helga's spine. Herr Hollis saluted in return. Helga noticed Tate's fists clench momentarily, but he quickly followed suit. Were she and Ruth supposed to do it too? She glanced at Ruth, wondering, but she didn't move and to Helga's relief it seemed it wasn't expected. The four men dropped their arms and the SA officers nodded and carried on down the street. Helga felt the relief wash through her, but instantly the fear of meeting another member of the SA or the Gestapo cut in again. Too afraid to speak, she just carried on walking, putting one foot in front of the other, holding Ruth's hand in her own.

In a few streets they arrived on a busy junction opposite a big, grey building. Herr Hollis removed his hat.

'That is the City Hospital, girls. That is where your mother's body was taken the night she died.'

They all stood on a patch of scrubby green land, in the shelter of another tall building, staring at the square, grey hospital through the incessant flow of cars, trams and buses and occasional carts going to and fro across the junction. Tate took off his flat cap and bowed his head, his cheeks wet with tears, and muttered a few words of prayer. An ambulance, its siren blaring, edged through the lanes of traffic and entered the building through an arched entrance in the centre. Was that where Mame's body had been taken, through that entrance? How did she get here? In an ambulance, or on some sort of

horse-drawn vehicle? It was impossible to imagine. Helga lifted
her eyes and saw a tall chimney rising above the hospital, a wisp
of white smoke coming from it and dissolving into the pale-
yellow morning sky. Was that where Mame was now?
Dissolved into the clouds, all around her in the atmosphere? If
she was, could she see them standing there in a desolate little
line, missing her, mourning her?

On the way home, they moved quickly, barely speaking,
avoiding Auguststrasse and the damaged synagogue. Tate and
Herr Hollis led them through different, quieter streets, hoping
to avoid another meeting with SA officers. Helga kept her eyes
on the pavement all the way, her ears attuned for the sound of
boots in front of her, dreading hearing the words 'Halt! Heil
Hitler!'

At last they were back in their own familiar neighbourhood,
crossing Leipziger Strasse and entering their apartment building. Frau Moshe was standing in the doorway of her apartment.
Her face registered relief when she saw them – she must have
been watching out for them.

'Come inside, little ones.' She drew the girls to her and
Helga gladly surrendered to her embrace. 'Come and warm
your insides. I have brewed some tea for you.'

'Go inside with Frau Moshe,' Tate said. 'I need to go
upstairs and speak to Herr Hollis about something.'

Nerves gripped Helga's stomach and she glanced at Ruth,
but Ruth didn't look concerned, even though Helga knew that
she had heard the conversation between Tate and Herr Hollis
too. She decided not to say anything about it just then. Instead,
she followed Frau Moshe into the apartment and sat down at
the kitchen table. Frau Moshe put mugs of tea in front of both
Helga and Ruth. Helga sat silently, sipping slowly, but the tea
didn't bring her the comfort she was expecting.

She just couldn't get those words out of her mind. *My wife
knows a woman who does this all the time...*

ELEVEN

HELGA

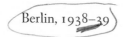
Berlin, 1938–39

Helga and Ruth would stand in the passage in the days that followed, listening through the closed door to the latest news. Tate would still mend clothes from the dining room table and customers would tell him what had happened to their friends and relatives; those who had been fortunate enough to have left Germany, those who had been taken away to concentration camps, those who had been arrested but miraculously released. The girls could see that Tate was becoming more and more withdrawn by the day. They would talk about it in anxious whispers when they lay in their beds at night.

'It's because he's worried, isn't it?' Ruth said. 'Everyone is leaving and now he has seen what is happening even Tate would like to go too. But we don't have any family abroad so he can't get the right papers. So, we are stuck here.'

'Oh, Ruthie, it's good we have each other.' Helga squeezed her sister's hand. 'I don't know what I'd do without you.'

Ruth turned and gave her a wide smile. 'But we'll never have to do without each other, will we? We've always been together and we always will be. We can count on that.'

'What do you think will happen to us?' Helga stared unblinking into the pitch-darkness of their bedroom, wondering even as she spoke why she had asked Ruth that question. She didn't even want to think about it herself.

'Tate will make sure we're all right,' Ruth replied, her voice softening. 'He always does.'

Helga wasn't going to say so to Ruth, but she wasn't as convinced as her sister that Tate would be able to make sure they were all right. Helga suspected that he was powerless, just as poor Mame had been. Was he still thinking about sending them away? Helga had never stopped agonising about it, but it hadn't been mentioned for a long time. Even so, was Tate making secret plans with Herr Hollis? If he was, he was certainly keeping them to himself.

Sometimes Helga and Ruth would sit with Tate at the table and help him with his work: pinning or tacking seams, measuring out hems, sewing on buttons. It helped to pass the long hours. By now they were tiring of reading to each other, reciting poems from school and trying to maintain any sort of study regime. Ruth was a far better seamstress than Helga, so Helga would sometimes put her work down and leave her and Tate to it. She would wander over to the window to kneel on the window seat and peer down into Leipziger Strasse.

From where she knelt, things seemed to be gradually returning to normal down in the street. Or at least many of the shops had been reopened and the place was getting busy again. But the street had changed. The shops were different now. Most had reopened with new names on the signboards. Names that were not Jewish names. It tore at her heart to see it, but as he had said would happen, Tate's shop was being renovated. An open-backed lorry was often parked up outside and Helga would watch the workmen go in and out, carrying planks of wood, tools, equipment. Over a period of a few days, the windows and doors were replaced and the BEIDER sign was broken up and taken down. Helga could hardly bear to watch as the beautiful black and gold sign that the family had been so proud of was smashed to bits with workmen's hammers, reduced to smithereens on the pavement. She couldn't bear to see the piles of black glass lying there: they represented everything that Tate and Mame had worked so hard for.

A new sign went up the next day: MULLER'S FINE LADIES' CLOTHING. It was no longer a tailor's shop but would sell off-the-peg clothes to middle-class German women. Daughters of the Third Reich.

Tate still went out a couple of times a week to get food. It was becoming more and more difficult as time went on; with so many Jewish shopkeepers having left the city, and all the restrictions on where he was permitted to shop, he had to resort to bartering for meat and vegetables and other essentials on the black market. In time, he was forced to sell pieces of Mame's jewellery just to put food on the table.

'Herr Hollis said he would help you,' Helga ventured one day when she saw the look on Tate's face as he took one of Mame's gold lockets from the box on her dressing table. Tate frowned when he realised she had been standing there in the doorway, watching him.

'What do you mean?' He slipped the gold chain into his pocket.

'I heard him say so. When we walked to the City Hospital.'

'Did you really? Ah, yes. That was for something quite different. I couldn't ask him to put his hand in his pocket for everyday expenses. We can get by with selling a few possessions and the sewing we're taking in.'

'But what was it for, Tate? Why did Herr Hollis offer to

lend you money?' Helga asked. She was dreading the answer but it had suddenly become important for her to know.

Tate shook his head. 'For something I really don't want. And I'm hoping never to have to pay for. Now, Helga my child, you don't need answers to all these questions. These are things for grown-ups to worry about. Not you. Now, off you go and find your sister and let me go out and search for something to eat for this evening's meal.'

Things were becoming very hard for Tate now, Helga could sense it. She knew it was dangerous for him to go out on the streets and each time he left the apartment to find food she was terrified that she would never see him again. To increase her fears, Frau Moshe often had fresh stories of Jewish people disappearing, of men being arrested by the Gestapo and sent to concentration camps, of others fleeing abroad as soon as their papers came.

One terrible evening, Helga's fears materialised. The harsh Berlin winter was finally on the wane and the trees in Leipziger Strasse were coming into leaf. The apartment was warmer now and there was no need to light a fire in the evenings. Helga and Ruth were waiting for Tate as usual. They began to realise that he was late returning home from his foray. He normally came back during the afternoon, but that day the clock in the kitchen ticked round to five o'clock and still he hadn't returned.

'He'll be back soon, there's no need to worry,' Ruth said, when Helga started to pace the apartment. 'He always comes back, doesn't he?'

'He's been lucky so far. Anything could have happened. He might have been arrested.'

Ruth stubbornly refused to give up hope and within half an hour came the sound of a key turning in the lock. Tate stumbled in through the front door and collapsed in the passage. Fear and pain washed through Helga at the sight of him. She glanced at

Ruth and saw her eyes were moist with tears. The girls ran to him.

'What happened?'

Tate shook his head. His face was covered in welts and bruises, his right eye bleeding. 'Some bully boys. Four of them. Hitler Youth, probably. Waiting for me on the street corner. They took the food I'd bought, they took the rest of my money.'

The girls helped him to his feet, through into his bedroom, where he lay down on the bed. They boiled water in the kitchen and ripped up rags to bathe his wounds. When he took off his shirt, there were marks on his arms and back too.

'It could have been worse,' Tate said as they cleaned his wounds. 'I'll be all right tomorrow, you'll see. But I'm sorry, tonight there will only be the leftover onions and potatoes from yesterday.'

They left him to rest and went to the kitchen to peel the vegetables for supper. But after a few minutes Tate appeared in the doorway. He was dressed in a clean shirt, but his face was covered in bruises that were swelling and blooming, reds and all shades of purple.

'I'm going down to see Herr Hollis, I won't be long.'

Helga carried on peeling her onion and listened to the door slam behind him. She was trying not to think about what Tate might be going to talk about with Herr Hollis.

She and Ruth worked on in silence. Ruth didn't once look up from the potato she was peeling. Helga wiped hot tears from her cheeks, not knowing if they were just from the onions. By the time Tate returned, the thin potato and onion soup was simmering on the stove. He sat down at the table.

'I have been making some arrangements with Herr and Frau Hollis,' he began and Helga's spirits plummeted. 'I've decided that it's not safe to keep you girls in Berlin any longer. Frau Hollis knows a lady. A kind German lady who can take you to safety in France. You can go on the train with her to Paris. There are good people there. Good, Jewish people who will take care of you. They are already looking after many Jewish children. I will come and join you as soon as I can leave Berlin, it shouldn't be too long.'

'But Tate!' Both girls threw themselves at him and he took them in his arms and held them tight.

'As you know, we don't have official papers,' he went on, his voice catching in his throat, 'but this lady can get some for you. You will just need to pretend to be her children for the journey.'

'Her children?' Helga saw Ruth's mouth drop open at his words, just as she knew her own had. A vision of Mame's face came to her, her strong, kind eyes, her warm, loving smile. How could they even think about being another woman's children? A German woman, a complete stranger too.

'I know it's difficult. It is difficult for all of us, but it's for the best. It isn't safe here any more. I should have done something months ago. I should have seen it coming, but I've been too trusting, as your dear mother always said I was. I've been hoping for something that isn't going to happen. I know now that I was wrong.'

'Don't send us away, Tate,' Helga pleaded, clinging to him. 'We want to stay here with you, whatever happens. We don't mind, as long as we're with you.'

'I am not sending you away from me, little one, I am sending you away from danger. It is all I can think of to do. I can't keep you holed up here at home for ever. And now this opportunity has come along. Herr Hollis has been kind enough to advance me the money to pay the lady.'

'When do we have to go?' Ruth asked. Her voice was deadly calm. Helga looked at her. Ruth was so much braver than she was, she always had been.

'In about a week's time. The lady needs time to get the documentation together. But let's not spend the precious time we have together crying. Let's look forward to being together somewhere else in the future. We all need to be brave right now.'

Helga dried her tears and forced herself to stop crying. If Ruth could bear this parting, she must too.

'Good girls, Mame would be proud of you.' Tate's face cleared with relief. 'Now, let us eat our soup and be grateful for the kindness of Herr Hollis and the others who are willing to help us in these terrible times.'

That evening, Helga and Ruth began to pack their little leather suitcases with as many of their clothes and belongings as they could cram inside them. Mame had bought those suitcases at the Wertheim department store when they'd last gone on holiday to the Baltic coast, several years before. She'd had their initials engraved into the leather and the girls were very proud of them. Packing brought back memories of those seaside trips: of sitting on blankets on the sand with Mame and Tate, of building sandcastles, of running in the bracing surf in their cotton bathing suits.

'Take a few pictures with you,' Tate said. He slipped a photograph of himself and Mame standing in front of the shop smiling proudly into the zip-up section of Ruth's suitcase. He put one taken of Helga and Ruth together at St Elizabeth's the term before they'd left into Helga's suitcase.

Ruth embraced the idea of going to France on the train with the German lady, as she always did new things. 'Come on, Helga, it will be an adventure. We've never been abroad before. You love going on train journeys, remember.'

But try as she might, Helga could not conjure any sense of adventure at the thought of being sent away from the only place she'd ever known and the only people in the world she'd ever loved. It felt as if they would be betraying Mame somehow, leaving the place she'd made home for them behind. But, as if reading her thoughts, Ruth tried to comfort her.

'Mame wouldn't want us to be unhappy, Helga. She would tell you to stop worrying and to make the most of it.'

Helga smiled and heard Mame's voice in her head telling her exactly that. Ruth was quite right, of course.

On the third day after Tate had first made the plans with Herr Hollis, a letter addressed to him was delivered to the apartment. It had the stamp of the Gauleiter's office along the top of the envelope. When Tate had read the letter, he'd slammed it down on the kitchen table. It was the first time, despite everything he'd been through, that the girls had seen him lose his temper. His dam had finally burst.

'What is it, Tate? What's happened?' Helga asked in alarm.

'They have sent me a bill for repairs to the shop. Many thousands of marks.'

Helga and Ruth stared at him, bemused.

'But why, Tate? What for?'

'For repairing the damage that those thugs did to the place back in November,' Tate raged. 'For doing it up for the benefit of some new owners. It's theft! It's robbery. I don't have that sort of money and, even if I did, I certainly wouldn't pay a pfennig to them. The injustice of it! They have killed my Jessica and they have ruined me. They are forcing our family apart. I will not have it. I will not!'

He got up from the table and pulled on his jacket.

'I am going out to see what I can do about this. Wait here, girls. Bolt the door and don't let anyone in.'

With that, he stormed out of the apartment. The girls followed him and locked the door behind him. They listened to his feet pounding down the staircase. He didn't stop at Herr Hollis's floor and he didn't stop at Frau Moshe's either. The front door of the building slammed shut. The girls ran to the window and knelt on the window seat just in time to see Tate emerge from the front porch of the building and head across Leipziger Strasse. Then he disappeared into a side street on the other side: he was heading towards the Jewish quarter.

All that day the girls waited for Tate to come back. They had no idea where he had gone or who he had gone to see. As usual they tried to entertain themselves with stories and games and songs, but soon they grew anxious with waiting. They didn't even go down to see Frau Moshe at lunchtime. She would be worried about them, they knew, but Tate had told them not to leave the apartment. They weren't going to break that promise.

The light was fading and Helga was kneeling at the window, watching the street with anxious eyes, when she finally saw Tate emerge from the side street and cross the road to the apartment.

'He's back,' she yelled to Ruth.

They ran to the front door and waited for Tate to reach the apartment. But they didn't hear his footsteps and they guessed he had gone to speak to Herr Hollis. When he finally knocked on the door, they ran to open it. A smile spread all over his face from ear to ear. He took the girls in his arms and held them tight.

'I have found another way! There is another way!' His voice was triumphant. 'There is a ship sailing to Cuba especially for Jews wanting to leave Germany and make a life in the United States. Herr Hollis has agreed to help and some of our kind friends in the Jewish quarter are helping too. It leaves in a couple of weeks from Hamburg docks. We are going to be on that ship, my darlings. We will all be together and we can start a new life in America, far, far away from this evil and murderous place that Germany has become.'

TWELVE

NAOMI

London, 1990

Several hours later, the boat docked noisily at Newhaven in the raw light of a cold dawn. Naomi stumbled with the other bleary-eyed foot passengers along the docks to the station platform and onto the waiting train. She found a seat in the corner of a carriage by herself and promptly went to sleep.

She must have slept for the entire ninety-minute journey because as she blinked awake, the guard was announcing that the train was about to arrive in London Victoria. Naomi stretched and yawned, gathered her belongings. The exhaustion of the long journey seemed to have seeped into every bone and muscle in her body.

She got down from the train, frowsy and crumpled from the journey, and with a shock she caught sight of Liam making his way down the platform towards her. He was wearing his old donkey jacket and jeans, his thatch of dark hair unkempt, five o'clock shadow on his chin. In his dishevelled way he was very good-looking. Her heart did a strange turn and she realised that she was actually glad to see him even after everything that had happened between them, all the difficult conversations they'd had.

He walked towards her. 'Hi!' she said. 'You didn't say you were coming to Victoria.'

'I wanted it to be a surprise.'

She felt his arms envelop her and he pulled her towards him and kissed her on the lips. Then he held her at arm's length. 'You look terrible,' he said, laughing.

'I know! It was a hell of a journey.'

'I'll carry your bag. You must be knackered. Do you want to grab a coffee before we get on the tube?'

She shook her head. 'Let's get home as quickly as we can.'

Her heart was sinking now. She hoped that Liam hadn't made plans to spend the day together. Hadn't he remembered that she'd come home to see her mother and that once she'd been to the flat and showered and changed, she would be heading off up to Primrose Hill?

As the tube train rattled towards Highbury Corner, Liam told her how he'd been spending his time over the past few weeks. He talked about some of the frustrations at work and told her some anecdotes about his pupils. He said he'd visited his father in Kilburn several times and talked about the TV programmes he'd watched. It didn't sound as though he'd been out much. She'd heard much of it already when they'd spoken on the phone, but hearing it again made her realise how lonely he must have been without her.

They emerged from the Victoria line and walked side by side from Highbury Corner to their flat in Upper Street. It felt strange coming back. As they entered the cluttered hallway, with Liam's and their downstairs neighbours' bikes blocking the threadbare stairs, she couldn't help thinking how cramped and depressing the building felt, even compared to the apartment in

Avenue Carnot. At least in Paris the road outside was fairly quiet and the view from her apartment windows was of cherry trees in blossom. Here, their windows looked straight out onto the main road, where buses and lorries thundered past day and night.

Up on the first floor, Liam opened the door to the flat and she realised instantly that he'd made a big effort for her home-coming. He'd vacuumed every room, there was no washing-up stacked in the sink and he'd even made the bed. Only a few weeks before it had been Naomi who'd kept the flat tidy. Liam's untidiness had always irritated her. He hadn't seemed to care whether he lived in squalor or not; in fact, he'd seemed oblivious to it.

'Impressed?' he asked with a grin.

'Mightily.' She strolled around her old home. Even the bath-room was shining and uncluttered. Beside their bed, on her side, was a huge bunch of red roses in a big jam jar.

'Are these for me?' She turned to him, surprised yet again.

He nodded, walked towards her and took her in his arms again. 'I've missed you so much.' He buried his face in her hair. 'I'm so sorry for how things were between us before you went.'

She pulled back – it was almost a reflex action – then imme-diately berated herself for not being able to yield to his touch. He was trying to make it up to her, she knew that, but she didn't feel quite ready to forgive him. He let her go and she sat down on the bed looking up at him, watching the disappointment cross his face.

'Thank you for the flowers, Liam. It's really lovely of you but let's just take it slowly, shall we?' she said. 'You said some pretty hurtful things before I went away.'

'I know and I'm sorry. You're right, I am trying to rush things. I've been so looking forward to seeing you this morning. Can I get you a coffee or a tea?'

'Tea would be great. I just need to jump in the shower now and then I'll head off up to Mum's. Remember?'

'Oh yes,' he said, his voice instantly cold. He turned his back on her and was already walking through to the kitchen. She heard him put on the kettle as she started to take off her travel-stained clothes.

'What's that all about?' he called from the other room. 'You said you couldn't tell me on the phone. You're not going to be long up there with your mum, are you? I thought we could go out for lunch.'

'I'm not sure how long I'm going to be, to be honest. It could take a while. Why don't we go out this evening instead?'

'Lunch would be better. I thought we could stay in this evening. Maybe get a takeaway and hire a video. Blockbuster's got some great new films in... So what *is* this secret thing with your mum?'

'It's tricky to explain.' Naomi wrapped a towel around herself. She went and stood in the kitchen doorway and watched him put teabags into the teapot.

'You know, Mum's past has always been a bit of a mystery to me.'

He turned. 'Has it? Didn't she come to this country on Kindertransport like your dad?'

'No. I'm sure I told you before. She came from America, somehow, after the war. But she started out in Berlin. I know that much.'

'Oh yes. You did mention that.'

'She was a bit funny about me going to Paris actually. I didn't think much about it at the time, but when I went to the flea market at Montmartre I found a picture of a French villa on an antiques stall. It was exactly the same picture as the one Mum has on her windowsill.'

Liam reached up and got the cups from the cupboard and set them on the side.

'So?'

'Well, I did a bit of digging...'

It suddenly felt odd telling him this momentous news when they'd spoken several times since she'd found the photo of the villa and throughout the time she'd been making her discoveries but she took a deep breath and blurted it all out in one go. When she'd finished telling him, he said what she'd realised he was going to say while she'd been relating her story.

'That's incredible, Naomi. Amazing that you found so much out about the place. But why on earth didn't you tell me about it?'

She swallowed. 'I'm not sure... I didn't feel ready to.'

She fell silent and contemplated her reasons. It was because of the distance that had grown between them since their arguments before she left, she thought. The things he had said to her then. And because, deep in her heart, she'd suspected he might not approve of her digging up the past.

The kettle boiled and she watched as Liam poured the boiling water into the china teapot and stirred it furiously with a spoon. She couldn't see his face but she could tell he was building up to something. When he turned to speak to her, the hurt in his face was plain to see.

'But why? Why couldn't you share it with *me*?'

She looked at him, guilt running through her. She didn't really know the answer to that question herself.

'It's such a big thing,' she stammered. 'And Mum has never talked about it. I can't explain why I didn't tell you at the time. But I'm telling you now, aren't I? I'm sorry.'

Liam pulled a chair out from the small kitchen table and sat down, his face in his hands.

'I just can't understand it. I know I was an idiot before you went away. I shouldn't have tried to stop you, it was really stupid of me. I just didn't want you to go away from me. I loved our life together. But now... if you couldn't even share something like that with me... I bet you told other people, didn't you? You mentioned someone at work.'

'Martine? Yes, I did tell her. I needed help with my search, that's all.'

'Anyone else?'

She hung her head so he wouldn't see her face and the colour creeping into her cheeks. How could she explain that she'd readily confided in Oliver Charles about it, when she hadn't wanted to trust Liam with the information?

'Anyone else?' he repeated. Miserably, she shook her head. She knew he wouldn't understand that she'd told her boss all about her search before she'd been prepared to tell him. He would jump to the wrong conclusion. But at the same time, she hated having to lie.

'I'm sorry,' she repeated. 'I should probably have told you before. But please don't take it like that.'

'It just makes me realise how far apart we've grown, these past few months. Ever since you started your job at that firm. Bit by bit, you've shut me out of your life.'

'That's not true, Liam,' she protested hotly. 'I can't help having to work long hours.'

He was silent, his face turned away from hers, thrumming his fingers on the table. Finally, he said, 'Let's talk about this later, shall we? Why don't you go and have your shower and get changed?'

He poured out the tea, slopping some on the table, and pushed a mug towards her.

Feeling wretched, Naomi took the tea and went into the bathroom. She coaxed the shower to its maximum strength, which was little more than a trickle.

When she'd finished and got dressed in the bedroom she went back into the kitchen. Liam had his leather jacket on. He was looking brighter now.

'I'll come with you up to Primrose Hill if you like?'

Her heart sank again. 'Oh, Liam, I'd better go on my own. It's a sensitive subject and it will be difficult enough as it is... Mum hates talking about her past. She'd prefer to bury it all.'

His face fell. 'Then why don't you just let her?'

'Because... because... I can't explain. It's important to *me* to know what happened to her when she was a child.'

'But why? That's her story, Naomi. If she wants to guard her past, surely that's up to her?'

She stared at him, resentment surging in her chest. What had it got to do with him anyway? Why would he interfere, try to stop her from doing this most important of things?

'You know,' Liam went on, 'Dad came over here from Ireland before the war. He had a terrible childhood. Abused by his father, poverty-stricken. He ran away and came to work in London on a building site. I've often wanted to find out more about his past, I don't even know which town he came from in the Republic. But he doesn't want to talk about it. It's too painful for him, even now. And I respect that.'

She felt a lump rising in her throat. How like Liam that was. And she knew it was genuine. 'But that's *your* decision,' she said, suppressing her tears. 'I'm not like you, I'm not so selfless. I want to know what happened to Mum. It's her history and it's my history too. And if I ever—'

She stopped herself quickly. Now wasn't the time to bring up what had been burning in the back of her mind for a long time, but which she'd never given voice to. If she ever had children of her own, she was going to say, she would want them to know Helga's history too. She and Liam had often talked about it in the past. It had felt safe to do so back then, it had felt so far off in the future, like a fantasy. Now, the way things were between them she didn't even want to say the words; but she knew, by the defeated look in his eyes, that he understood anyway. Slowly, deliberately, he took his jacket off and put it on the back of the chair.

'I'm sorry. It's none of my business. You go and see your mum on your own. I've got some marking to do anyway. I'll see you later on.'

By the time she'd reached Primrose Hill, Naomi had managed to put the painful exchange with Liam behind her. It had run through her mind all the way there on the bus. She'd sat in her favourite seat on the front of the top deck as the double-decker made its ponderous way through Islington, around the back of King's Cross station and on up to Camden Town. She couldn't stop going over and over how Liam had tried to stop her doing all the things she'd wanted to do recently. But why had things soured between them so? Looking back, she realised that he'd been right in a way about when things had started to go wrong. They *had* been drifting apart since she started her job in the City. From that point on, they'd started moving in different circles, spending less time together, moving away from each other. It had happened so gradually that she'd barely noticed, but in that time they had grown fathoms apart. Could those fathoms be bridged? Did she even want to try now?

She reached her mother's house and stood staring at it for a moment, trying to compose herself. Everything was so confusing at the moment. She pushed the doorbell and listened to the familiar sound of it ringing in the kitchen in the back of the house. Then silence. She pushed the bell again. Perhaps Helga was out shopping, or out for a walk with Kitty? It was possible, on a Saturday morning. Maybe they'd even gone out for lunch together. After another minute she rang again.

She was just looking for her keys, about to unlock the door herself, when the sound of footsteps came from inside the hall. Then, to her astonishment, the letter box opened.

'Is that you again, Kitty?' It was her mother's voice. Imperious, annoyed even.

'No, Mum, it's me!'

'Oh, Naomi!' Helga sounded shocked. 'What on earth are *you* doing here? Why didn't you tell me you were coming home?'

The letter box snapped shut, then came the sound of the lock on the other side. The door opened and Helga stood there in the hallway, looking a little shamefaced. Naomi stepped inside and put her arms round her mother and they hugged.

'I was just making some coffee,' Helga said, drawing away. 'Why have you come back? Everything's all right in Paris, I assume?'

Helga was peering at Naomi and she noticed with a shock that her mother looked drawn and tired, dark circles smudging the skin under her eyes. She wore no make-up and her hair was unbrushed, grey streaks and roots showing. She must have missed a couple of appointments at the hairdresser. This was so unlike Helga, normally so well turned out, such a stickler for doing things properly, looking her best.

Helga quickly turned and started to walk down the passage.

Naomi followed her through to the kitchen. 'Paris is great, Mum. But is everything all right with *you*?'

'Of course. Everything's fine.' There was that frosty tone again. 'Why shouldn't it be?'

'You look a bit... well, a bit under the weather, that's all. Not quite your usual self. Are you quite sure you're OK?'

'Absolutely.'

'So, what was all that about Kitty? Why on earth were you talking through the letter box?'

'Nothing. It was nothing,' Helga said briskly. 'Now, do you want some coffee?'

'It's OK, thanks. I had some tea at the flat.' Naomi sat down at the table. 'So, why didn't you want to talk to Kitty, Mum?'

Helga sat down opposite her and sighed. 'Well, if you must know, we had a bit of a misunderstanding, that's all.'

'Misunderstanding? But you two have always been so close. It must have been serious, Mum, if you're not speaking. What happened?'

Helga drew herself up and pursed her lips.

'I don't really want to talk about it. Now, why don't you tell me all about Paris? And why are you in London? Are you just back for the weekend?'

'I came back because I wanted to talk to *you*, Mum.'

Helga's face fell. 'Talk to me? Why? Is there something you need to tell me? What can be that serious that you couldn't tell me on the phone? You're not ill, are you? You're not—?'

'No! No, Mum, nothing like that. Look,' Naomi plunged on quickly, before her nerves could overcome her.

'This is going to be difficult to tell you and you might be a bit annoyed with me, so I'll just get on and say it. I've been doing some digging in my spare time. I looked into the history of the villa in the photograph I found. You know, the one I told you about, the day I arrived in Paris—'

She stopped. Her mouth felt dry. Her mother was staring at her now, dark eyes fixed on her face. Those eyes were full of terror. What was she so afraid of? Then Naomi herself began to falter. Should she go on? Perhaps Liam was right after all. Perhaps she should just let it rest. She swallowed hard. She couldn't just give up now. Not now she'd come this far. She took another deep breath.

'I went there, Mum. To the Villa Helvetia. I got the train out to the suburbs and I found it. I nearly missed it though. It's changed so much from the photograph. It's a police headquarters now.'

'Police headquarters?' Helga snapped, regaining some composure. She frowned. 'Look, I don't know anything about any police headquarters in a Paris suburb. How would I know anything about that? I told you before...'

But although she'd managed to get back to her imperious

manner, her eyes were still full of terror and her lips were wobbling. Naomi's own heart was beating fast. She shouldn't be surprised; she'd half expected this to happen. But how could she get past this? Her mother's reaction had made her more certain than ever that her history was bound up with that building.

'I know,' Naomi said finally, trying to keep her voice steady. 'You told me that you'd never been to Paris. But I couldn't help wondering why you have that postcard on your windowsill, Mum. *Please* tell me the truth. You see, I found out what that place used to be just before the war.'

She stopped and waited for the reaction. But Helga didn't reply; her eyes were snapping now and she blinked rapidly as if she was startled by a bright light.

'My friend at work, Martine,' Naomi went on, 'introduced me to her grandmother. She is very old now and she remembers the war. She told me that she used to visit the area before the war. Mum, she told me that the Villa Helvetia was an orphanage for Jewish children.'

Still Helga didn't respond. She just carried on staring at Naomi, frowning deeply, as if she couldn't understand what was being said, or as if what her daughter was saying was deeply troubling to her.

Spurred on by the silence, Naomi persisted. 'I just wondered if you might have known someone who'd stayed there... or even—'

'That's enough!' Helga slammed her fist down on the table, making Naomi jump. 'You can stop with your questions. I simply won't listen to this nonsense any more.'

THIRTEEN

HELGA

Berlin, 1939

In the few days that followed, Tate was in and out of the apartment several times a day. As well as his usual forage for food, he was busy arranging visas for Cuba, tickets for the boat train and for the voyage on the *St Louis* itself. Although his face was heavy with exhaustion each time he came home, he had a new spring in his step and hope in his eyes that Helga hadn't seen for a long time. Not since months before Mame was taken from them.

The day Tate finally came home with immigration papers for Cuba for all three of them, he was smiling brightly. Helga's heart soared to see him so happy and with the knowledge that they would all be leaving Berlin together.

'Come and look, girls,' he called. 'Here are our passports to freedom.' He had laid the official-looking documents out on the kitchen table.

Helga and Ruth stared at the papers in wonder.

'I got them through some of my contacts in the Jewish quarter. They were cheaper than the official channels, but these papers have been issued by the Cuban authorities, signed personally by the director general of the Cuban Immigration Office.'

Helga glanced at the certificates. Indeed, they did look official. Her own said,

Fraulein Helga Beider. Minor, Jewish Female. DOB 27 June 1927. Official landing certificate for the Republic of Cuba. To be exercised at the Port of Havana, for entry before 1 July 1939.

It was stamped with an official-looking stamp, CUBAN IMMIGRATION OFFICE, and signed with a flourish by 'Manuel Benítez Gonzales, Director-General'.

'Oh, Tate, that's wonderful!' she said, hugging him round the waist, her eyes brimming with tears.

Ruth grabbed her by the hand and Tate with her other hand and all three went through to the living room and danced a jig round the room together, eventually collapsing breathless in a heap and laughing uncontrollably. They hadn't done that for months either, not since well before Mame was taken from them.

As they lay there on the floor laughing, Helga felt a sudden tug of emotion at the thought that they would soon be leaving their home behind them, leaving Berlin, where she and Ruth had spent their whole lives and where they had last seen their mother. Despite her passing, they still felt Mame's constant presence with them in the apartment, talking to them as they prepared food, as they sat at the table and read books, practised their mathematics and handwriting. Where would she go when they left? Would she stay here in the apartment, missing them? Would they be leaving her behind for ever?

Tate stroked her hair and lifted her chin. He was looking into her eyes, smiling. 'Mame would want us to do this, little one. If you listen, she will tell you that herself. And she will come with us too. She will always be with us, every step of the way.'

'Tate is right, Helga,' Ruth said. 'Mame wants us to go. She is happy for us.'

Helga swallowed her tears and smiled back at her father and sister. Suddenly, leaving Berlin behind seemed the right thing to do. But within a few minutes, another prickle of worry had entered her mind.

'But what about Frau Moshe?' she asked in a panic. 'Can she come? If they are taking lots of Jewish people on the ship, surely there will be room for her too?'

'I have asked her, little one, but she wants to stay here, I'm afraid.'

Later, when Helga and Ruth went down to Frau Moshe's flat, the old lady greeted them warmly as usual.

'Let us make a start on today's vegetables,' she said, her face wrinkling into a smile. She wiped her hands on her apron.

'Your father brought these yesterday.' She went to her larder and came back with a string bag full of muddy kale, which she dumped on the table. 'I will fetch a bowl of water.'

Helga couldn't contain herself. 'Frau Moshe, you know we are going to go to Cuba on a ship soon, don't you?'

Frau Moshe didn't reply at first. Instead, she turned back from the sink with a bowl of water and crossed the kitchen with it, putting it down on the table. Her face was impassive.

'I know. Your father called in to tell me yesterday. That is very good news for you girls. I will miss you both, but I'm very glad that you are getting away from Germany.'

'But what about you? Don't you want to come too?' Helga asked, panic rising again. 'Tate can get you tickets.'

The old lady sat down heavily on a kitchen chair. 'I cannot go, my child.'

'But why not?'

'This place has been my home my whole life, Helga,' Frau Moshe said. 'My Aaron brought me to this apartment as a young bride. I need to wait here for him to come back. I need to look after his home for him.'

Helga and Ruth exchanged worried looks.

'But it isn't safe for Jewish people in Berlin,' Helga said. 'You are always telling us that, Frau Moshe.'

'I told you that because I want you two girls to have a chance of a better life somewhere else. For me, my life is nearly at an end. I have no fear for myself. After all, what can the Nazis do to me, an old lady? They could send me to a work camp, as they have so many of our men, but they won't get much work out of me.'

Helga's lip wobbled. She didn't know what to say. She thought of Professor Heinrich being punched and kicked by the mob, of poor Mame and of all the other innocent people killed on Kristallnacht. Frau Moshe knew all of this only too well.

'But Frau Moshe—' she began.

'Be quiet, Helga,' Ruth snapped. 'It is up to Frau Moshe. If she wants to stay behind, it is up to her.'

'Quite right, Ruthie,' said Frau Moshe with a wry smile, squeezing Ruth's hand on the table. 'I'm not afraid of Herr Hitler or his SA bully boys, or of any of them. They can do what they like to me, but I'm going to stay here and wait for my Aaron. I know that one day we will be together again.'

Finally, the morning they were due to leave arrived. Helga had hardly slept all night and, when chinks of dawn light appeared between the curtains, she ran to the window to kneel on the window seat and watch the first rays of the golden sunlight rise over Leipziger Strasse for the very last time, a lump in her throat.

They had a breakfast of their last loaf of unleavened bread and hot tea in silence in the kitchen, each nursing their private thoughts. When they had eaten, Tate said, 'Come along, girls, fetch your luggage. We need to start walking to the station.'

Tate locked the flat and they walked downstairs with their cases. Frau Moshe was already waiting for them in the lobby.

'Take good care of each other,' she said. She ruffled the girls' hair. 'Here, I've made you something for your journey.' She slipped each of them a newspaper parcel. 'Lebkuchen. A little treat.'

'Lebkuchen?' It had been months and months since either girl had tasted those cookies. How had Frau Moshe managed to get the ingredients? 'Thank you, Frau Moshe,' they chorused. Helga could hardly bear to say goodbye to their kindly old friend. Her eyes misted with tears as Tate opened the door and ushered them out of the building.

Then they were out on the pavement, holding their suitcases, and the door to the apartment block clicked shut behind them.

'Come, cross the road now, girls. We need to hurry to the station.'

They followed Tate across the road and, once on the other side of Leipziger Strasse, Helga turned to take a quick look at her old home before they slipped into the side street. That glimpse would remain forever etched on her memory. Those six blank windows in a row along the top of the old familiar building, behind which her whole life to date had unfolded.

But there was no time for sadness or reflection. They hurried through the backstreets and the walk reminded Helga of the day they'd walked with Herr Hollis to the City Hospital. Her heart was in her mouth, in case any SA officers in their brown uniforms stepped out in front of them. She had to keep reminding herself that even if they did, it would be all right. Tate had official papers and travel permits, they were allowed to be out on the street today.

They crossed the Spree River on the old familiar bridge, just as they used to when Mame was taking them to school in the Jewish quarter, then turned to walk beside the water to the central station, Hauptbahnhof. Tate walked ahead, carrying a knapsack and lugging his own suitcase along beside him, and she and Ruth followed with their own. Helga's suitcase was heavy and the leather handle slippery in her sweaty hand. Now that the sun was rising in the sky, the city was heating up in the early-summer air. As they neared the station steps, Helga noticed with dread that there were uniformed police and soldiers checking papers in front of the entrance. A slow-moving queue of people with luggage shuffled towards the desk to be stamped through.

Tate joined the back of the queue and Helga and Ruth fell in beside him. They inched forward behind another family towards the station entrance. Looking around her, Helga noticed that, like themselves, almost all the others in the queue were Jewish families. They must be bound for the boat train for Hamburg docks in order to board the *St Louis*. Just like them, these people were seizing this late opportunity to leave Berlin.

There were a few men like Tate amongst the travellers, but many were elderly and there were many mothers travelling alone with their children. Some of these were very young, clinging to their mothers' skirts, others were older children like Helga and Ruth, and there were also several teenagers. Some women were even pushing prams as well as hauling suitcases. All were dressed smartly in jackets and hats for the journey, carrying an assortment of luggage: holdalls, knapsacks, boxes tied up with string and whatever else they could carry with them.

As the family neared the front of the queue, Helga glanced

up at Tate, who now had his papers at the ready. His face was filmed with sweat again and he was shifting nervously from foot to foot. Up ahead, there were two guards flanking the officers who were checking papers. These guards had Alsatian dogs on chains, straining at their collars. They snarled and snapped at the people in the queue as they moved towards the station. As they got nearer to the front of the queue, Helga stopped looking around her and kept her head down. She could see the boots of the guards ahead – they were so shiny, they looked like mirrors.

The family in front of them was finally stamped through. They moved aside and headed towards the station entrance. Then suddenly the Beiders were at the head of the queue and the two uniformed officers were right in front of them, staring at them coldly. One officer snapped his fingers.

'Papers.'

Helga lifted her eyes timidly. The officer was tall and well-built. Under his grey cap, he had flaxen hair. It was exactly the same colour as Fraulein Ingrid's hair and his eyes were the same shade of pale blue as Helga's beloved teacher's eyes too, but this man's eyes were as cold as ice.

Tate's hands were shaking so much the papers fluttered in them. He handed them to the guard. There was a long, breathless pause as the officer stared down at the papers, frowning. He shuffled through them, checking them rigorously. Then he looked up and scrutinised Tate.

'Yacob Beider?'

'Yes, sir.' Tate bowed his head respectfully.

'And your daughters, Ruth and Helga?'

'Yes, sir.'

The officer looked at each of them long and hard, then scrutinised their papers again. Then he looked up again and fixed his cold blue eyes on Tate's face.

'You are travelling with two young daughters. But where is

your wife? The mother of your girls? Does she not travel with you?'

One of the dogs snarled and its chain rattled on the paving stones.

'My wife passed away, sir. In November.' Tate's voice was little more than a whisper.

'Speak up, man.'

Tate cleared his throat. 'My wife is dead, sir.'

There was another pause, then the officer muttered something into his colleague's ear. He stamped the papers and handed them back to Tate while the other officer picked up the telephone on the desk and spoke into the receiver.

'You may proceed to the boat train,' he said, then looked past them and snapped his fingers. 'Next!'

With quaking knees, they walked forward, past the snarling dogs and in through the station entrance. Then they were hurrying across the cavernous, echoing concourse. As they ran, Helga noticed that there were many more SA officers parading with dogs. She tried not to look at them; their presence made her stomach turn with fear.

'The boat train is at platform nine,' Tate said. 'We'll have to hurry.'

The train was full when they reached it, the engine at the front letting off steam that billowed across the platform. They walked along the platform towards the front of the train and Tate peered in through the windows, searching for a place to sit. At last, he spotted some seats in a carriage about halfway down. They clambered on board and dragged their luggage behind them. Helga and Ruth found separate places in different parts of the carriage, but Tate remained standing in the corridor.

A whistle blew and the train started off with a jerk, then settled into a slow rhythm, bumping and grinding its way out of Berlin station and on through the centre of the city. From where she sat in the middle of the carriage, Helga could only see the tops of the buildings – warehouses, offices, apartment blocks – as they slid past. She caught Ruth's eye across the overcrowded coach. Was her sister thinking the same as her? Was she wondering too if this was the last time they would ever see the city that was their home? She glanced in Tate's direction and saw that he was smiling at her through the packed bodies of others standing in the aisle.

The three-hour journey from Berlin to Hamburg docks was punctuated with some unscheduled stops in the middle of the countryside. Every station platform was lined with SA guards with dogs. Every ten minutes or so between stations the train would screech to a halt and guards would board to check passes. Once, a middle-aged man was bundled off the train and into a waiting truck. He went quietly. As Helga watched him cross the field escorted by two officers, she wondered why he wasn't making a fuss.

At last, the train trundled into Hamburg docks and shuddered to a final stop with a triumphant blast of its horn. Everyone got to their feet, gathered their luggage and got off the train in a crush. People were in joyous mode now, but the waiting SA guards forced them to walk in a column to the quayside, where they waited in line to have their papers checked once again. Helga and Ruth walked either side of Tate.

'Not long now, girls. Look up ahead,' he said. 'There's our boat, the St Louis.'

A thrill went through Helga at the sight of the smart liner, with its white paint and rows of portholes and three funnels. It was moored up amongst hulking cargo boats that were being loaded and unloaded by great mechanical cranes. The deck of the St Louis was already crowded with passengers, standing at the rails, watching others walk up the companionway that ran between the quayside and the boat.

The queue for checking papers moved forward maddeningly slowly. In front of them was a woman with a small boy who kept staring back at the girls as his mother ushered him forward. Behind them was an elderly couple struggling along with their heavy luggage. The stout old lady with her grey hair reminded Helga of Frau Moshe and she felt a pang of sadness remembering. Why couldn't Frau Moshe have come with them? Why had Dr Moshe been taken away by the Nazis? It was all so unfair.

At last, the woman and the small boy had been processed and were waved through by the officers checking papers. There were two guards again, sitting at a trestle table, just like at Berlin Hauptbahnhof. Tate handed them the papers and the guards scrutinised them for a breathless few minutes. As they waited, there came the sound of tyres on cobbles and, with alarm, Helga saw an army lorry draw up on the docks beside the ship. The officer spoke quickly to the guard beside him, then looked up at Tate.

'Yacob Beider?'

'Yes, sir.'

'We have orders for your arrest. They telegraphed us from Berlin. You owe the Gauleiter of Berlin reparations for damage to your shop in Leipziger Strasse. You have filed false declarations with the authorities.'

'That's not true, sir...' Tate began, his voice tremulous. Suddenly confusion broke out all around them. Soldiers swarmed out of the army lorry and surrounded the queue. Tate was seized by two of them and in the next second, they were dragging him away. Dogs were barking. Helga lunged towards Tate, trying to grab his jacket, but a guard pushed her aside roughly and she fell sprawling to the ground. She scrambled up straight away, screaming for her father.

'Tate! Tate!' Ruth was screaming for him too.

'Go on the ship, girls. Get on the ship!' Tate called frantically as he was dragged away. 'Let them go on the ship, please. I beg you. The officer has all their papers.'

Then he was gone, disappearing between the taller soldiers and those who closed in behind them. The last glimpse the girls had of their father was of him being pushed roughly up and over the tailgate and bundled into the lorry. Helga and Ruth clung to one another, engulfed in terror. The wind had gone from Helga's body and she felt limp, unable to move. She couldn't breathe and she couldn't speak. Where was Tate going? When would he be back? All she knew was that he'd told them to get on the boat. It was the one solid thing in this sea of confusion. She knew they had to do that.

The guard who'd spoken to Tate had been conferring with his colleague. Now he got to his feet, came out from behind his trestle table and addressed the queue.

'These two young girls have papers for Cuba. They cannot travel alone, they are minors. One of you must volunteer to chaperone them on the journey or they cannot board the ship.'

The old man who'd been standing behind them in the queue stepped forward. 'We will take them, sir. My wife and I will vouch for them. We will take them on board. Come, girls. Come with us.'

Helga clung to Ruth, both sobbing as they followed the couple up the gangplank and onto the ship. It was the moment they had all looked forward to for days, but now shock and panic clouded Helga's vision and all her surroundings seemed blurred and unreal. At the top of the companionway, they were jostled by crowds of other passengers and almost pushed apart, but she held on to Ruth's hand fiercely. Shoved forward by the press of bodies, they found themselves standing at the ship's rail. With her heart empty, Helga clung to the bars and watched as the gangplank was cranked up on its chains and stowed away.

Soon the ship was casting off and moving slowly away from the dock wall. With a blast of its horn it started to chug away from the quayside and to weave its way through the busy waters of the docks between the other ships moored there – cargo ships, passenger ships and great forbidding warships flying the swastika. Once clear of obstacles, the *St Louis* gathered speed and made its way towards the River Elbe and the North Sea. Helga's heart was filled with unbearable longing for Tate and Mame. She was convinced that she and Ruth were leaving them behind for ever.

The shock and the grief of that realisation blinded her eyes with tears and as the ship chugged on, down the long river and eventually out to sea, she saw her last glimpse of her homeland through a veil of tears.

FOURTEEN

NAOMI

London, 1990

When Naomi left her mother's house, her mind was fizzing with frustration. She felt thwarted too; as if she'd reached a complete dead end in her search. Despite Naomi's further gentle attempts, Helga had firmly declined to be drawn about her childhood or what had happened to her during the war. She'd still refused to admit that she knew anything about the Jewish orphanage at Villa Helvetia in Montmorency. But there had been one telling moment: at one point when Naomi had mentioned the Villa Helvetia, Helga countered by saying, 'I've never been to Montmorency.'

Naomi had stared at her. 'You said Montmorency. How did you know it was there?'

As quick as a flash, Helga said, 'Because you said so, at the beginning,' and she'd sounded so convincing that for a moment Naomi had believed it to be true; but looking back over it afterwards, she was sure she hadn't mentioned Montmorency herself.

This time there was no doubt in Naomi's mind that her mother was bluffing. But she was no further forward. How could she ever get Helga to talk about it? It felt as if she'd tried everything.

She walked away along Gloucester Avenue towards Regent's Park Road and reaching the end of her mother's terrace, she glanced back at the tall house. To her surprise, there was Helga standing at her bedroom window. She must have gone upstairs to watch Naomi walk away. That wasn't like her. Was she regretting the fact that she hadn't been more forthcoming? That there seemed to be a widening gulf opening up between them, when once they'd been so close? Suddenly, Naomi felt very lonely. First the tense words with Liam and then the difficult and fruitless conversation with her mother. It felt as though the relationships that had once been the most important ones to her were falling apart.

On an impulse, she turned back and waved with both arms, walking backwards for a few paces. There was a brief pause, then Helga held a hand up in response. A lump rose in Naomi's throat. She turned away again and carried on walking, head down, thinking back over the stilted conversation they'd had, sitting in Helga's kitchen.

She shuddered, thinking of Helga thumping on the table to put an end to her questions. Naomi had been shocked into silence and seeing her mother's obvious distress had provoked a twinge of guilt in her heart.

'Do you mean to say,' Helga had gone on, her voice shaking, 'that you came all the way back to London on that hideous overnight boat train just to ask me these ridiculous questions?'

Naomi nodded, unable to meet her mother's gaze, staring at a knot in the pinewood table.

'I knew that it wouldn't be easy to talk about, Mum, so I wanted to be with you when I told you what I'd found out.'

'And what exactly *have* you found out?' Helga's voice was fierce now. 'Nothing that concerns me! What a waste of time and expense, Naomi. You could have told me about all this on the phone. I can tell you now, you've taken yourself on a wild goose chase. I have nothing to tell you about that place. Nothing at all.'

Naomi opened her mouth to say she didn't believe her, but looking up and seeing the anger in her mother's eyes, the flush on her cheeks, she quickly decided there was nothing to be gained by persisting with the subject of the villa at that point. So, instead, and to try to calm things down, she'd changed the subject completely. She'd begun to talk about Paris, how she was loving being in the city, and about how much she was enjoying the work too.

'Somehow life in Paris seems a lot more leisurely than life in London,' she finished.

'It sounds as though they work you quite hard, though,' Helga observed. 'You said the other evening that you were in the office until quite late.'

'Sometimes, it's true. But it doesn't really feel like work, somehow. My boss always works late himself and it's so inspiring to work with him, Mum. I'm learning so much. I really don't mind working a few hours extra.'

Helga peered at her. 'You're looking quite well on it, I must say. Far better than a few months ago when you were working all hours in the London office. You looked as pale as a ghost then.'

Naomi recalled Liam's reaction to how exhausted she'd looked when she'd got off the boat train only a few hours previously. A shower and a change of clothes must have worked wonders.

'And how is Liam getting on?' Helga asked as if reading her thoughts. 'I take it he'll be going over to visit you before long?'

'He's well, thanks. And I expect so.' Naomi bit her thumbnail, thinking back over their brusque exchange. 'We just haven't got round to organising it yet.'

She knew her voice sounded flat and non-committal as she said those words and, normally, Helga would have picked up on that and quizzed her about it. But not today. She was different today, out of sorts and clearly thrown off course by the exchange about the villa. Naomi was relieved in a way that she was too distracted to cross-examine her about Liam.

'So, what have you been doing with yourself lately, Mum?' she asked, once again in an effort to change the subject.

'As a matter of fact, I've been going through some old photographs and putting them into albums,' Helga said, brightening a little. 'I found lots of very nice ones of you when you were small. Lots of good ones of your father too. Now I'm not so busy, I thought it was high time I got them out and organised them all.'

'Can I see them?' Naomi asked, surprised. What had brought this on? Helga had always been unsentimental about the past, at least the bits of the past she'd disclosed to her daughter – the years since she'd come to this country and met Naomi's father.

'If you like. I'm sure you've seen most of them before, but they've been gathering dust in a box upstairs for years now. The album is up in my bedroom, I'll bring it down.'

She pushed her chair back and got up stiffly from the table.

'I could come up with you, Mum, to save you doing that.'

'No,' Helga said quickly. 'Don't come up, my bedroom is a bit of a mess. There's stuff all over the floor. I'll go and fetch it, you stay here.'

She swept out of the kitchen without a backward glance. From the tone of her mother's voice, Naomi knew that she couldn't push the issue. But still, that too was strange, she reflected. Helga normally kept her bedroom immaculate and well organised. Why was it suddenly a mess? Or was she worried about Naomi seeing the photograph of the villa on the windowsill and bringing the subject up again?

Soon Helga reappeared, carrying a large, navy blue, leather-bound album.

'It's good-quality, isn't it? I got it from a little stationer's shop on Camden High Street – I wanted something special.'

She set it down on the table and turned to the first photograph. 'That's me,' she said, 'In New York. That must have been taken just after the war. I was probably about seventeen.'

'Oh, Mum! I've never seen that one before. How fascinating, how young you look!'

Naomi leaned forward to take a closer look. She was stunned by the photograph, by the skinny, white-faced girl with the sad eyes under dark brows, her face framed by unruly black hair. It was almost like looking at an image of a younger version of herself. Although she'd never been that thin, or quite that sad either. But it wasn't just the photograph itself that shocked her, she was also amazed that Helga had shared such a personal memory with her after the exchange they'd had about the Villa Helvetia.

'Were you on a trip to the city?' she asked. She knew that Helga had lived with an old couple on the outskirts of New York for several years, but other than that she knew very little about her mother's time in America.

Helga shook her head. 'No, that was when I had my first job. I went into the city every day at that time. I was working as a secretary in an insurance agents' a few blocks away from Central Park. A group of us used to go there at lunchtimes – one of my colleagues took that picture.'

'How long were you there, Mum? I mean, when did you come over to England?'

'Oh, not too long after that photo was taken. Once I'd saved enough for my sea passage, I took off.'

'But why, Mum? What was it that made you come to London?'

There was a short pause and Helga's eyes, which had become warm and lively for a minute or two, took on that wary, evasive look again.

'Oh, itchy feet, I suppose. I wanted to see the world...'

She turned the page quickly and the girl on the bench was gone.

On the next page were images that Naomi had seen before. Her parents' wedding in the synagogue in Finchley. Helga looked happier, more confident, in these and her cheeks had filled out in the intervening years. Then came the pictures of her parents' honeymoon in Bognor Regis, the two of them standing awkwardly on the quayside, sitting fully clothed on the beach, then endless pictures of herself as a little girl and growing up. She was alone in some, in others with one or other of her parents and in yet others with schoolfriends. Seeing so many images of her beloved father brought tears to her eyes; bitter-sweet tears of love and happiness, tinged with the sadness of losing him.

She'd seen most of these pictures before and although they brought back wonderful memories, it was the one of Helga in Central Park that really intrigued her. It was the only one that was new to her that day and the fact that her mother had been prepared to talk about it gave her hope that if she persisted, she might find out more. So, when they'd finished looking through the album and Helga had closed it up, she said, 'I don't suppose you have any more pictures of your time in America, do you, Mum?'

Helga shook her head. 'Not so many people had cameras back then. We weren't snapping all the time like people do now.

I didn't have much money and nor did any of the people I knew.'

Naomi took a deep breath. 'And what about from before the war? In Germany, when you were a child. Do you have any photographs that were taken then?'

Helga's smile froze and she frowned deeply. Her lips began to tremble and for a moment Naomi thought she was about to cry or become angry again. Her mother shook her head slowly, but she didn't reply.

'Might you tell me a bit about it one day, Mum?' Naomi went on in a gentle voice. 'I'd like to know what happened to you... to your family. It's important to me.'

Helga was silent, her head bowed. Then when she lifted it, she said in a bitter voice, 'Why can't you people just let the past rest?'

'I'm sorry, Mum,' Naomi said, seeing the instant distress in Helga's eyes. 'I didn't mean to upset you.'

And after that, the conversation had become even more stilted and difficult until twenty minutes or so later, when it had dwindled to nothing, Naomi had got up to leave.

But now, as she neared Regent's Park Road, she couldn't get those strange words out of her mind: 'Why can't you people just let the past rest?'

Who were *you people*? It was not just her, then? And then suddenly it became clear to her. The strange shouting through the letter box, the unexplained disagreement with Kitty. Was this what it was about too? Had Kitty also tried to ask Helga about her childhood?

She made a decision then. There was only one way to find out. Instead of turning left towards the bus stop, Naomi turned in the other direction: she began to walk purposefully along Regent's Park Road towards Kitty's flat.

FIFTEEN

HELGA

The MS St Louis, 1939

Helga stood on the deck of the *St Louis*, squeezing her sister's hand, watching from the rail as a sturdy black pilot boat guided the majestic liner between the other vessels and towards the entrance to Hamburg harbour. Her chest was heavy with emotion and her heart was aching for her father and mother and everything they were leaving behind. Gradually, through the tears and confusion, and above the excited chatter of passengers crowding around her and Ruth, pressing them against the rail, she became dimly aware of the blaring of trumpets and the thump, thump, thump of drums. A brass band was playing on the dockside as the ship set sail. She turned and smiled at Ruth, holding her gaze. They were completely on their own now. Their strong, unbreakable bond was even more important. And she knew she needed to keep her sister safe.

People had crowded on deck to watch as the boat put distance between itself and the land that had once been their home. Daylight was fading and lights were coming on in the buildings, their reflections glittering on the water as the dockside receded into darkness. The imposing clocktower and station, the warehouses and shipping offices that lined the waterfront, hung with red and black Nazi regalia, gradually faded into the distance and the advancing dusk. They sailed past barges loaded with sand and gravel, forbidding gunmetal warships bearing Nazi insignia, and lines of towering cranes at the harbour mouth. The ship gathered speed and soon they were out of the harbour and sailing down the wide River Elbe, towards the North Sea, one hundred kilometres downriver. People drifted away from the rails and the crowds on the deck gradually thinned out. Helga wondered what would happen now.

'Come on now, girls.' It was the kindly voice of the old man who had brought them on board. 'We must find our cabins. Do you have the papers your father gave you?' He put a hand on each of their shoulders.

Helga glanced at Ruth, whose face was streaked with tears and as pale with shock as she knew her own must be. Her sister was still clutching the papers and passes that Tate had thrust into her hands as he was dragged away. Slowly, with a reluctant gesture, she handed them over to the old man.

'Thank you, my dear,' he said, examining the papers under one of the deck lamps through thick glasses. 'By the way, we are Herr and Frau Weiss. We come from this city. The city of Hamburg. What are your names, girls?'

Helga told him their names, but Ruth stayed silent, her eyes cast downwards.

'You must be very shocked by what happened to your father.' Frau Weiss spoke up then, her voice kindly. She held out a leathery hand out to take Ruth's. 'It must have been a terrible shock for you both when he was taken away like that. We do understand. Our own dear son was taken by the Gestapo like that too, just a couple of months ago. But please don't give up hope. This will all come to an end one day and then your father will come and find you, you'll see.'

'And in the meantime, we will help you,' Herr Weiss said. Like his wife's, his voice was friendly and gentle, but that was of little comfort to Helga. She tried to smile, to acknowledge his kindness, but her heart was breaking and she knew her sister's was too.

'Now, come along with us,' Herr Weiss said, glancing at the papers again. 'Bring your suitcases. We will find your cabin and get you settled. Second-class deck, I see – that's a couple of decks down from here.'

Obediently, and because there was nothing else they could do, they followed the old couple – whom Helga noticed had no luggage with them – slowly down a metal stairway, inside the boat and along passages deep inside the ship, where doors to cabins opened off on either side. The second-class decks were crowded with families hauling their luggage along too, examining their tickets and searching for their accommodation. There was an air of excitement all around them; people were chattering and exclaiming, happy to be on their journey at last, away from the country where they had suffered rejection and persecution.

'Ah, here it is. Cabin number B54.' Herr Weiss stopped in front of a white-painted metal door and pushed it open. Inside the narrow cabin were three bunks: two on one side and a single, low one on the other. On the far wall were a washbasin and a chest of drawers, and high up above that a round porthole let a wide shaft of moonlight flood in. Herr Weiss switched on the light.

Helga stared miserably at the narrow single bunk and her eyes filled with tears again. How different they would feel if Tate hadn't been taken from them, if he was here to share the escape he'd worked so hard for, had sacrificed so much for. She could hardly bear to imagine where he was now. And although she screwed her eyes shut to stop the images, still they came. She had a clear picture of Tate, sitting miserably on a hard bench on the back of a lorry, his shoulders hunched. He was jolting along with a group of other Jewish men, a cold-eyed Nazi standing over them, pointing a gun at them, a sardonic smile playing on his lips.

'Get yourselves settled in here, girls. We are just up on the deck above,' Herr Weiss said. 'The steward took our luggage along, but we need to go and find our own cabin now.'

Helga stared at him silently, wondering what she and Ruth should do now. Ruth stared too.

'We will come and fetch you before suppertime,' Herr Weiss said, seeing their confusion. 'I need to speak to the captain first to make sure you can come and eat with us in the first-class dining room.'

With reassuring looks, Herr and Frau Weiss backed out of the cabin and the door clanged shut behind them. Helga and Ruth put their leather suitcases down on the floor and sat down side by side on the lower bunk.

'They've taken him to one of those camps, haven't they?' Ruth said. 'Like Doctor Moshe. Like all the others. We'll never see him again.'

Helga put an arm round her sister's shoulders and although she was terrified of exactly the same thing, she told herself she had to try to keep both their spirits up.

'We don't know that, Ruthie,' she said. 'Tate will come and find us in Cuba. He knows where we're going, after all. When he's released, he will follow us. Let's not give up hope. Let's try and think about the future, just like Frau Weiss said.'

Ruth looked at her miserably, her pale cheeks streaked with tears. 'What will happen to us, Helga? Who will look after us now? Who will protect us now Tate has gone?'

'We have each other, we can look after each other. And

people are kind. Look how kind Herr and Frau Weiss are. And this ship is full of Jews just like them and just like us. We're not alone now.'

Ruth lay down on the lower bunk and stared above her. 'I'm scared, Helga. What if there are Nazis in Cuba? What if it's just the same there? What if there are SS and brownshirts and Gestapo and Hitler Youth there too?'

Helga glanced nervously at the door. Even though she'd just said they were amongst friends, she was so used to being afraid that it was an automatic reaction. The passengers were all Jewish, but what about the crew? She thought she'd seen some hostile looks from deckhands as they'd walked through the ship a few moments before. Still, she didn't want to alarm Ruth even further.

'There won't be.' She lay down beside her sister on the bunk and felt for her hand. 'It will be safe there. That's why Tate wanted us to go there. He told us all about it, didn't he? They are welcoming Jews from Germany. Otherwise, we wouldn't have got papers to go there. And this ship wouldn't be going there full of Jewish people.'

'Perhaps,' whispered Ruth. 'But what will it be like without Tate to look after us? We've only got a few reichsmarks, that won't last long.'

Helga was silenced by that comment. She had some money in her purse but she remembered Tate saying that even if he had any money, they couldn't take much out of the country and that he would have to get a job as soon as they arrived in Cuba.

'Frau and Herr Weiss will look after us. Don't worry, Ruth,' she said, trying to stifle the thoughts.

'But they don't know us. Why would they do that?'

Helga shrugged. Once again, she had no answer to that question.

'Perhaps they'll put us in a home!' Ruth burst out. 'They're bound to do that, aren't they?'

Helga swallowed, fear prickling her skin, making goose-bumps rise on her arms. All the saliva dried out of her mouth. She hadn't thought about that but surely Ruth was right. They would be taken by the authorities and put into an orphanage as soon as they arrived in Havana. This was too much. She gripped her sister's hand and let the tears come. They both lay there sobbing together until the motion of the ship and the repetitive thrum of the engines soothed them into a restless sleep.

There was a knock on the door and Helga stirred herself to answer it. Lights were on in the passage and Frau Weiss stood there. Helga blinked. The old lady was dressed in finery – a black chiffon dress with a fur stole round her shoulders. There was a string of pearls around her neck. She looked as if she was going to a party.

'My husband has spoken to the captain and explained your circumstances. Captain Schroder was very sympathetic and said that you're welcome to dine with us in the first-class dining room.'

'We need to get up and go to supper, Ruth,' she whispered. 'Frau Weiss is here to collect us.'

She'd anticipated resistance, but Ruth got meekly out of bed.

'Have you got anything clean to change into, my dear?' Frau Weiss said. She seemed more worried about what they wore than about being late. Without saying anything, Ruth went to her suitcase on the other bunk and pulled out a mint-green cotton dress. Helga had a matching one in her own suitcase. Mame had sewn them the previous summer. Helga pictured her under the lamp in the corner of the living room, patiently sewing the elaborate smocking on each dress by hand. Ruth began to take her clothes off.

When they emerged from the cabin a few minutes later, their hair was brushed, their faces scrubbed and they were dressed in their identical green dresses, although they were a little crumpled. Frau Weiss's eyes lit up in relief: 'You look perfect, girls.' She took both of them by the hand. 'Now come, let's hurry along.'

Herr Weiss was standing patiently beside the elaborately carved double doors when they arrived outside the dining room a few decks above. A liveried steward held the door open for them and a loud hubbub of conversation engulfed them. As they entered the room, Helga gazed around her in awe. It was huge and sumptuous, like a ballroom, lit by glittering chandeliers, with huge, framed paintings and gilded mirrors decorating the walls. All the tables were set with linen tablecloths and silverware and were already occupied. It was a sight that she could never remember having seen in her life before. Every table was occupied by a Jewish family, chattering excitedly. Like the Weisses, the others were dressed in their best clothes and jewellery and relaxing with cocktails as they waited for their meals. Waiters buzzed around with silver trays of drinks and a string quartet played classical music on a little podium on the far side of the room.

The head waiter approached and bowed, his eyes flitting over the group. Helga shrank back as she met his gaze. She recognised that look. She'd seen it so many times before on the streets of Berlin from angry citizens, directed towards Mame or Tate or even herself and Ruth. A narrow-eyed mixture of loathing and disdain. But, catching Helga's eye, the man quickly smiled, then bowed towards Frau and Herr Weiss and ushered them all through the tables towards an empty one opposite where the orchestra was playing.

The waiter pulled out the chairs for each of them, they sat down and he fussed around, spreading napkins on their laps, handing them menus printed in flowing writing. Frau and Herr Weiss ordered schnapps cocktails.

Frau Weiss's eyes were shining with nervous excitement as she looked around the vast room.

'Did you ever see the like, Werner? We haven't sat down in a restaurant like this since the early thirties.'

But Herr Weiss's eyes were downcast. He spoke in a low voice. 'Did you see the way that man looked at us, Rachel?'

'I didn't notice anything. Why?'

'Hush. Don't speak so loud! He's a Nazi. Just like a lot of the crew members. I've noticed murderous looks from a number of them already.'

Nazis? Fear washed through Helga. Hadn't they left that behind? She glanced at Ruth, whose own eyes were wide with fear too.

'Oh, nonsense! You're exaggerating. The Hamburg America Line have welcomed us Jews. They put on this voyage especially for us. Why would they allow Nazis on board?'

'The captain told me as much when I went to enquire about the girls dining with us. The company doesn't have a choice. They have to have Party members on the ship, it's the law. They're here to report on us and on anyone who doesn't fall into line. And they're probably plotting against us even as they have to serve us – they're doing it through gritted teeth.'

Frau Weiss's incredulous eyes opened wider. 'Oh, Werner! Don't spoil things, please.'

'But what I say is true, Rachel,' he hissed. 'The whole world is against us, whipped up by those devils. Paying for a passage on a luxury ship to the other side of the world doesn't mean we've got away from the hatred.'

'Nonsense! Please calm down. We're leaving all that far behind us now.'

But she suddenly looked uncertain. Helga wondered if she was thinking of the son they'd left behind.

'If you don't believe me, ask the captain. He told me so himself. He was trying to warn me, I think. He's a decent man. A good German. Have you noticed that there's no Nazi regalia anywhere in this dining room?'

'Of course. That's why I can't believe what you're saying to me now.'

'It's the captain's orders. And even the Nazi Party can't overrule him on certain things to do with the running of the ship. Look over there, next to the orchestra. See behind them on the podium, that sheet draped over a statue? That's a bust of Hitler under that sheet. Can't you see? They covered that up on Captain Schroder's orders too – he told me so himself.'

'Hush! The waiter's coming back now.'

Herr and Frau Weiss straightened themselves up and smiled sheepishly as the waiter approached with a silver tray and served their drinks in crystal glasses. Helga took her water and sipped it miserably. She was very thirsty.

'Are you ready to order, sir?'

Herr and Frau Weiss looked down at their menus and Helga saw that Herr Weiss's hands had started shaking. She looked at her menu too and then saw why. Underneath the nautical anchor sign of the Hamburg America Line was a stylised swastika. She watched as Herr Weiss's face grew red with anger and found herself hoping fervently he would keep his rage in check – she didn't want to see him arrested and dragged away too. But when he finally looked up, his face was composed and smiling. Helga relaxed.

'Schnitzel for us all please, fried potatoes and black bread on the side,' he said.

'Very well, sir.' The waiter snatched up the menus. Helga was relieved that she hadn't needed to make a decision about the food. She was so hungry, but still the thought of Tate, travelling on the back of a truck, hungry and terrified, haunted her mind and she wouldn't have felt happy ordering for herself.

Even so, when the food arrived she tucked in guiltily and she noticed Ruth doing the same. It was the first proper meal they had tasted in months and it was all Helga could do to stop herself gulping it down greedily.

When the meal was over, Frau Weiss guided them back to their cabin.

'I will come and fetch you in the morning in time for break-fast. And after that, we will look round the ship. Now, get into bed, there's good girls. It's very late and you must be exhausted.'

'What will happen to us when we get to Cuba?' Ruth asked suddenly and Frau Weiss's smile instantly faded away.

'Please don't worry about that yet, my dear. We've got weeks to work that out. My husband will speak to the captain. You will be taken care of, you can be sure of that.'

'They won't put us into an orphanage, will they?'

'Oh, my dear!' Frau Weiss came inside the cabin and shut the door behind her. 'Come here.'

Awkwardly, she pulled the two girls to her and held them tight. Helga allowed herself to be drawn in and buried her face in the folds of Frau Weiss's evening dress. It smelled musty and of strange, spicy perfume. She felt the lump rising in her throat and the rush of emotion. But how she wished it was Mame or Tate, or even Frau Moshe who was hugging them tight, instead of this kindly stranger.

'I know it's very hard for you both, but Werner and I will do our best for you. So please, settle down now and get into your beds and try to get some sleep. My husband said that we will be calling at Cherbourg tomorrow morning. That's in France, you know. That will be exciting, won't it?'

Helga stared at her silently. How could anything be exciting the way she and Ruth were feeling?

Frau Weiss drew away from them and backed towards the door, putting her hand on the handle.

'Now, I'll see you in the morning. Do try to get some rest.'

After the door had closed behind her, Helga and Ruth sat down side by side on what would have been Tate's bunk.

'She doesn't know what to say to us, does she?' Ruth murmured.

'She's trying to be kind – they both are.'

They held hands and sat there in silence as the great ship sped on westwards through the darkness, rising and falling gently with the ebb and flow of the currents in the North Sea. Through the porthole they could see the twinkling stars. They could hear the rush of the waves against the hull, the low rumble of the ship's engines, the thump, thump, thump of the propellers. The sounds of other passengers enjoying themselves floated towards them on the warm night air. The strains of music from a distant ballroom, the laughter of people on deck, the chatter of the family in the next cabin, the wail of a baby from along the corridor.

'Everyone sounds so happy,' Ruth said.

Helga thought about her words for a moment. 'But they can't all be, can they?' she replied. 'I mean, not really...'

'Perhaps not,' Ruth admitted.

'They're all Jewish, after all. They're all running away from Germany.'

Helga thought of Frau Weiss, dressed in jewellery and clothes that must have been hanging in her wardrobe in moth-balls for years, trying to forget the traumas of recent years by immersing herself in the luxury on board, of the pleasure of the voyage and the hope that it might bring. After all, she'd just left Germany, where her son had been taken to a concentration camp. Despite what she said about not giving up hope, she must be thinking she might never see him again.

'Perhaps they're just trying to forget,' she said, squeezing Ruth's hand. 'Let's try to get some sleep, shall we?'

SIXTEEN

NAOMI

London, 1999

When Naomi reached the bottom of the spiral staircase and knocked on the front door, Kitty's dog barked from inside the basement flat. She was breathless from the short but fast walk from her mother's house and the tense exchange they had just had. She looked around her at the small, white-painted court-yard as she waited for Kitty to answer. Bursting with colour and immaculately kept, with honeysuckle and clematis trained up trellises on either side of the door and bright red geraniums in terracotta pots all around, it seemed to be a perfect reflection of Kitty's vibrant personality.

The door opened and the big white dog with her silky coat bounced into the courtyard, almost knocking Naomi over. Kitty followed close behind with a waft of expensive perfume. She was wearing a blue striped chef's apron over a silk blouse.

'Millie, calm down!' She grabbed the dog's collar. 'Naomi, darling! I didn't expect you – I thought you were in Paris.'

'I am... I mean,' Naomi laughed, her tension evaporating, 'I'm just home for the weekend.'

'Well, come on in. I was just tucking into a late lunch, but you must come and join me.'

'Oh, I'm sorry. If this is a bad time...'

'Of course not.' Kitty held the door open for her and she stepped inside.

'It's just... Well, I've just been to see Mum.'

'Ah.' Kitty heaved a sigh. 'I thought that must be it.'

'She seemed a bit out of sorts, to tell you the truth. And she said that you and she had had a... well, a falling-out.'

'Oh, I wouldn't say that, darling. Not a falling-out exactly...'

'Can you tell me what it was about? Mum said some odd things that didn't make much sense.'

'Come, sit down.' Kitty pulled a chair out for Naomi at the dining table in the window. The table was laid with a linen cloth and silver cutlery. A salad bowl, cold meats, a large quiche and a bottle of sparkling wine. Kitty did things in style, even when she was alone.

'I'll nip to the kitchen and get another plate and some cutlery. There's plenty of grub. I just popped round to Cullen's and got a few bits of salad. Sit down, Millie!'

The Afghan slunk behind a chair and lay down with a grunt. Naomi smiled, noticing two cats draped on the chair, a tabby lying along the back and the other, a British Blue, curled up on the cushions. Kitty bustled back and started putting slices of cold meat, quiche and salad on the plate she'd brought for Naomi. She poured her a generous glass of champagne too.

Kitty took a mouthful of her own quiche, then put her knife and fork down, dabbed her mouth with a napkin and took a glug of wine.

'So, can you tell me what's happened between you two?' Naomi asked.

Kitty seemed to be trying to avoid the subject. 'Oh, Naomi,

darling, I'm not sure it's going to help. I've tried several times to make contact with your mother since we had our little misunderstanding, but she seems dead set against speaking to me at the moment.'

'Can you tell me what the misunderstanding was about?' Naomi repeated.

Kitty toyed with her glass and, for once, she hesitated. Uncertainty crept into her eyes. 'It's difficult, darling. I don't want to breach any confidences, or to be disloyal to your mother. Now, do tuck in... and don't forget the bubbly. It's really very good.'

Naomi didn't really feel like eating, but to oblige Kitty she took a mouthful of the succulent quiche. It had crumbling pastry and was very rich, oozing with cheese and cream. It took several moments before she could speak again.

'I don't want you to say anything you'd feel uncomfortable saying about Mum, but it's such a shame that she's not talking to you. You've always been such good friends and she seems very lonely at the moment. She's not at all herself. You know, I think it's because I've been asking her about her past. She doesn't like talking about it, but I think it would help both of us if it was out in the open.'

'I agree. She clams up whenever it's mentioned. But whenever she's ready to talk to me again, I'll be right here waiting for her – I've told her as much.'

Naomi took a sip of the sparkling wine. As Kitty had said, it was very good and even as she swallowed that first mouthful, she felt it relax her tense shoulders and limbs.

'I don't suppose your "misunderstanding" had anything to do with you asking about Mum's past, did it?' she asked.

Kitty stopped chewing and took another sip of her own drink. 'Well, as a matter of fact, it did... But why do you ask that?'

'Because of something she said to me earlier, and because I

came home specifically to talk to her about it, so it's been on my mind. You see, when I was in Paris, I stumbled across an old photo – I've got it with me actually.'

Naomi took the framed photograph of the Villa Helvetia out of her bag and handed it to her. Kitty took it and frowned as she peered at it through her long eyelashes. Then she looked up at Naomi, her frown gone.

'It's the same as the one she has in her bedroom!'

Naomi nodded. 'And I couldn't resist trying to find out about the villa while I had the chance.'

'Go on...'

So, for the third time in the space of a few hours, Naomi recounted what she'd found out about the villa in the photograph. Kitty watched her as she spoke, her blue eyes widening with surprise, every so often interjecting, 'That's incredible', or 'How amazing, darling'.

'And when I told Mum what I've just told you,' Naomi finished up, 'she simply refused to admit to knowing anything about it. I'm convinced she's not telling the truth. But she seems so unhappy. So troubled. It might sound selfish, Kitty, but as I get older, and as she does too, I'm beginning to feel that I really need to know about it.'

Naomi felt Kitty's hand slide over hers on the table and fought back the tears.

'And it might help Helga to talk about it too. You're right, Naomi. It was Paris that upset her. She got very emotional one day, totally out of the blue. It was the first weekend you were there. So anyway, I asked if it would help to talk about what happened to her during the war and she completely clammed up.'

'So she *was* in Paris during the war, then? Was that what it was about?'

Kitty hesitated and dropped her gaze. 'Look, darling, I can't tell you exactly what she said. She needs to tell you herself when she's ready. Your questions are definitely affecting her.'

'So why don't we both go and talk to her, then?' Naomi asked. 'We're the two people who love her the most. If we go together, and persuade her, she might talk to us.'

Kitty shook her head. 'I don't think that would work...' She thought for a moment, then went on, 'Look, I think that this is for you and Helga to work out between you. I know it sounds tough, Naomi, and I'm more than happy to help you, but she wouldn't thank me for interfering.'

'Perhaps, but I'm not sure what I can say to persuade her that I haven't said already.'

'Maybe you should just leave it for a while. Let the dust settle. Perhaps she was taken off guard when you went round earlier?'

They ate in silence for a few minutes, the carriage clock ticking on the mantlepiece. Naomi thought over what Kitty had said and a wave of sympathy for her mother went through her. Perhaps she'd been wrong trying to force the issue like that. Especially when Helga wasn't prepared. After all, she hadn't even known Naomi was coming home.

After a time, Kitty put her knife and fork down. 'I've got some eclairs for dessert. Would you like one?'

Naomi shook her head. 'Thank you, but I couldn't eat any more. I'm really full up now and I should be getting home, I suppose.'

After she'd thanked Kitty and said goodbye, and was walking to the bus stop, Naomi's mind returned to the situation with Liam. Perhaps she should just go home, make her peace with him and invite him out to Paris the following weekend. It didn't sound such a bad idea, she had to try something. By the time she'd reached the end of the road her mind was made up: that was what she would do. She even began to walk with a spring in her step.

But when she reached the end of Gloucester Avenue, she paused and glanced down the road towards Helga's terrace. A wave of sadness washed over her at the thought of Helga there all alone in that big house, flicking through the photograph album, nursing her memories. Sudden guilt overwhelmed her at the thought that it was she who had caused her mother all that pain. Perhaps Liam was right about digging up the past after all. Perhaps she should just drop it and move on. What good could come of it anyway, when Helga herself was so adamant that her secrets should be guarded?

On an impulse she turned back the way she'd come and walked quickly along Kitty's road, past Kitty's flat, to a flower shop a few doors along. She bought a large bunch of white lilies mixed with roses and scribbled a note on the little card that accompanied them.

The woman in the flower shop said the delivery boy would take them to Gloucester Avenue as soon as he got back from his current round. Naomi paid her and retraced her steps to the bus stop.

Forty minutes later, she let herself into the flat on Upper Street. 'Liam?' she called, but the place was empty. Disappointed, she wandered through the small rooms looking for evidence of where he might be. Liam's jacket had gone and so had his knapsack. There was a note on the kitchen table, beside a pile of neatly stacked exercise books.

Dear Naomi,

Dad called. He sounded miserable and needed some shopping, so I'm going up to Kilburn to help him out. I think I will stay up there tonight after all. Probably best if you and I give each other some space for a while to work all this out. Give me a call when you're back in Paris.

I'm sorry things have turned out this way,

L

She sat at the table reading the note over and over again. It had come as a shock after she'd just spent the whole bus journey looking forward to seeing him and planning what they would do together in Paris but deep down, she wasn't surprised. She looked around her at the tiny kitchen, where they used to enjoy cooking meals together and spend long evenings eating, drinking and laughing with friends. That hadn't happened for a long time, though.

With a deep sigh, she rummaged in her bag for the timetables for the boat train. There was no point staying here on her own, she needed to return to Paris.

SEVENTEEN

HELGA

London, 1990

Helga stood at her bedroom window watching Naomi walk away from the house, towards Primrose Hill. Her heart was heavy with regret, her emotions in turmoil. In some ways, watching Naomi was like watching her younger self walking along that street; slim and light on her feet, her dark hair bouncing around her shoulders. But not in other ways. Naomi walked with the purposeful stride and confidence she'd always had, growing up in a secure, loving home with no major traumas in her life. Helga knew she'd never actually walked quite like that herself, weighed down as she'd been since such an early age with pain and regret.

Her daughter had taken her completely by surprise when she'd turned up out of the blue earlier. Helga shuddered, passing her hand over her face in embarrassment, thinking about how she'd behaved when Naomi rang the doorbell. How stupid and presumptuous she'd been, thinking that it was Kitty!

Naomi must have thought she'd taken leave of her senses. If only she hadn't shouted at her through the letter box like that. She'd given away that she and Kitty had had a disagreement and Naomi was naturally curious as to the reasons. Helga was sure that Naomi hadn't been convinced by her bluster about their 'misunderstanding'. She wasn't surprised. Her daughter was bound to wonder what had happened; Kitty and Helga had never previously exchanged a cross word. Not since they'd first met, decades before.

Helga happened to glance down at the windowsill. There was that photograph staring up at her. The one that had caused so much trouble already. The faded black and white picture of that white-painted Parisian villa with its balconies and eaves and beautiful shady gardens. What a dreadful quirk of fate that Naomi had stumbled across an identical photograph in an antiques market on her very first day in Paris! If only she hadn't started prying, digging up the past. It was incredible that in such a short space of time she'd managed to uncover the inescapable truth. The truth of what the Villa Helvetia had been before the war: an orphanage for Jewish children.

With a heavy heart, Helga turned away from the window and picking her way between the remaining family photographs, still laid out on the bedroom floor, she sank down heavily on the edge of the bed. She tried to focus her mind – she needed to think about what Naomi had told her, to digest it, to plan how to deal with it.

Her mind wandered to the encounter Naomi had described having with her colleague's grandmother. What was her name again? Madeleine somebody? Helga bristled, remembering. She must be one of those prying Parisians who used to walk along beside the fence along rue de Valmy and peer into the garden, staring at whoever was inside. If they happened to catch the eye of one of the staff or children, they would instantly look away guiltily and hurry on their way. All the townsfolk were the same. They must have known what was happening in Nazi Germany. They were clearly aware that there was a group of Jewish children living there in their midst, but did any of them ever lift a finger to help when the final reckoning came? No, they looked the other way and did nothing at all to stop it happening.

As memories threatened to overwhelm her, Helga put her face in her hands and let the tears trickle out between her fingers. She felt trapped, like a cornered animal. How would she be able to guard her secrets now? The people she loved most in the world, Naomi and Kitty, were closing in on her. Why did they want to prise open the innermost secrets of her past? Why did they need to know?

Despite herself, she missed Kitty's easy companionship, their frequent lunches and trips to the shops. Life seemed quite empty without it. Would it really be so difficult to take up her friend's repeated offer of reconciliation? The last time she'd phoned, Kitty had even reassured her that she would respect Helga's wish to remain silent. She'd promised that she would never ask again about Helga's past, if they could only go back to their old companionship. But Helga wasn't sure she could trust Kitty any more. The unspoken rules implicit in their friendship had gone for ever. The joy of being with Kitty had been that she used to take Helga out of herself, away from all her memories. She and Kitty were so different – Kitty was full of fun and the joys of life, untainted by the war and by haunting memories.

She sighed, looking down at the photographs spread out on the floor. She'd been looking through them, pausing to reflect over each memory, earlier, when the ring of the doorbell had given her a start. She'd been sorting them into date order and putting them in envelopes, ready for when she'd bought another album. The first one was full now. It had been a slow process, sifting and classifying the photographs, but she'd almost finished.

She needed to carry on, but the turmoil of the past hour had dampened her enthusiasm for the task. So, shutting the bedroom door on her memories, she went downstairs to make herself a quick lunch – tea and a cheese sandwich – which she ate alone at the kitchen table. What a shame Naomi hadn't stayed to lunch, Helga thought; but then again, she hadn't exactly been asked to. Their conversation had just fizzled to nothingness and it had become so awkward between them that Naomi had finally said a stiff goodbye and taken her leave.

Helga climbed the stairs again, went into her bedroom and stood looking down at the photographs. There were many snaps of Naomi as a child, her big smile beaming out from various different backdrops. There were also dozens of photos of Helga and her husband on numerous foreign holidays, arm in arm at the Parthenon in Athens, sitting together on a camel in the desert in Egypt, standing side by side in front of the Taj Mahal.

She leaned over and switched on the transistor radio beside her bed – she needed something to distract her while she carried on with the task. Then she got down stiffly onto the floor and knelt in front of the photos.

It was just coming up to three o'clock. The sound signals on the radio beeped the hour and the newsreader relayed the headlines. Nelson and Winnie Mandela were visiting the Netherlands, a famous opera singer had died; Norman Lamont, Margaret Thatcher's chancellor, was predicting recession. Helga listened with half an ear. She smiled fondly as she picked up a photograph of Naomi in her school uniform, standing on the front steps of the house on her first day at secondary school, and dusted it on her sleeve. Then, before she'd had a chance to write the date on the back, another headline from the radio made her drop the photo.

This week we have been reporting from Berlin, where on Wednesday, troops from the East German Border Guard began

the long task of dismantling the Berlin Wall. Later in the
programme, we'll have a special report from our Europe editor.
He will be looking back over the tumultuous events of the past
few months in that city...

She couldn't imagine what Berlin was like now and she
didn't want to see pictures of it in the newspaper or on the television either. She didn't want to be reminded of those streets,
where in her memory the swastika had flown on blood-red
banners and flags and where she and all those she'd loved had
been persecuted, killed or hounded out of their homes. Not that
it would be the same city now anyway.

The newsreader had moved on now, talking about the
impending recession, but after that the broadcast switched to
the voice of the East German editor, who was reporting from
the Berlin Wall, the rumble and crash of heavy machinery in
the background.

I'm now standing on Bernauer Strasse in the Mitte district of
Berlin, along which the Berlin Wall has run for over four
decades. Behind me, the sound you can hear is the demolition
of the Berlin Wall, that symbolic and physical barrier that has
divided this city in half, between the communist regime of the
East and the freedom of the West.

People in East Berlin have been allowed into the Western-
controlled areas of the city through the checkpoints for several
months now. In this report I will be interviewing members of
the Kramer family who had been separated for decades and
who are now reunited at last. One half of the family has
resided in one of the roads just behind the commercial and
shopping street, Leipziger Strasse, since before the two halves
of the city were separated.

Leipziger Strasse! Just the name of her old street sent chills through Helga's body. She was back there then, kneeling on the cushions of the window seat, Ruth beside her, their warm breath clouding the glass. They were staring down at the shivering cables of the trams as they rattled to and fro through the shopping district, watching the ant-like people moving in and out of the shops along the street, the great Wertheim department store, its imposing pillars garlanded with flags, its name lit up in neon lights. What was it like in that street now, after the Allied bombing raids of the 1940s, after decades of austerity under communist rule?

She couldn't listen any more, she got up and switched the radio off. Then, as if in a dream, she went to the trunk at the end of her bed, opened the lid and took out the box, where there was still one photograph she hadn't laid out with all the others on the floor. With trembling hands, she took it out of the box, as she had so many times down the decades, and stared at it for a long moment. Everything about that photograph was familiar to her: the imperfections of their skin, the way Ruth's smile tilted a little to the left, the way that stray wisps of her own hair stuck to her cheek were all etched on her mind. She traced her finger around the outline of her sister's face, feeling the texture of her hair under her fingertip, the softness of her skin, the curve of her lips.

The loud ring of the doorbell interrupted her again, making her jump out of her reverie. Who on earth could that be? Could it possibly be Naomi again? Surely not. It was a couple of hours since she'd left.

Her heart beating a little faster than usual, she hurried down the stairs. This time she wasn't going to shout through the letter box. Whoever it was, she would make sure she held on to her dignity. If it was Kitty... well, if it happened to be Kitty, she would just have to listen to what she had to say.

She crossed the passage and stood behind the door, pausing for a second, trying to dampen down the nerves that were screaming at her not to open it. After a couple of deep breaths it was clear that the nerves weren't going to go away, so she pulled back the bolts and unlocked the door.

A young man stood there, a huge bunch of white lilies mixed with roses in his arms.

'Mrs Rosen?'

She nodded and felt a broad smile cross her face as she held her arms out to receive the flowers. She buried her nose in the blooms: they smelled so good.

'Who are they from?' she asked.

'I'm not sure, I'm afraid, they didn't tell me at the shop. But... oh, here's a card.'

He handed her a small envelope with her name written on the front. She thanked him and stood in the doorway, waiting for him to retreat away down the steps, before she went back inside and closed the front door. She was still smiling. A smile that spread right through her body and warmed her heart.

She went back into the kitchen, sat down at the table and opened the little envelope. A card embossed with silver flowers dropped out. She picked it up and her heart leapt. It was Naomi's writing.

Dear Mum,

I'm so sorry I upset you. I really didn't mean to hurt you. I understand that bringing up the past is very painful for you and that I was wrong to try to look into it in Paris without your knowledge. If you don't want to talk about it, I'll respect that. I hope you'll forgive me.

I hope you don't mind but I went to chat to Kitty. I'm so worried about you. You don't seem yourself at the moment. It's your decision, I know, but please talk to her, Mum. She misses you and she loves you. She's your best friend and she only wants the best for you. We both do!

And I hope you like the flowers too. I'll be going back to
Paris tomorrow, but I'll give you a call very soon,

All my love,

Naomi

Helga read the note over and over with mixed feelings. Part of her, the proud part, was outraged and embarrassed that Naomi and Kitty had been discussing her like that. But another part of her was touched by Naomi's words and the message they conveyed. Something in that note had touched her heart to the core and even as she sat there, staring at her daughter's words, she could feel the ice in her heart slowly start to melt. Again and again, her eyes skimmed over the words, 'She only wants the best for you. We both do!' They really touched her to the core.

Blinking the tears away, she unwrapped the flowers and found a vase under the kitchen sink. She snipped away the longer stems with the kitchen scissors and arranged the stems in the vase. Then, carefully, so as not to spill the water, she carried it up to her bedroom and set it down on her dressing table.

She sat down in front of it and took a long, hard look at herself in the mirror.

'Your hair is a mess, Helga. And you've been feeling sorry for yourself. We can't have that,' she said aloud to herself, but it was Mame's voice in her ears.

She took up her hairbrush and started to tidy her hair. There was nothing she could do about the grey roots today. She would have to phone Luigi's on Monday. He would be closed for the weekend now. Then, for the first time in many days, she opened her make-up bag and began to put foundation on her face. Within ten minutes she'd applied blusher, eye make-up and lipstick, and was looking like something approaching her old self again. Feeling a little cheered by that, she went to the wardrobe and found a pair of linen trousers and a pale-blue blouse – clothes that were comfortable but suited her and made her feel good. When she'd changed into them, she stood in front of the long wardrobe mirror and examined herself. *That's much better, Helga*, Mame's voice said in her head. *You're ready to face the world again.*

She picked up her handbag and keys, threw a jacket over her shoulders and hurried down the stairs and straight out of the house, locking the front door as she left. At the bottom of the front steps she turned right and started to walk briskly along Gloucester Avenue towards Primrose Hill, just as Naomi had a couple of hours before.

EIGHTEEN

HELGA

The MS St Louis, 1939

Despite her shock and turmoil at the events of the previous day, Helga slept soundly, that first night in their cabin on the *St Louis*, rocked by the gentle rolling of the ship and soothed by the sea air wafting in through the porthole. She had curled up with Ruth on the lower bunk for comfort, as she often had throughout the terrifying months hiding in the apartment after Mame died, and they had drifted off to sleep together.

When she awoke that first morning, for a moment she wondered where she was. Then the thrum and vibration of the ship's engines, and the voices of other passengers talking in the corridor as they walked past the cabin, reminded her she was on board the liner that would take them across the Atlantic. But in the same instant she had a flashback to Tate being dragged away from the boat queue by the Nazi officers. A feeling of intense loneliness and abandonment swept through her as she remembered that incident, and that Tate wasn't with them on the voyage.

Her body and mind felt heavy with sleep and she sensed that Ruth had slept soundly too. She sat up and stretched. At that moment, Ruth stirred and opened her eyes and Helga saw her sister's expression change as she went through the same thought process that Helga herself had gone through a few seconds before. Without saying much, they both untangled their limbs and got out of bed. They dressed in their mint-green dresses once again and washed the sleep out of their eyes in the washbasin. Then, cautiously and hand in hand for safety, they ventured out of the cabin together for the first time, to visit the ladies' washrooms along the corridor. There, they both marvelled at the marble showers and the sparkling clean, flushing lavatories.

Helga wondered what to do next but, as if to solve the dilemma, there was a knock at the door.

'Are you awake, girls?' It was Frau Weiss again. 'Herr Weiss and I are going up to the dining room for breakfast now. Would you like to come with us?'

Helga glanced at Ruth, whose face was registering relief just as she knew her own was.

'Yes please, Frau Weiss,' Ruth called, and pulled the door open. This morning Frau Weiss was not wearing her evening finery, just a simple white blouse and black cotton skirt. Today she looked old and tired.

'Come on, follow me then. I hope you slept all right?'

Up in the dining room they were joined by Herr Weiss and shown to the same table they'd occupied for dinner. The scene was much as it had been the previous evening, only this time there was no orchestra playing. Instead, there was piped music coming from loudspeakers – old-fashioned, thumping German band music. It reminded Helga of walking along Leipziger Strasse with Mame and Tate, before things got so difficult for them, and listening to the sounds that drifted out of the beer halls and cafés. She swallowed, pushing away the memory.

They ate boiled eggs and bread, and drank orange juice, while Herr and Frau Weiss ate toast and drank coffee from a steaming pot. The waiters brought warm French pastries to the table too – croissants and pains au chocolat. Helga had never tasted either before. They looked and smelled delicious, but she eyed the basket and shook her head quickly. Ruth did the same and Helga instinctively knew that Ruth was thinking exactly as she was. It was one thing eating plain food – they needed to eat, she reasoned – but how could they allow themselves to tuck into luxury pastries when Tate was surely starving and suffering back in Germany?

After the meal, Frau Weiss said, 'Come, girls, let us have a look around the ship. Herr Weiss and I had a wander around after we'd said good night to you yesterday evening. It's quite magnificent and you'll love it, I'm sure.'

Helga looked at Ruth with questioning eyes, but Ruth shrugged as if to say, 'What harm could it do?'

So, they followed Herr and Frau Weiss out of the dining room, along the gilded corridors and through the public rooms of the ship, staring about them in wonder. Helga had never seen anywhere quite as magnificent or luxurious. They wandered through graciously furnished staterooms where chandeliers hung from the ceilings, tinkling gently with the movement of the ship, a huge, galleried 'social hall' where passengers were being served coffee by bustling waiters, past the gilded double doors to a cinema. They peeped into luxuriously furnished smoking rooms, ladies' rooms, cocktail bars, a gymnasium, then finally wandered outside onto a huge sports deck on top of the ship, where the funnels of the great liner loomed above them. Some of the young men and women passengers were playing deck games, laughing and joking, the wind in their hair and the morning sun in their eyes.

'It's good to see the youngsters enjoying themselves, Werner,' Frau Weiss remarked. 'They have been through so much these past years at home.'

Herr Weiss mumbled his agreement, then motioned them towards the rails.

'Come here, girls,' he said, leaning over and pointing out to sea, 'if you look out on this side, you can just about see the French coast. We are approaching Cherbourg. We are putting in here to take on some more passengers.'

They went over to the rail to stand next to Herr Weiss and both shaded their eyes. Helga could just make out the shape of the land; a long, grey strip shrouded in morning mist, but second by second, that strip was getting closer and more distinct.

'How do you know all this, Werner?' Frau Weiss asked.

'I got talking to one of the stewards while you were fetching the girls,' he said.

'Why were you speaking to a steward?' Frau Weiss asked in a low voice, frowning and glancing around her. 'You said last night that they weren't to be trusted.'

'Hush, Rachel. Not all of them are Party members. Some are loyal to the captain and are sympathetic to us Jewish passengers.'

'But how you do you know that?'

'I have my ear to the ground. The steward I spoke to more or less told me as much.'

'Oh dear,' said Frau Weiss miserably, 'I thought we'd be getting away from all that...'

'I'm afraid not. The Third Reich won't let us go as easily as that, Rachel.'

The old couple fell into an unhappy silence. Helga was confused. Surely they were leaving because they weren't wanted in Germany? So why didn't the Nazis just let them go in peace? Why were they still watching them and making things difficult for them? Would they still be watching them even in Cuba? She glanced at Ruth, who looked at her and shook her head, mystified too; but neither of them dared speak up or ask any questions. Helga bit her lip, her stomach tightening with anxiety. Who would protect them against these campaigns of hatred in that far-off land, if Mame and Tate were no longer there to stand up for them?

But the French coast was becoming more distinct and they could soon see the green fields and sandy beaches and then the town of Cherbourg with its walled harbour, where fishing boats and small craft bobbed about on the water, and cars and lorries moved along the waterfront. A little black pilot boat came speeding out to meet the ship and Helga and Ruth watched with other passengers at the rail as a uniformed sailor climbed a ladder on the side of the ship and disappeared inside the bridge.

'That's the pilot. He's come to guide the ship into the harbour,' Herr Weiss explained.

The ship moved forward towards the harbour and the crew weighed anchor just outside. Then a flotilla of small boats loaded with boxes and sacks came out from the quayside and the cargo was loaded onto the lower decks by the crew.

'They're taking on more supplies for the long voyage,' Herr Weiss said.

After that, more boats arrived and passengers began to board the lower decks by a gangplank lowered on chains. Helga craned over the side to see them. Men, women and children were coming on board, hauling their luggage, just as they had done at Hamburg.

'The steward told me that many of these people are refugees from the Spanish Civil War,' Herr Weiss explained. 'You know, they are actually *fighting* the fascists there.'

'Hush, Werner,' Frau Weiss said. 'Please don't let anyone hear you. We don't want any trouble.'

After the passengers from Cherbourg had boarded, had

their papers checked by officers of the crew and disappeared below deck with their luggage, the little boats peeled away from the side of the ship and sped back to the quay, while the gangways were stowed by the crew and the engines of the *St Louis* began to rumble once again and the deck to tremble under their feet.

The ship was moving out to sea again and the four of them stood at the rail, watching as the French coast gradually faded from view.

'We won't be putting in anywhere else until we reach Cuba,' Herr Weiss said, and nerves swirled around in Helga's stomach. What would happen to her and Ruth when they did reach Cuba? She could hardly bear to think about it.

Passengers who had been watching the new arrivals board from the rail drifted away and Herr and Frau Weiss also left the girls and went inside to their cabin.

Helga and Ruth stayed out on deck. It was good to feel the bracing sea air in their faces, to watch the seabirds circling in the blue sky and lean on the rail at the stern and watch the huge white furrow left by the great ship in the calm blue waters. Soon, there was no land to be seen anywhere. Just blue, blue ocean, stretching as far as the eye could see, melting into the blue sky at the horizon.

'Did you hear what Herr Weiss said? The next time we see land, it will be Cuba,' Ruth remarked, shading her eyes and staring westwards.

Helga felt a fresh tingle of nerves at the thought. It was like being cast out into the unknown.

'How long will it take, do you think?' she asked, and Ruth shrugged. Neither of them had any real idea. Tate had talked about days, weeks at sea, but they hadn't really taken much notice. They had just been looking forward to leaving Germany behind them and travelling to a far-off, exotic land, starting a new life with him. If he was with them on the journey, what did it matter how long it took?

'Look over there!' Ruth had turned away from the rail and was pointing at some activity that was taking place on the deck near the bow of the ship. Uniformed crewmen were erecting a huge, framed structure that took up a large portion of the foredeck.

'That's the swimming pool!' Helga said. 'Let's go and look.'

Several other youngsters were flocking around the crew now, amongst them many young children, who ran about the deck, shouting and jumping in excitement. Helga and Ruth hung back shyly.

The huge, rectangular frame was soon in place and then the crewmen rolled out the pale-blue rubberised lining of the swimming pool and secured it to the frame. One of them unreeled a giant hose and began to fill the pool with water. The children watched in wonder.

'Do you think *we* could swim in there?' Ruth asked. Helga knew exactly what she was thinking. Should they be swimming and enjoying themselves amongst these riotous children when Tate was suffering?

'We don't have our swimming costumes,' she said.

'Of course,' Ruth replied in a flat voice and Helga saw the look of disappointment cross her face.

'Our old ones wouldn't have fitted us anyway,' Helga murmured, thinking how much taller they had both grown since they'd gone on that last family holiday to the Baltic coast. But although they were taller now, they were also much thinner.

'Do you remember swimming in the sea?' Ruth asked. She must be thinking exactly the same thoughts. 'And how Tate would carry us on his back and drop us in the water? And how Mame used to stand at the edge of the waves shouting at him to be careful?'

'She didn't want to come in because she'd never learned how to swim, poor Mame!'

Helga laughed, remembering the fun they'd had that summer, and Ruth laughed too. Then they stopped themselves and Helga saw the tears in Ruth's eyes at exactly the same moment that she felt them prickle her own.

'Come on, shall we go to the back and watch the seagulls again?' she asked, suddenly wanting to get away from all the raucous children. They must be too young to understand what was happening or be on the ship with their families, so what went on in the outside world didn't matter. It must feel like an exciting adventure to them.

Over the next couple of days, while the boat crossed the choppy waters of the Bay of Biscay, it was impossible to use the swimming pool and a tarpaulin was rolled over the top to stop daredevil children from trying. Many people retired to their cabins, seasick, and the dining hall was half-empty. But Helga and Ruth and Herr and Frau Weiss did not succumb to sickness and soldiered on. They would eat their meals, then take a turn around the deck, if the doors weren't barred due to bad weather. Then they would retire to their cabins until the next meal.

Helga and Ruth would sit on the lower bunks and either read the couple of books they'd slipped into their suitcases or talk. Most of their conversations were about the past. Both girls wanted to fix in their minds the good times, when Tate's business was thriving, they were enjoying life living in the apartment in the bustling centre of Berlin, they were happy at St Elizabeth's school and Mame was a constant, joyful influence in their daily lives. They didn't talk about the future at all, it was just too daunting to contemplate.

Helga found these days of limbo on the Bay of Biscay, while the ship rolled and pitched frighteningly, monotonous but

strangely soothing in a way. It was good to have nothing to do
and no decisions to make, and to have time to reflect on their
situation. But on the third day the sun broke through the clouds,
the ship moved on into calmer waters and passengers emerged
from their cabins and hurried out on deck, anxious for fresh air
and sunshine after the rough seas of the past days.

The crew rolled back the swimming pool cover and once
again excited children flocked to it. Just as before, Helga and
Ruth stood there watching, hanging back from the crowd, afraid
to be part of so much exuberance. But the pull of the swimming
pool was too much for them to resist for long, despite the deep
sadness that consumed them both.

So, the morning after the weather changed, after breakfast
the two of them ventured shyly out onto the upper deck. They
stood hand in hand and watched in awe as mothers and their
young children and older girls and boys splashed about in the
water, enjoying the sparkling morning sunshine. A tall, slender
girl, a little older than themselves, came up and stood beside
them. She was wearing a red and white striped swimsuit and a
white rubber swimming hat pulled down over her forehead. She
was carrying a red and yellow beach ball.

'I've been watching you two,' she said. 'My name is Eleanor,
by the way. Why don't you come in the water?'

When they explained that they had no swimming costumes
with them she said, 'We can lend you some! My little sister has
a spare set of bathers and so do I. Come on down to our cabin
and I'll find them for you.'

Ruth and Helga exchanged uncertain looks.

'Come on! You're staying on B Deck, aren't you? I've seen
you in the corridor. We're just a few doors along from you, near
the washrooms.'

The older girl was so forceful and confident that they automatically followed her down the metal steps and along the
endless corridors back to B Deck. She reminded Helga of some

of the more assertive senior girls at school. Eleanor didn't seem to mind that she was barefoot, was just wearing a bathing costume and that her pale skin was covered in beads of water.

While they were walking, she kept glancing back over her shoulder and asking them a stream of questions.

'I saw what happened in the queue for the boat in Hamburg, by the way. That was your father, wasn't it, who they took away?'

'Yes,' Helga mumbled miserably.

'Why did they take him? Do you know?'

Helga hung her head.

'Not really.' Ruth supplied this answer.

'They took our papa too,' Eleanor said, pausing on a metal staircase, her voice suddenly serious. 'He was a lawyer. He didn't come home from work one day and we found out the Gestapo had arrested him in his office. We've never seen him since.'

Helga stared at her, hardly able to believe that this attractive, outgoing girl, who at first had appeared not to have a care in the world, must have suffered just as they were suffering.

'It was over a year ago now,' Eleanor continued. 'Mother managed to find out that he'd been taken to Sachsenhausen concentration camp. We hoped and prayed for him to come back. Mame wrote letters to everyone she knew, but it was no use.'

She turned away then and carried on down the stairs in silence. At the bottom, she opened a door to let them through into the next passage.

'How come you're leaving Germany?' Ruth asked.

'Mame has relatives in America. They arranged everything for us. Mame says that one day, when Papa is released, he'll be able to join us in New York.'

'New York?' asked Helga, surprised. 'So, you're not going to Cuba?'

Eleanor shook her head. 'We're stopping off there, but we have visas for the United States. Most people on this ship are trying to get to the States eventually. Didn't you know that?'

Helga and Ruth stared at each other, alarmed, but they didn't want to admit their ignorance.

They had reached B Deck now and there was a short commotion as a group of people came out of the door and the girls had to stand aside to let them through. No, they most certainly did not know that. Had Tate known that? Had getting to the United States been his ultimate plan? He'd never told them so and none of the papers he'd shoved in their direction when he'd been arrested had mentioned the USA. Or at least Helga didn't think they did. As they followed Eleanor along the passage, past their own cabin to a door a few metres on from theirs, Helga resolved to check the papers when they got back to the cabin. That all-too-familiar feeling of confusion and abandonment swept over her yet again.

'Here we are,' Eleanor announced. 'You'd better stay out here. Mother and my little sister Sara are sick, so they don't want any visitors. I'll get the bathing suits.'

With that, she disappeared inside the cabin. She emerged two minutes later, triumphantly holding up two swimming costumes, one pink and the other bright yellow.

'They both belong to my sister. She doesn't need them at the moment and she's more your size than I am.'

'What's wrong with your mother and sister?' Helga asked.

'Mother is still seasick, even though things have calmed down now, but Sara has a bad cough. She's not allowed to go out on deck or she might get a chill. Now, you'd better go inside your cabin and put those costumes on. Hurry up though, I'm getting cold, hanging about down here. And bring towels.'

Once Helga and Ruth had wriggled into the unfamiliar bathing costumes, they slipped cardigans on over them, picked up their towels and went with Eleanor back along the passages, up the flights of steps and out onto the deck. Soon they were lowering themselves into the cool waters of the giant pool, trying to avoid the boisterous splashes of the younger children and bumping into the grown-ups who were swimming to and fro, face-down in the water so they couldn't see where they were going. It felt so good, almost like freedom, Helga thought as she and her sister splashed about. And most of all, to see Ruth grinning and laughing brought joy to her heart, a feeling she'd long forgotten.

'Thanks so much for this,' she said to Eleanor as they took a breather at the side of the pool.

'You're more than welcome,' Eleanor said. 'It's good to have fun.'

Yes, it was good to have fun. Helga felt buoyed by the notion and promised herself she would try harder.

Later that afternoon, when they went down to the cabin to change, Helga got her suitcase and took out the papers that Herr Weiss had given back to them after they'd first boarded the ship. She spread them out on the floor and she and Ruth knelt down and scrutinised each one. The papers were just as she remembered: official landing certificates for the Republic of Cuba, stamped by the Cuban Immigration office and signed by Manuel Benítez Gonzales. There were also tickets for the passage on the *St Louis*, the Hamburg America Line, from Hamburg to Havana, Cuba.

'Tate never said anything about America,' Ruth said, staring down at the papers, searching in vain for any clue to their intended final destination.

'No. He didn't.'

'He just kept saying that he would be able to get a job in Cuba and we would be safe there,' Helga remembered. 'So that's probably where he meant us to stay.'

NINETEEN

HELGA

The MS St Louis, 1939

That afternoon was the first of many that Helga and Ruth spent in the pool on the upper deck with Eleanor. She took them under her wing, and they were glad of someone older to take charge of them and tell them what to do. They didn't mind that she was bossy; in fact, it made things easier for them. Helga sensed that Eleanor was missing ordering her younger sister about and that she and Ruth were substitutes. But it didn't matter. They were just glad to have someone to look out for them who seemed to care about them.

Gradually, as the great ship sped further across the Atlantic, putting more distance between itself and Europe, the atmosphere on board grew more relaxed. Those people who'd shuffled up the gangplank in Hamburg, cowed through years of persecution, who'd found it difficult to smile and relax at the start of the voyage, seemed to be soothed by the sea air, by the gentle motion of the ship, by the good food and luxurious conditions on board and the attentiveness of the stewards. Most of the crew, despite what Herr Weiss had said about some of them being Nazi Party members that first evening, were hardworking and kind to the passengers.

Helga noticed that Frau and Herr Weiss seemed altered by the voyage too. They would spend their afternoons out on the top deck reclining in deckchairs, reading, or watching the youngsters play in the pool. They too seemed less suspicious and insular than when they'd first come on board. But Helga couldn't help worrying about what Eleanor had said.

Most people on this ship are trying to get to the States eventually.

Was that where Herr and Frau Weiss were headed? Did this mean they weren't going to be there to look after her and Ruth in Cuba after all?

One evening at dinner, Helga decided to pluck up her courage and ask this question. She was terrified of what the answer might be, but she and Ruth needed to know.

She waited until the first course had been served and the waiter had bustled away. Then she took a deep breath.

'Herr Weiss, do you and Frau Weiss have visas for the United States?' she asked in a loud, clear voice. The old couple stared at her, their expressions frozen. Herr Weiss put his knife and fork down on his plate and dabbed his mouth with his napkin. Helga noticed that his hands were shaking.

'As a matter of fact, we do, my dear. We managed to get them in Hamburg before we sailed.'

'So, is that where you're going, then, Herr Weiss? Not Cuba at all?' Helga persisted, her lips trembling.

'We're not quite sure what will happen, to tell you the truth, Helga, my dear,' he replied. 'Nothing can be certain in these difficult times.'

'But you said you would look after us,' she said, and

although she was trying to be brave, she could feel her eyes pricking with tears.

'What are we going to do in Cuba if you aren't going to be there?' Ruth chipped in.

Frau Weiss was twisting her napkin, looking at her husband with anxious eyes.

'I'm so sorry, girls,' Herr Weiss began. 'There seems to have been a misunderstanding. I'm afraid we didn't say we would look after you in Cuba, we simply said we would escort you on board the ship in Hamburg, because of the sad and unfortunate circumstances you found yourselves in.'

'But you said... you said...' Ruth stammered. Like Helga, she was clearly racking her brains to remember exactly what they *had* told them when they first came on board. Everything had happened so quickly, it was hard to remember. Then it came back to Helga in a rush.

'You said that our father would come to find us and that until then you would look after us.'

'Oh dear. I'm so sorry for any confusion, Helga, my dear,' Frau Weiss said. 'But Herr Weiss and I have always planned to go to America. My sister is there, you see. In Chicago. She sent us money and helped us get visas after our dear Joachim was taken away by the Gestapo. We must have assumed you had US visas too. We really didn't mean to mislead you, not for one second.'

'Look, when we get to Havana, we will do everything we can to help you,' Herr Weiss said. 'We won't be going straight to Chicago, we will have to wait for our passage in Havana. We could be there some time. It will all be all right, you'll see.'

But Helga wasn't so sure. After dinner that night, instead of going back to their cabin she and Ruth went out on deck and stood at the rail under the stars in the warm evening breeze. There were others out on deck taking the evening air. Couples walking about arm in arm, groups of men smoking and talking amongst themselves.

They stared down into the blackness of the ocean and listened to the rush of the ship through the waves and the rhythmic pounding of the engines propelling them relentlessly westward.

'This ship is going so fast,' Ruth said. 'It won't be long before we've reached Cuba. And then what will we do?'

'I don't know,' was all Helga could say. She had no idea and was desperately thinking of some words of comfort for her sister. 'We'll have each other though, won't we?' was all she could think of.

'Why don't we ask the captain?' Ruth said.

'Ask the captain? What would he know about it?'

'I don't know. But he's in charge... He seems a kind man, that's all. He might be able to help us somehow.'

Helga thought about this. She knew that Herr Weiss had been to see Captain Schroder on the first evening, to ask if she and Ruth could eat their meals in the first-class dining room, and that he had agreed instantly. And Ruth was right: he did have kind eyes. He was a well-built man with an imposing moustache, who clearly commanded the respect of the crew and staff on board. When he made his way across the dining room to take his place at the top table at mealtimes, he nodded and smiled at the passengers. Which was surprising, if she thought about it. They were all Jewish and he was not. And, according to Herr Weiss, he was brave enough to stand up to the Nazi Party members in the crew and was keeping them in check.

'Perhaps,' she said tentatively. 'It's a good idea, Ruthie, but maybe we could do that when we get nearer to Cuba. In the meantime we can try to work out what to do. I'm sure we're going to be all right.'

But whenever she thought about approaching the captain to ask him to help them, Helga's tummy went weak with nerves.

He looked so important and so busy. How would he react to two young girls, travelling alone, coming to speak to him to ask for his help?

So, for the time being they did nothing about it and allowed themselves to be caught up in the shipboard routines. Three meals a day with Herr and Frau Weiss at the same table in the first-class dining room and afternoons with Eleanor and the other children out on deck or swimming in the pool. Sometimes, when they tired of the pool, they would wander round the ship as they had on the first day; they would peep inside the bars and function rooms and watch the other passengers relaxing and chatting together. Helga and Ruth were both aware that this would all come to an end all too soon, but until it did, they had little choice but to surrender to the rhythms of the journey.

On the first Saturday morning, Frau Weiss knocked on their door as they were in their cabin getting ready for breakfast.

'I've come a little early this morning because I wanted to let you know that after breakfast, Herr Weiss and I will be going along to a Jewish service. I just wondered if you wanted to come to pray with us?'

'To pray?'

'Yes, dear. Captain Schroder has arranged for Jewish prayers to be held in the social hall. It will be a little like going to the synagogue at home.'

'But we haven't... we haven't been to a service for a really long time,' Helga faltered, thinking of the burned-out synagogues they'd passed in Berlin after Kristallnacht, the blood-red writing proclaiming 'Juden Raus'. An involuntary shiver went through her.

'Of course not. None of us have been able to worship as we wanted to. But we can on this ship. You might want to come along and say a prayer for your father?'

'Yes,' Helga said immediately, and Ruth nodded too.

So, after breakfast, they went with the old couple through the ship to the vast social hall on A Deck. The ship's corridors were crowded with passengers flocking to the service, clearly the first opportunity most of them had had to openly worship for months, even years.

The huge hall was packed with worshippers. The men wore skullcaps and prayer shawls, the women their best outfits. The gallery above the hall was lined with crew members and, as she glanced up, Helga noticed the waiter who'd served them on their first evening. She saw a look of derision in his eyes and quickly looked away. It took her back to the streets of Berlin in the months before they had to leave, where looks of hatred were the currency of daily life. She'd been a little reluctant to come along when Frau Weiss had first suggested it, but now, after seeing that man's look, she became determined to pray for Tate.

A rabbi was standing at the front of the hall. He began saying prayers in Hebrew. Helga listened to his voice intoning the sacred words. When she closed her eyes, she was back in the synagogue of her childhood, with Tate and Mame sitting either side of herself and Ruth. The memory was almost too much to bear and once again sadness overwhelmed her and tears started spilling from her eyes and running down her cheeks. She bent her head and said silent prayers for Tate, asking God to watch over him, to make sure he was safe and to bring him back to them as soon as he could.

Much of the long journey passed in a blur for Helga. One day melted into the next, as the ship ploughed on towards the Caribbean Sea and the weather grew steadily warmer.

Each day was punctuated by the same comforting routines and the two girls went through them automatically like sleep-walkers. They knew that the end was in sight and were dreading what would happen when it did come, but they were powerless to stop it. One afternoon towards the end of the voyage, Eleanor's sister, Sara, was well enough to join them on deck. Unlike her older sister, Sara was a shy, quiet girl and, although she had recovered from the worst of her chest infection, she was still plagued by a cough that racked her chest. She didn't seem bothered by the fact that her older sister had collected two new, younger friends while she was ill; in fact, she accepted the situation without comment.

'Would you like your costumes back?' Helga asked tentatively, feeling a pang of guilt that she and Ruth had been using the young girl's clothes while she was in her sickbed, but Sara shook her head.

'Mame says I mustn't go in the water,' she said. 'Not until my cough has gone.'

So she sat in a deckchair at the side of the pool, wrapped up in a winter coat, despite the sunshine and the warm breeze, watching the others enjoying themselves without a trace of envy. She was obviously used to being the sick one, sitting on the sidelines while others played. Helga felt a twinge of pity for this pale, thin slip of a girl. Sara reminded her of how she and Ruth had looked only a few weeks ago. Comparing Ruth to Sara now, though, Helga could see how the sea air and sunshine and plentiful food had put flesh on her sister's bony frame and colour in her cheeks, and she knew that it had done the same for her too.

Every time they caught sight of Captain Schroder either in the dining room or going about his business elsewhere on the ship, Ruth would nudge Helga and whisper, 'Why don't we ask him now?' But Helga would always shrink from approaching him. There was no possibility of speaking to him in the dining room. He was always either making purposefully for his table, or stopping to exchange pleasantries with one of the passengers. It was so exposed there, so public. And on the other, less frequent occasions that they saw him on deck or in one of the public rooms, they were both too shy to speak to him.

'Let's wait and ask him when we get to Cuba, Ruth,' Helga suggested one day, when they'd spotted him going into the bridge and yet again just couldn't bring themselves to approach him. So even though they knew that they were just putting it off, they agreed to leave it until they were in port.

At last, ten days after they'd boarded the ship in Hamburg, land came in sight, appearing as a slight thickening of the far horizon. It was dusk by then and the tantalising sight was soon cloaked in darkness. The engines changed their tone and the ship slowed down. Someone said that the land they could see was the Bahamas.

The excitement on board was palpable. There was to be a last-night ball in the social hall that evening for the grown-ups and Frau Weiss had been getting excited about it for days. She dressed in the black dress she'd worn for dinner on the first evening and came to say good night to Helga and Ruth in their cabin.

'We'll be landing in Havana first thing tomorrow morning,' she said.

Helga's heart sank, knowing that soon it would become clear what was going to happen to her and Ruth.

'Please don't worry, girls,' Frau Weiss said, seeing their expressions of doubt. 'Werner and I will make sure you're all right. You'll see... Now, please stay in your cabin tonight and get some rest. I'll see you tomorrow morning at breakfast. Now, I mustn't be late for the ball!'

She was clasping her hands together, her cheeks bright with rouge and excitement, and despite their fears for the next day Helga and Ruth couldn't help getting caught up in Frau Weiss's mood. They had plans of their own for the evening.

After Frau Weiss had bustled off, Helga and Ruth got dressed again and let themselves out of their cabin. Eleanor was already waiting impatiently in the corridor for them, as they'd planned earlier on when they'd been swimming. She held up a finger to hush them.

'Where's Sara?' Ruth asked.

'She can't come, she's feeling ill again.'

They crept through the back corridors of the ship to the passage that ran behind the gallery of the social hall. To their delight, the door to the gallery was unlocked and they crept inside and stood in the shadows out of the glare of the lights. Below, in the main hall, under the light of the glittering chandeliers, couples, dressed in their finery, were already spinning around to the music of the small orchestra. The sound of the waltz they were playing filled the air. To Helga, standing there in the gallery between Eleanor and Ruth, it looked like a scene from a fairy tale.

'It's wonderful,' Helga breathed, smiling at Ruth. 'It's just like Berlin.' It reminded her of Leipziger Strasse again, when they used to watch couples circling the dance halls opposite from their front windows.

They stayed there and watched for several dances, caught up in the romance and excitement of the evening. Herr and Frau Weiss spun round beneath them at one point and Helga and Ruth smiled at each other at the sight of the kindly old pair who'd gone out of their way to help them. They were obviously enjoying themselves and Helga was surprised to see that they danced beautifully together.

But the spell was broken when the door behind them opened and a harsh voice said, 'Oi, what are you kids doing here?'

They wheeled round guiltily. One of the stewards was standing in the doorway, his face red with anger. 'Get straight back to your cabins or you'll regret it, I can tell you.' He held the door open and motioned them through. As they ran past him into the corridor, Helga heard him say under his breath, 'Filthy little Jews.'

The shock of hearing it hit her like a physical blow. She hoped that Ruth and Eleanor, who were slightly ahead, hadn't heard it, but it brought the fear and pain of those last months in Berlin back to her with full force. She realised that what Herr Weiss had said about Nazi Party members amongst the crew must be true.

She barely slept that night, knowing that it was the last night on board the *St Louis* and wondering what the morning would bring. She and Ruth had agreed that after breakfast they would go along to the captain's office and ask for his help. They had packed their little suitcases and their mint-green dresses were laid out on Tate's bunk, ready for the morning. Ruth slept soundly beside her. Helga wondered how she could sleep with all the uncertainty the morning would bring hanging over them. But then, Ruth hadn't heard the steward say those terrible words. The words that had shaken Helga to the core.

She must have drifted off to sleep eventually, because she woke to the sound of the ship's siren blowing.

'What's that?' Ruth sat up, her eyes wide with alarm.

'I think I heard someone say they would sound the siren when Havana came into view.'

'Let's go out and see!'

They dressed quickly and left their cabin. Other passengers were up and about too and they followed the excited throng outside.

Passengers were crowded on deck to watch the land they'd pinned their hopes and dreams on for many months come closer. The weather was balmy, even in the dawn, and the sea was already deep blue and the island they'd long imagined as a haven of peace and beauty lived up to their expectations as it rose out of the mist in the shimmering heat of the sunrise.

'It looks like a fairy-tale island,' Ruth said, her eyes dreamy.

The two girls stood at the rail watching as the ship drew closer. A large, tropical, green land emerged from the mist; they could see the glimmer of a lighthouse on a cliff as they approached and, as they got closer to the port, the gleaming white buildings that lined the waterfront and the spire of a cathedral behind them.

A small boat came out from the harbour to meet the *St Louis*, just like at Cherbourg, and when it reached the ship a dark, uniformed man climbed on board and disappeared into the bridge.

Soon after that, the ship's engines slowed even further and there was a commotion as the crew weighed the anchors. A murmur went through the crowd. 'What are they doing?' 'Why are we stopping here?'

'Maybe we have to go to shore on little boats?' Ruth suggested. 'Perhaps that's why we've stopped.'

Through the restless crowd, Helga spotted Herr and Frau Weiss. They both looked tired and a little bewildered. Helga and Ruth pushed their way through the people towards them.

'Do you know what's happening?' Helga asked Herr Weiss and he shook his head.

'I spoke to one of the officers, but he had no idea. He said they are going to serve breakfast, so people can eat before they go ashore. That's why we've come to find you. Come on down. Then afterwards we can collect our luggage and disembark.'

They went down and ate breakfast in the almost-deserted dining room. When they were finally alone, Ruth said, 'We need to go and see the captain now, Helga. Herr and Frau Weiss won't be able to help us, will they? They don't seem to know anything about Havana, and they might get on another ship to America straight away.'

Helga reluctantly agreed and they hurried along to the captain's office. They knew exactly where it was – they'd watched him go in and out enough times when they'd been too afraid to approach him. When they neared the room, they noticed that the door stood ajar and hesitated, wondering what to do. Nervously, Helga put her hand on the handle to push it open. Upon hearing voices inside, she froze. The captain was speaking to someone and the words she heard sent chills right through her.

'I am trying to think of a way of delivering the news to the passengers that won't cause a riot but there's no easy way to tell them that the Cuban president has withdrawn the landing permits from all those passengers who don't have a visa for the States.'

'So, what will they do, sir? What will the shipping line do?'

'At the moment I've no idea but it makes my blood boil that these poor people have come halfway across the world to get away from a murderous regime only to be turned away. Those permits were issued by the Cuban authorities and the passengers paid good money for them.'

'Shall I close the door, Captain...?'

Helga and Ruth looked at each other, wide-eyed. They heard footsteps cross the room towards the door and before it slammed shut they turned on their heels and ran down the passage towards the staircase to their cabin.

TWENTY

NAOMI

Paris, 1990

It was well after midnight when Naomi let herself into the apartment building on Avenue Carnot. She tried her best to be quiet, but crossing the hallway, her heart sank as lights flicked on in the concierge's residence. Before Naomi could reach the bottom of the staircase, the apartment door clicked open and the concierge put her head out. She was dressed in a mauve dressing gown and slippers, her grey hair in curlers, covered by a hairnet. She looked around, blinking in the harsh light.

Naomi was exhausted after her journey back from London. She was in no mood to talk to the old woman, who was always keen to find out what she was up to and to tell her snippets of information about other residents of the apartments, none of whom Naomi had ever met properly. Naomi realised that coming back from London late on Saturday night when she'd foolishly mentioned that she wouldn't be back until the same time on Sunday would give the old woman a lot of material for gossip.

'Bonsoir, madame,' Naomi said, passing quickly.

'Everything OK, mademoiselle?'

'Yes. Everything's fine, thank you.'

She hurried past and went quickly up the stairs to the apartment. The place was stuffy after being shut up for two nights. She threw open the windows and leaned out, listening to the night-time sounds of the city: the horns of vehicles on the Champs-Élysées, the wail of police sirens from distant suburbs, the hubbub of people in a pavement café along the avenue. How different it was here from London and the cramped flat on Upper Street with buses and lorries rattling the windows as they rumbled past.

Exhausted, she brushed her teeth, crawled into bed and closed her eyes.

Eventually drowsiness overcame her and she slept heavily for hours. When she finally awoke, late on Sunday morning, it felt cooler than the night before. It was raining and the rain was blowing in through the open windows, soaking the clothes that she'd left on the chair beside the window. With the change in the weather, her mood this morning was even more bleak. She wondered if it was even worth getting up, she felt so low. But eventually, hunger and the need for a shot of caffeine drove her out of bed. She showered, dressed in some fresh clothes from the wardrobe and went out to a nearby boulangerie for croissants. She brought them back to the flat to eat – she didn't want to sit alone in a café today, feeling as she did. So she brewed a coffee in the kitchenette and sat at the coffee table, out of the reach of the rain, to have her breakfast. When she'd finished, washed up and tidied the flat, sorted out her washing to take to the launderette the next day, the rest of the empty day stretched out before her. She wondered how to fill the hours alone.

She thought of Martine and remembered how the older

woman had told her to phone at the weekends if she was ever at a loose end. She found the number Martine had given her on a scrap of paper in her bag and dialled. The phone rang for a long time. She was about to give up and replace the receiver when, to her surprise, Martine's grandmother answered.

'Oh, Naomi, how wonderful to hear from you. No, I'm afraid Martine isn't here today. She's actually gone into work.'

'Oh!' That was a surprise. Martine virtually never worked at the weekends.

'And how are you, Naomi? I so enjoyed our talk when you came round to visit.'

'I'm very well, thank you.'

'Did you manage to speak to your mother about Mont-morency? Martine told me you'd gone home for the weekend and I guessed you might mention what you'd found out about the orphanage to her.'

'I tried, Madame Clément, but she really didn't want to talk about it. The fact that I'd been looking into it really upset her, I'm afraid.'

'Oh, my dear, I am so sorry to hear that. But perhaps your mother just wants to forget about it. Some terrible things happened during the war. Lots of people simply don't want to remember.'

'I know.'

'It's hard, I'm sure, when you'd like so much to find out about it, but sometimes we just have to let the past rest.'

'You're right, Madame Clément. And I've already decided not to bring it up with her again.'

'Probably for the best. Now, why don't you try calling Martine at the office? She won't be back until late this after-noon, she said.'

'Yes... perhaps I'll do that.'

When she'd put the phone down, she thought for a moment. Why had Martine gone into work? She was normally very protective of her free time. Perhaps someone had called her in to help out on something urgent? Guilt crept through Naomi as it dawned on her that perhaps Oliver had called Martine in to work on Naomi's own case. Maybe there had been a development that couldn't wait until Monday.

Curious, she called the office number and Martine answered.

'Naomi! Is that you? Are you calling from London?'

'No, I'm in Paris. I came back early.'

'Really? Everything's OK, is it?'

'Yes... well, sort of, I suppose. But why are you at work?'

'Oh, Oliver needed some help with something that came up on Friday evening on the case. He had meetings with the clients yesterday. Some new documents have come to light. He needed some help analysing them and putting arguments together.'

'That sounds intriguing. Do you want me to come in and lend a hand?'

'I can manage, but if you *want* to come, there's still quite a bit to get through.'

'I don't have anything else to do today... I'd be glad of the distraction, actually.'

'Well, all right, that's very kind of you, but only if you're sure.'

Five minutes later Naomi was on her way, hurrying through the rain up Avenue Carnot, dashing across all the main roads that intersected around the Arc de Triomphe, then walking briskly along Avenue Kléber towards the office. She'd brought her umbrella and, although it was raining, the air felt warm and Paris was sparkling and as beautiful as ever. Gradually the rain began to ease off and, before she got to the end of Avenue Kléber, the sun had come out and steam was rising from the pavements. She put her umbrella away and turned her face to the sunlight. It felt good to be back here and she was looking forward to getting to the office, catching up with what had happened on the case and seeing her friend.

Martine was poring over papers in her smoke-filled office and looked up from her work when Naomi walked in. She smiled broadly and came out from behind her desk to kiss Naomi on both cheeks.

'Bonjour. So lovely to see you and so unexpected too! What happened at home? You are all right, aren't you?' Martine examined Naomi's face anxiously.

Naomi sat down in the chair opposite Martine's desk. 'I'm OK, thanks.'

'But something must have happened,' Martine persisted, 'for you to come back a day early. Did you broach the subject of the orphanage with your mother?'

Naomi told Martine what she'd told Madame Clément less than an hour before.

'Oh, I'm so sorry, Naomi. All that digging... You must feel so deflated.'

'I do a bit.'

'Perhaps she'll come round if you give her time, though?'

Naomi shook her head. 'I don't think she will. In fact, it made me realise how painful even thinking about the past is for her. It seems cruel, now, to persist with it.'

Martine pulled a face in commiseration. 'But at least you got to see your boyfriend?'

'That didn't go so well, either. That's why I'm back. Oh, Martine, I've made such a mess of everything.'

'Of course you haven't. You mustn't think like that. Life is complicated and sometimes it's hard to find your way through. It doesn't mean you've messed up.'

Naomi smiled. 'You're very kind, but at the moment it feels as though I have...'

She paused and thought about Martine's words, then her

eyes wandered to the pile of papers on Martine's desk and she remembered why she was there.

'Look, don't you want some help with the work?'

'OK, if you really don't mind helping out. Let me explain what's needed.'

Naomi listened carefully while Martine explained the latest development in the case and showed her the documents that the clients had found in one of their archives right at the eleventh hour.

'These could make all the difference to our case. Oliver is really excited about it. He said he thought our evidence was not robust enough and we were having to be very inventive with legal arguments before these documents came to light.'

'Is Oliver here too?'

'Of course! You know *him*. He wouldn't expect others to come in to work and not put in the hours himself.'

Naomi smiled, thinking about Oliver's work ethic, his commitment to the case. Then she remembered with a rush how he'd asked her to dinner only last week and how it had been a little awkward between them when she'd left that evening. She'd been so wrapped up in worrying about her mother and about Liam for the past twenty-four hours that she'd put Oliver and the conversation they'd had that evening right to the back of her mind. But now, involuntary thrills ran right through her at the thought that he was in the office, of seeing him again.

She took the papers Martine had given her and crossed the hallway to her own office. She sat down at her desk and was soon absorbed in the new documents. Her mind immediately began running over the possible legal arguments they presented. She was so engrossed that she hardly noticed the passing of time. She had no idea how long she'd been reading when she was startled by a knock at the door. Oliver put his head round it.

'Hello, stranger!' he said, smiling broadly, 'Martine told me you were here. I'm so glad you came in, I couldn't wait to tell you the latest developments.'

Naomi looked up from the papers and smiled back. 'Martine gave me the background. I'm now working through some of the later documents for her.'

'Why don't we talk over a late lunch? Some of the restaurants are closed, it being Sunday, but I know a really nice one in one of the backstreets that's always open. How about it? Martine is ready for a break too.'

'All right,' Naomi replied, feeling a confused mixture of emotions. She still felt a little awkward after Oliver's dinner invitation, not quite knowing what to make of it. Despite that, she was genuinely pleased to see him and glad to be spending time with him and with Martine. It was a real contrast to the hurt and turmoil she'd been experiencing after her time in London.

At lunch, in a tiny, intimate bistro in a low, cellar-like room off a side street, they ate ragout and drank red wine and Oliver explained some more details about the new evidence that had turned up.

'The pressure's really on now. We need to get depositions filed at the court next week, so these papers have come very late in the day, but they contain so much useful evidence, they really are a lucky break for the client.'

'Indeed,' Martine said. 'And it's really great that Naomi's been here to help us today.'

Oliver smiled warmly. 'It is. Thank you so much for coming in, Naomi. It's very generous of you and I'm so pleased you did. It will really speed things up with three of us working on it.'

There was no time to talk about anything other than the work. Naomi was glad that Martine was there, partly because she enjoyed her vivacious company but also because it meant that there was no question of any awkwardness between herself and Oliver. When they walked back to the office, Naomi felt a glow of warmth from the food and wine and being with like-minded people. She realised how glad she was that she'd come back to Paris early.

They worked until six o'clock, then Martine came through to Naomi's office and said she needed to go home to check on her grandmother.

Naomi stirred and looked up from her work. 'Gosh, is that the time already? I suppose I'd better be getting back too. I need to sort myself out for the morning.'

'Of course. You should get home and get some rest. I'll see you tomorrow, then,' Martine said, waving as she left.

Naomi was just packing up her things and getting ready to leave when Oliver appeared in her doorway.

'Ah, I see you're going. I was about to leave myself,' he said. 'I couldn't interest you in that dinner now, could I?'

Naomi felt her cheeks growing warm and busied herself with putting the documents away in the filing cabinet.

'That's a nice idea, Oliver, but I'm not at all hungry, I'm afraid. The lunch was pretty huge.'

When she found the courage to look up at him, she saw disappointment on his face. 'How about a quick drink then?' he asked.

'All right,' she said quickly. She didn't really want the evening to end and to go home alone to an empty flat. How wonderful, to spend it with Oliver.

They walked side by side to one of the bar-brasseries on the Trocadéro.

'How did your visit to London go?' Oliver asked, when they were seated at a table and had ordered Kir Royales from the busy waiter.

'Oh, it was a bit of a disaster actually,' she said, finally dropping her guard as she realised that she was glad of an opportunity to talk to someone.

'Oh, really? What happened?' His eyes were full of concern.

So she told him all about the conversation with Helga and about how strangely her mother had been acting.

'I'm really worried about her,' she said when she'd finished. 'She's even fallen out with her best friend. They've never had a cross word before. Kitty – her best friend, that is – told me that me coming to work in Paris had stirred up everything for Mum. That it all traced back to the war, some-how. But Mum wouldn't say much to Kitty, either. She's so sad and so lonely at the moment. I'm really not sure what to do.'

Oliver took a sip of his drink. 'It must be very hard for you both...' Then, after a pause, he said, 'And you still think she was at the orphanage in Montmorency when she was a child?'

Naomi nodded. 'I know that she originally came from Berlin. I had thought she was evacuated to the United States, but now I think she must have been in Paris at some point, judging from her reaction and the fact she keeps a photograph of the Villa Helvetia on her bedroom windowsill. It obviously means something to her.'

'Berlin, you say?' Oliver looked at her sharply.

'Yes. Didn't I tell you that last week?'

'I don't think so. I think you just said she came from Germany.'

He shook his head as if in disbelief and stared down into his glass.

'Is something the matter?' Naomi asked.

Oliver took another, longer sip of his drink. 'I've done a lot of research myself into Jews from Berlin, as a matter of fact.'

'Oh, really? I didn't realise you were Jewish, Oliver.'

'I'm not, but Evelyn was. You see, her whole family had lived in Germany before the war. They were all from Berlin. Generations of Heinrichs and Rosenthals. Both sets of grandparents were native Berliners and her mother and father were both born there, only half a mile apart.'

'That's an incredible coincidence,' Naomi said, sipping her drink.

He went on turning his glass around absently, looking into the swirling liquid.

'It is, but, since there were one hundred and sixty thousand Jews living in Berlin in the early thirties, it's not *that* much of one, really. The two families were friends. Her father's father was a professor of economics. Very eminent he was too, Professor Heinrich. But he lost his job when the Nazis passed a law that only Aryans could teach at universities.'

'That's terrible,' Naomi murmured, thinking about Helga. Had it been like that for her too? She'd never said what her father had done for a living, although Naomi's own father had once mentioned that he thought Helga's father had been a tailor. 'I read about the Aryanisation programme once,' she added.

'It was criminal, actually,' Oliver said vehemently. 'An act of hatred. Both Evelyn's parents were talented musicians and both were sent by their own parents to stay with relatives and attend music school in London. This was some time in the mid-thirties. They were sent away to escape the Nazi regime. They were both in their late teens at the time.'

'What happened to your wife's grandparents?'

'Nobody really knew for a long time. Her parents never heard from any of them again. After both her parents had passed away, though, Evelyn became more and more curious about what had happened to her grandparents. It became really important to her. Especially when she got ill and realised she had only a short time to live herself. We did a lot of research in the months leading up to her death. What we discovered was truly sobering.'

'What did you find out?'

'We never really found out what happened to her father's father, but the others were all taken to Auschwitz eventually and perished there during the war.'

'How terrible,' Naomi said, seeing the tragedy on his face. The memory of the research was clearly also bringing back memories of Evelyn's last days.

'So, you see,' he said earnestly, looking into her eyes, 'I understand exactly what you're going through with your mother. I can see why you're so eager to find out her story.'

'Well, I was,' Naomi said, twisting her own glass by the stem. 'Until yesterday. But now I'm trying to stop thinking like that. I've realised that if she wants to let the past rest, I need to respect her wishes.'

'That's very compassionate of you, Naomi. Very understanding. But it must be difficult.'

'It is a bit,' she said wistfully, then drained her glass.

'Would you like another drink?' he asked.

'I'm not sure. I should be getting home really.' She stifled a yawn.

'Of course. I'm sorry for keeping you. It was really good of you to come in today, especially after your long journey.' He signalled to the waiter to bring the bill.

'I was happy to,' she said, meaning it.

The waiter hurried over with the bill and there was a pause in the conversation as Oliver paid.

'Please, let me contribute,' Naomi said, getting her purse out, but Oliver shook his head.

'Another time, perhaps.'

'Definitely,' she said.

They walked out into the warm evening.

'Let me find you a taxi,' Oliver said, 'It's very late now. I don't want you walking home on your own.'

'Oh, it seems perfectly safe on the metro. And it's not far at the other end.'

'It might look safe, but there's no point taking chances,' he said. 'There are some very odd types about in Paris at this time of night.'

They walked down towards the Trocadéro, where there was a taxi rank. Oliver spoke to the driver of the first car in fluent French and the man nodded. Oliver opened the door for Naomi.

'Well, good night. It's been a great day for the case and thank you so much for coming for a drink with me, too. It's been wonderful to talk.'

She returned his smile, which reached right to his eyes. She was pleased to see him smiling again. When he'd been telling her about Evelyn's parents, she'd been dismayed to see him slip back into that look she'd seen before at the office: bewildered and alone.

'Good night then. See you tomorrow.'

As the taxi drew away from the rank, leaving Oliver standing there, smiling and holding his hand up in a wave, she waved through the back window of the car too. Then she saw him turn round and, shoulders hunched, begin his walk home.

The taxi sped along the floodlit avenues towards Charles de Gaulle–Étoile, its tyres rumbling on the cobbles. Naomi reflected on what Oliver had revealed to her about his late wife's background. Why hadn't he mentioned it last week when she'd told him about Helga's past? Perhaps he hadn't felt able to, perhaps it was too painful to talk about, but the traumas of the weekend and the fact that Naomi had been open with him about the difficulties she was having finding out about her mother's past had brought it all to the surface. Either way, she was glad he'd told her. It gave them something else in common and the rapport between them was even more firmly established as a result.

Back at the apartment, she called Helga to let her know she'd arrived back in Paris safely. The conversation was rather stilted, but Naomi had expected that. Helga thanked her for the flowers and the note, but was clearly finding everything overwhelming and seemed anxious to end the call. Naomi shrugged to herself as they said goodbye, puzzled, thinking that perhaps her mother needed a little more time before she called her again.

She picked up the receiver again to call Liam, then hesitated. Was now really the right time to call? Nothing was to be gained by speaking to him, she decided. And because he had said that they both needed some space, perhaps it was too soon to call him anyway, despite his request in his note for her to do so. If he really wanted to speak to her, perhaps he should be the one to initiate the conversation.

TWENTY-ONE
NAOMI

Paris, 1990

For the rest of that week, Naomi went into the office early and left late. She tried to put everything that had happened at home at the weekend to the back of her mind. Liam didn't call her and she didn't attempt to call him either. She worked tirelessly on the case and she and Oliver spent many hours together discussing the evidence and the legal arguments and how best to present it to the court. It became routine for them to work until around seven, then adjourn to one of the intimate restaurants a short walk away and eat supper together. It felt so natural to do so and Naomi enjoyed Oliver's company so much that she was surprised when Martine took her aside one Friday afternoon and shut the door.

'People are talking, you know,' Martine said, leaning against her desk, drawing on a cigarette.

'Talking?'

'Yes. Hadn't you realised?'

Naomi shook her head. 'What do you mean?'

'I mean about you and Oliver. They are saying that... well, they are saying that you are getting fond of each other. In short, they are gossiping about it.'

Naomi stared at her in disbelief. 'But why? There's nothing between us. It's a strictly professional relationship.'

Martine laughed and blew smoke in the air. 'They have seen the way he looks at you. And you do seem to get on very well.'

'Well yes, we do. We have lots in common. But that doesn't mean—'

'I know, I know. But just think how it looks from the outside for a moment. You are closeted there in the office together for hours on end. You spend every lunchtime together. You eat together in the evenings...'

Naomi sat down heavily and put her head in her hands. 'I hadn't thought of it like that at all,' she said, appalled to think that everyone in the office had been speculating about the two of them.

'Are you quite sure?' Martine asked in a teasing voice. 'In your heart of hearts?'

'Well, I do admit that I admire him and that we seem to be on the same wavelength...' Naomi said slowly.

'And you are on the rebound from your boyfriend... and Oliver is lonely.'

Naomi looked up, surprised at her friend's words. 'I'm not on the rebound, Martine. We haven't split up. We're just giving each other some space, that's all.'

'OK. I'm sorry, I thought, from what you said when you came back from London, that it was all over between you.'

Naomi shook her head. 'Things didn't go well at the weekend, but it doesn't mean it's over.' But even as she said those words she wondered if she had been fooling herself and

Martine's instinct was right. Perhaps, in all but name, it was over.

'All right,' Martine said slowly. 'So, even more reason to be careful with Oliver, then. It's just that he's still grieving and I don't want him to be hurt again.'

'He won't be hurt because like I said, there's nothing between us. I can't believe it. This is really embarrassing...'

Martine was eyeing her sceptically. 'You're more naïve than you look, Naomi. But like I say, please be careful. For your own sake and for his.'

Naomi went back to her office in a shocked daze and started to pack up her things. There had been no mention of the evening to come yet, so she thought she would just leave the building discreetly, without saying anything. But before she'd managed to put all her files away, Oliver knocked on the door and stepped inside.

'I thought we could pop along to Le Pain et Le Vin again. How about it?' he asked, smiling.

'I'm really sorry, Oliver, but actually I can't this evening, I'm afraid,' she said, unable to look him in the eye.

'Oh!' He instantly looked crestfallen. 'Of course. I shouldn't have presumed...'

She didn't know how to respond and wished he would just go and leave her on her own, but he stood there, watching her. Finally, he said, 'If I were you, I'd take a break over the weekend, Naomi. I've been working you far too hard this week. And taking your company for granted after work too. But we're ahead of the game now. There's absolutely no need for you to come in tomorrow.'

'Oh, but...' she stammered. She hadn't meant to imply that she wasn't prepared to work on Saturday.

'Have a very nice weekend, then,' he said, a formal edge to his voice. He'd recovered his composure now and was smiling politely. 'And do get some well-earned rest.'

He left and a few minutes later Naomi left the building too, saying a hasty, embarrassed goodbye to the receptionist. She walked quickly home along Avenue Kléber under darkening skies, running over and over the humiliating conversation with Martine, going hot and cold with shame, wondering how she could have been foolish enough to make herself the target of office gossip.

When she reached Avenue Carnot, she let herself into the apartment block and went slowly up the stairs. She realised how exhausted she was, by the long week and the shock of Martine's revelation. Liam had hardly crossed her mind during the whole of that time, she realised with surprise.

But now another, different wave of shock went through her as she reached the top of the stairs and saw that the door to her apartment was ajar. She rushed forward quickly and pushed it open, and was astonished to see through a crack in the door that the lights were on in the living room. Her heart was beating fast as she pushed the door open and went in. Her mouth dropped open in surprise when she saw who was sitting on the settee, flicking through a magazine. Her dark hair betrayed no greys and had been cut since the weekend; she was wearing make-up again and a stylish grey jacket and trousers.

'Oh, hello, Naomi. The concierge let me in. She said you'd started coming home later in the evenings this week, so I was about to give up waiting and call your office to see where you were.'

'Mum! What on earth are you doing here?' Naomi rushed forward and put her arms round her mother and held her tight for a long moment.

'Kitty persuaded me to come,' Helga said when they'd disentangled themselves. 'She's with me in Paris, in fact, only she's waiting back at the hotel. She thought it best for me to come and see you on my own to start with. I owe you an apology, my darling.'

'You don't need to apologise, Mum. It's me who should be apologising to you.'

But Helga shook her head. 'I've been too afraid to face the truth, but I think it's time for me to do that now. You have every right to know about what happened to me during the war, so I came here to tell you myself.'

TWENTY-TWO

HELGA

The MS St Louis, 1939

When Helga and Ruth ran away from the captain's cabin that morning, skidding along the passage towards the deck, they were in a panic, not knowing where to go or what to do. They were stunned by what they'd just heard: the conversation through the open door, the unmistakeable anger in the voice of the captain – *it makes my blood boil that these poor people have come halfway across the world to get away from a murderous regime only to be turned away.*

How could they go straight back to the dining room and tell Herr and Frau Weiss what they'd just discovered by chance because they were eavesdropping – that those on board were going to be denied entry to the very country they'd scrimped and saved to enter, which had been their only beacon of hope in a hostile world?

So, instead of going to the dining room, they ran as fast as their legs would carry them down the metal staircase and along to their cabin. Once inside, they threw themselves down on the bunks and caught their breath, let their pounding hearts slow down.

'What's going to happen to everyone?' Ruth said at last. Helga shook her head in bewilderment. There were over nine hundred Jews on board this ship, pinning their hopes on getting into Cuba. Their very lives depended on it. Many of them had relatives waiting for them in Havana. What would happen to them all? Chills went through Helga as a terrible thought occurred to her: what if the ship was ordered to go back to where it had come from? Back to Germany, to face once again the violence and hatred?

'Herr and Frau Weiss are expecting us in the dining room with our suitcases, perhaps we'd better get them and go up?' Ruth's voice broke into Helga's thoughts.

'But you heard what the captain said, Ruth,' she said. 'There's no point taking our cases upstairs. Let's stay here. We don't want someone else to come in and take over our cabin, do we?'

Ruth shook her head. 'I suppose not. But Herr and Frau Weiss will be expecting us.'

They continued to sit there together on the bunk in shocked silence, the sound of gulls on the water and the nervous conversation of passengers from the decks above floating to them through the open porthole. But within a few minutes their dilemma was solved; there was a knock at the door and Frau Weiss entered, her face flushed and anxious.

'I've no idea what is happening, girls. It's all very confusing. The captain has just made an announcement that the ship must wait at anchor here on the edge of the harbour while the Cuban authorities carry out some checks and deal with some paperwork. All sorts of official-looking men have boarded the ship. No passengers are being let off for the time being.'

Helga and Ruth exchanged worried glances, but they remained silent. Neither wanted to worry Frau Weiss by telling her what they'd heard. They didn't want to be the bearers of such important and such devastating news. Was there even a possibility that they'd misunderstood or misheard what the captain was saying, Helga wondered. On the other hand, perhaps the captain had been mistaken and things would work themselves out. He would surely do his very best to help everyone on board.

The turmoil and confusion carried on throughout that first day. The ship remained anchored there on the edge of Havana harbour, unable to dock. Later in the morning, Helga and Ruth, together with Herr and Frau Weiss, went up on deck. It was already crowded with worried passengers, clamouring for information from the crew and stewards, who were unable to tell them anything. A series of motor launches sped to and fro from the docks, bringing various different officials to the ship to speak to the captain. Later, in the afternoon, about ten uniformed Cuban policemen boarded and patrolled the decks with their guns drawn and pointed them aggressively at the restive passengers.

'They have orders to make sure that no refugees leave the ship,' Herr Weiss explained.

The hours passed and still there was no resolution. The captain remained closeted in his cabin while more officials came and went, as well as civilians in suits, whom Herr Weiss said were from the shipping line; but still no passengers were allowed off the ship.

As the day wore on, a series of boats of assorted sizes and shapes began making their way across the harbour to the ship's side. When they drew aside, the people on board them would shout up at the decks and wave furiously, and often individual passengers or whole families would rush to the side and wave back in return.

That evening, dinner was served as usual in the dining hall, to a subdued group of passengers. Herr and Frau Weiss hardly spoke and when they did it was mainly to exchange worried thoughts.

'They're going to send us back to Germany. The lot of us, Werner. What will we do?'

Herr Weiss reached out a hand and gently took his wife's in it. 'Don't fret, Rachel, please. Until we know what is going on, we can't worry like that. The captain will make sure we land safely, you'll see.'

But Frau Weiss was not to be comforted. She pushed her food away and dabbed with her napkin at the tears streaming down her face. Helga and Ruth watched her silently, not wanting to give voice to their own fears, which mirrored Frau Weiss's. Helga felt Ruth's hand creep into hers in her lap and she squeezed it tight. Ruth was as afraid as she was, she knew that, but at least they had each other.

On the second day, Eleanor and Sara came to their cabin after breakfast.

'Come on, we might as well go and swim,' Eleanor said. She looked just the same as she ever did, smiling and confident, while Sara as usual hung back shyly. 'There's nothing else to do while we're waiting.'

So they went up to the pool, pushing their way through the crowds of passengers on deck, past the policemen, who stared at them, unsmiling, as they went through, and joined the other children in the swimming pool. There, they splashed the day away under the fierce Caribbean sun, just as they had before.

That day, for the first time since they'd met Eleanor, her mother emerged from her cabin, pale and thin from weeks of sickness. She had made her way up to the deck to sit in the sun by the pool. She seemed disoriented and confused, and happy to leave Eleanor to mind Sara and take charge of things generally for the family.

So, the days passed like that. The girls tried to pretend that things were just as they had been on the voyage over, even though the ship was still and the engines were silent; they went to meals in the dining room, which still seemed to be operating as normal, although both the staff and stewards were quiet and anxious; they spent their time playing in the pool or lying in their cabin. Sometimes they would look out of their porthole at the regular flotillas of small boats surrounding the ship – the people on board them waving up at the decks, holding up children and animals.

'They are families of people on board. They've come to give their loved ones hope and strength,' Herr Weiss told them.

At mealtimes, as the days wore on, he gave them a running commentary of what was happening.

'The captain is trying to negotiate with the authorities. Apparently, President Brú issued a decree while the ship was on its way from Hamburg, withdrawing all the Cuban visas that had been issued to German Jews.'

'It's just terrible, Werner. People paid good money for those visas. What are we all going to do?'

But unusually, he had no answer.

'Captain Schroder is trying to get the shipping line to bring some influence to bear,' Herr Weiss said the next day. 'It's all down to money, apparently. If they were prepared to put up several hundred thousand dollars, it might be possible. But the owners of the shipping line aren't prepared to help out. What do they care about a cargo of Jews?' he added bitterly, his face creased with anxiety.

Another day, at lunch, he said, 'I've heard that Captain Schroder has been talking to aid agencies – the Jewish relief committees in the United States.'

And, 'They're flying people down from New York apparently,' he said the next day. 'Perhaps they'll be able to help.'

Whenever Helga and Ruth went out on deck to get to the swimming pool, they noticed that the atmosphere on board the ship was becoming ugly. Skirmishes broke out between passengers and crew, sometimes too between passengers and the Cuban police. Once, on their way back to their cabin from the pool, they witnessed two policemen breaking up a group of angry passengers at gunpoint. Helga followed Ruth to their cabin, her heart pounding. She'd been dreading reaching Havana and not having anywhere to stay, anyone to look after them, but this terrifying, lawless limbo felt even worse.

'You look worried, Helga,' Ruth said.

'Aren't you worried too? Those terrible fights breaking out everywhere. It frightens me.'

'Me too,' Ruth admitted, but then squared her shoulders. 'But we must be brave. I'm sure that's what Mame and Tate would tell us. We have each other and that makes us doubly strong.'

Helga smiled, reassured. How brave Ruth was. How she wished she had as much courage as her sister.

After four days of uncertainty, the morning came when Frau Weiss knocked at their door. It was still before breakfast and the girls were just getting dressed. When Helga opened the door, she sensed immediately that something had happened. Herr Weiss stood behind his wife in the shadows. This was very unusual; she normally came down to fetch the girls by herself. Herr and Frau Weiss were both dressed in their best clothes. As soon as Helga saw the expression on their faces, her heart sank. Frau Weiss had guilt written all over her face and Herr Weiss was looking studiously down at the floor.

'Helga, Ruth... my dear girls. I'm afraid we've come to say goodbye,' Frau Weiss began, twisting her hands together in embarrassment.

Helga's mouth dropped open. 'Goodbye? What do you mean?'

'Well... oh dear, this is so difficult. The captain has managed to negotiate with the Cuban authorities for those who have US visas to leave the ship. We're going to be allowed to wait there for our onward travel. So, I'm sure you'll understand, we must take up this opportunity and go ashore. Werner... oh dear. You explain to the girls, can't you?'

Herr Weiss stepped forward and stood beside his wife. Now he looked them both in the eye. 'My wife is right. We're very sorry, but we must take this last chance to get to Chicago. We're both elderly and our health is failing fast.'

'But... but...' Helga stammered. 'You're not leaving us behind on this ship, are you?'

'There are many kind people here who will help you and take care of you. I'm so sorry, girls, but we can't take you with us. We've pleaded with the captain and his officers, and with the Cuban officials on board, but it's impossible. The Cuban president has withdrawn all the Cuban visas issued to German Jews, as you know. Only those with US visas are allowed to disembark.'

Tears sprang to Helga's eyes and she saw that Ruth, standing beside her, was crying too. 'Please don't leave us behind, Herr Weiss. We have nobody to look after us. You've been so kind – how can you just leave us like that?'

'Oh dear.' Frau Weiss stepped forward and put one arm round Helga and the other round Ruth and pulled them both to her. Helga buried her face in Frau Weiss's shoulder and smelled her musky perfume. For a split second, it could have been Mame she was clinging to, or even Frau Moshe. Someone caring and kind who'd shown them love but who they now had to get used to doing without. She couldn't hold back the tears. Ruth and Frau Weiss were crying too.

'Now, now, Rachel... We need to say goodbye now or we'll miss the launch,' Herr Weiss broke in.

Frau Weiss pulled back from the girls, drying her eyes.

'Can't we come up on the deck with you to say goodbye?' Ruth asked, her voice choked. Herr and Frau Weiss exchanged worried looks.

'It's probably better to stay down here,' Herr Weiss said.

'No! No!' Ruth protested. 'We're going to come up with you.'

Reluctantly, Herr and Frau Weiss allowed the girls to follow them upstairs to the deck, where a little crowd had gathered beside the rail. A small group of people were queuing to climb down the accommodation ladder into a launch that was drawn up alongside. Their suitcases were being roped down by the crew.

'Look!' said Ruth as they approached, pointing to the gaggle of people. 'It's Eleanor!' and the two of them left Herr and Frau Weiss's side and ran towards the little crowd, where Eleanor, Sara and her mother were shuffling forwards with their suitcases. Eleanor was supporting her mother with one arm and looking round anxiously behind her as they moved forward.

'Eleanor!' Helga yelled through her tears. 'Are you leaving too?'

Eleanor left her mother's side and ran towards them. Helga saw from her face, blotched with tears, that she too had been crying.

The three of them embraced while Sara looked on shyly and their mother stood beside their luggage looking helpless.

'I'm so pleased you came up,' Eleanor said. 'I wanted to stop by your cabin and say goodbye but Mother said the launch was about to go and that there was no time.'

There was only time for a brief hug. 'Look after yourselves,' Eleanor said. 'You are both strong, just remember that. If you ever make it to New York, come and find me.'

Then the stewards were beckoning and Eleanor's mother was calling her to come. Helga stood beside Ruth and watched as the three of them made their way to the rail and began to climb down the ladder. Then it was Herr and Frau Weiss's turn. Herr Weiss took Helga's hand first.

'Now, I've spoken to the captain about you and he's going to make sure that you're cared for and that you have somewhere to go to when the ship docks. There's a good chance that he will be able to negotiate for the rest of the passengers to come ashore in Havana very soon. Don't give up hope, girls. In a couple of days, you could be with us again.'

Then he shook both their hands, almost formally, but Helga saw the tears in his eyes as he turned away. As her husband moved forward, Frau Weiss clung to each of them in turn, tears streaming down her face.

'I'm so sorry, my little ones. God will take care of you. I will pray for you every day.'

And then she was gone, being helped down to the launch by two stewards, her brightly coloured scarf fluttering in the warm breeze, her hair escaping from its pins.

'Let's watch them go.' Helga took her sister's hand and they pushed their way through to the rail. The launch, with its cargo of twenty or so lucky passengers, their luggage stacked at the back, pulled away from the side of the ship, turned about in a great circle of white foam and headed towards the dockside.

Most people on board didn't turn back to look at the ship, but two did. Helga and Ruth waved at the disappearing boat until their arms ached and the elderly couple waved back at them; and as it drew away, Helga could still make out Frau Weiss's red scarf as the boat grew smaller and smaller, then eventually melded into the colours of the docks in front of it.

. . .

When the *St Louis* finally left Havana harbour two days later, Helga and Ruth clung to each other. They were alone again now and, although nearly all the passengers who had set off from Hamburg all those weeks ago were still on board, waving goodbye to the ones the two girls had come to know and love had hit them hard.

After the Weisses and Eleanor and her family had gone, things seemed even more desperate and the loss of their friends and protectors brought home afresh the other losses that were still raw in their minds. The two girls didn't feel like swimming now that Eleanor wasn't there to encourage them. The deck was so crowded with angry passengers, officials and policemen, they decided it was best to stay in their cabin most of the time and only go out when they needed to.

On the evening of the Weisses' departure, when the dinner gong sounded Ruth said, 'Do you think it would be all right to go to the dining room? I'm feeling a bit hungry now.' They had been so downcast that they hadn't ventured out of their cabin to eat at all that day.

'I'm not sure. We're supposed to be in second class, aren't we? It was only because Herr Weiss asked the captain that we were allowed in the first-class lounge.'

'It will be all right,' Ruth said. 'Herr Weiss said he had spoken to the captain this morning.'

Helga agreed reluctantly and let Ruth take the lead when they arrived at the dining room. Ruth went straight to the table they'd always occupied with Herr and Frau Weiss and sat down. Helga followed suit a little nervously, but no one seemed to take any notice of them – everyone was too preoccupied with their own troubles. But when the captain entered, he made his way between the tables. To Helga's astonishment he came straight over to where they sat.

'He's going to tell us to leave,' she whispered to Ruth as he approached, her cheeks burning with embarrassment and shame.

'Of course he's not. Look, he's smiling.'

'Good evening, frauleins,' he began. 'We haven't met before, but I've just come to reassure you that I'm going to do everything I can to ensure you have somewhere to stay when the ship docks so you needn't worry. Herr Weiss told me all about your circumstances.'

'Thank you, sir,' both girls said in unison, then Ruth asked, 'When *are* we going to dock, Captain?'

The captain shook his head slowly and his smile vanished. 'I'm sorry to say that I don't know the answer to that question. I'm doing my best to negotiate with the authorities and I will continue to do so but if it proves impossible, we will travel up the coast of the USA and seek refuge there. You know, Florida is only a few hours' sailing from here.'

'Florida?' Helga repeated. 'Are we going there?'

She'd seen pictures of Miami Beach in one of Mame's magazines once. The miles of white sand, the happy people splashing in the shallow sea, the grand hotels with their rows of beach umbrellas, the swaying palm trees.

'Let's see. Now, do come and see me in my office if you need anything and the stewards will continue to serve you in first class. So, you don't need to worry about that.'

With that, he nodded briefly to both of them and moved away. They watched him winding his way between the half-empty tables towards his own.

After that conversation with Captain Schroder, they were not surprised the next morning after breakfast when the ship's engines began to rumble and the floor underneath them began to vibrate. They went out on deck and stood by the rail with hundreds of other passengers as the ship finally pulled away from the harbour edge where it had been moored for a week.

The gleaming buildings of the quayside gradually faded away into the mist.

A flotilla of small boats that surrounded the ship and followed it as if escorting it away from the island were left behind too and soon the ship was sailing alone on the high seas under the scorching sun, heading north towards Florida. From the cabin porthole Helga watched them, her heart lifting a little, thinking of Florida, its white beaches, its palm trees. Perhaps she could dare to hope? Perhaps things might be brighter from now on?

TWENTY-THREE

HELGA

The MS St Louis, 1939

Now they were all alone, the girls stayed in their cabin and only came out at mealtimes and to use the bathroom. They sensed unrest and danger amongst the passengers and were even more wary of the crew than they had been before. Since leaving Havana they had been shocked to see stewards openly insulting Jewish passengers, swearing at them and pushing them, allowing their Nazi sympathies to surface just as if they were back in the Third Reich.

It seemed that now the ship had been turned away from Cuba those malign influences had resurfaced, emboldened, because the tide of world opinion seemed to have turned against the passengers. Leading the assault was the steward who had verbally abused Helga the night of the farewell ball. She'd never mentioned that to Ruth, but now her sister could see it for herself so there was no sparing her feelings any more. All of this reminded them only too painfully of those months of abuse and violence they'd endured in Berlin.

So, instead of spending time on deck, they stayed in their stuffy cabin. There, they knelt side by side on Tate's bunk and watched the gentle progress of the ship through their porthole. Within a few hours of setting sail from Havana, the flat, emerald-green coastline of Florida with its white sand beaches and swampy inlets came into view. Then, as the sun went down, staining the landscape pink and red, and the sky grew dark, they could see the lights of a big city, twinkling in the distance.

'That must be Miami,' Ruth said. 'Do you think we'll land there?'

'Maybe...'

They watched and waited, holding their breath, to see if the ship would turn towards the land, but to their dismay they sailed on past. 'It doesn't look as though they are going to let us dock there either.'

For three days the *St Louis* sailed slowly northwards up the eastern seaboard of the United States, but at no point did it make the long-awaited turn towards land. Helga had no idea where they would end up. Their only source of information was listening to the rumours that circulated amongst the other passengers. Whenever she and Ruth went up to the dining room they would hear whispered snippets of information.

'Someone said that the Dominican Republic agreed that they would take us in, but we're travelling north, so obviously that didn't happen.'

On the second day, another passenger said, 'I heard that the captain has telegrammed President Roosevelt and asked if we could land in New York.'

'*He* must give us refuge, surely? How can the United States refuse us in our time of need?'

'I heard they have a quota of refugees for the States and they won't take any more,' another passenger chipped in.

'It's a scandal. The whole world is turning against us...'

'There's always Canada. I heard the captain is asking every country that he can.'

Every mealtime the stories were slightly different, but all along the same lines. Desperate attempts were being made to find a place that would welcome almost a thousand Jews fleeing persecution, but their limited options were gradually running out. Making his way through the tables at mealtimes, the captain looked more and more drawn and preoccupied as the days drew on. Sometimes he didn't come to the dining room at all.

On the fourth day, during the afternoon, as Helga and Ruth were watching through their porthole, the engines changed tone and the St Louis slowed. They sensed the shift of direction as the ship changed course.

'We've turned away from the coast,' Ruth said as, through the porthole, the land gradually tilted and disappeared from view.

And as the ship completed its long, sweeping turn and settled back on a steady course, heading east directly away from the coastline, Helga realised that it was true. That all they could see from their portside cabin window was flat, grey ocean under a steel-grey sky, stretching as far as the eye could see.

'We're heading back to Germany,' Helga said, shock choking her voice. 'What are we going to do?'

Ruth didn't answer and Helga wondered if she was having the same thoughts as she was; it was crazy, but she'd suddenly wondered whether somehow, going back to Germany might mean that they could be reunited with Tate. She told herself to stop thinking like that. How could anything have changed that much in the four weeks or so that they had been away? The Nazis would still be in charge, Tate and so many others like him would still be imprisoned in concentration camps and her own and Ruth's lives would be in danger just as they had been before. After all, some of the Nazi Party stewards on board were treating the passengers just as they liked now. Scolding herself for even considering that any good might come from the ship turning towards home, she squared her shoulders and reminded herself that she needed to face up to reality. She must prepare for what they would have to deal with when they got back to Hamburg, whatever that might be.

After dark, they went up to dinner. The mood was gloomy, but just as before the rumours were running wild. Some people were saying that the ship had been ordered back to Hamburg by the shipping line, but others were more hopeful. 'The captain would never let that happen. Just think of what he's done for us so far,' someone said.

The days dragged past and the monotony of the Atlantic crossing was punctuated with spikes of terror for Helga, as she thought about what might happen to them when they reached Europe. Her imagination ran riot. If she'd been anxious about having nowhere to stay in Cuba, she was triply anxious about returning to Germany. Would she and Ruth be sent to a concentration camp just like Tate? Did they even send children to those places? She was acutely aware that with every passing moment the ship brought them closer and closer to their fate. She was so worried that she even stopped eating. Ruth did too and she watched her sister's face grow thinner and paler without the sunshine and nourishing food that had sustained them on the westward journey. Looking at Ruth was like looking into a mirror. She knew she must look the same.

One day, after breakfast, Captain Schroder approached their table. 'I haven't forgotten about you, girls,' he said, with a reassuring smile. 'You might have heard – I've been very busy cabling to all the governments of Europe to find as many passengers as I can safe refuge when we dock.'

Helga looked into his kind eyes, knowing that her own must be full of hope.

'I have refused to return the ship to Germany, so you don't need to worry about that.'

Helga let out a breath of relief.

'Where are we going then, Captain?' Ruth asked.

'I've had some success with Britain and France. Those governments have each agreed to take several hundred passengers. I haven't found places for everyone yet, I'm sorry to say. All the children on board will remain with their parents, but you two are a special case.'

The two girls looked up at him, holding their breath.

'My officers and I are contacting aid agencies in several countries – France, the Netherlands, Belgium – to see if they can help you.'

The two stared at him, not knowing what to think. Was that good news? Helga wasn't quite sure what an aid agency was. She assumed it was some sort of charity.

'Please don't look so worried.' The captain smiled. 'I'm not going to give up until I've found somewhere safe for you. That's why I came to talk to you. I'll let you know as soon as I have some news.'

But several days passed and the atmosphere on the ship grew more restless. People sensed that the end of their long journey was close and, although most passengers were landing in countries that would welcome them, they still had no idea where they would be staying. All they knew was that it wasn't where they'd set out for with hope in their hearts all those weeks before. Helga and Ruth grew more and more anxious.

They'd heard whispers that they would see land within a day. Had the captain found somewhere for them? Had he forgotten about them? As they sat at breakfast, barely able to eat and having all but given up hope, the captain stopped at their table.

'I have some news for you, girls. Tomorrow we will be docking in Antwerp,' he said.

They stared at him.

'That's in Belgium,' he explained. 'And I've finally found somewhere for you to go. The aid agencies have put me in touch with a foundation in France. This foundation is already offering home and refuge to many Jewish children from Germany. I've arranged for them to take you when we dock.'

Helga wondered what exactly a foundation was, but she didn't dare ask. Was it an orphanage? She remembered how she and Ruth had dreaded Tate sending them away to an orphanage, all those months ago in Berlin, but now the prospect didn't seem quite so frightening. Tears sprang to her eyes as the tension and stress she'd been battling for so many weeks suddenly dissipated in a rush.

The captain carried on smiling gently as she wiped her tears away. 'Now, I'm afraid I'll be very busy when we land, so I might not be able to come and say goodbye,' he said. 'But I wanted to let you know that when you walk off the boat, there will be a lady waiting there for you. She will be holding up a sign with your names on it. She is a volunteer from the foundation and she will make sure you get on the right train.'

A train?

'Where will the train be going?' Ruth asked the question that Helga's mouth was already open to ask.

'Oh, didn't I say? Paris. You'll be going to Paris. The suburbs, actually. That's where the house is where you'll be staying and there are kind people there. They will take care of you, you'll be safe.'

'Thank you, Captain,' Helga said, relief flooding through her, thanking God for the captain and his kindness. At last, light at the end of the tunnel!

'Good luck, girls, and God bless you both. Now, I must get back to the wheelhouse. It will be a busy few hours, overseeing our arrival into Antwerp.' With a slight bow of his head, the captain left their table and made his way out of the dining room.

The young woman holding the piece of card on which was written in large black capital letters HELGA & RUTH BEIDER was wearing a red, short-sleeved dress and a wide-brimmed straw hat. She was studying the crowd descending the companionway anxiously as Ruth and Helga descended with their suitcases.

'Come on, she's over there!' Ruth tugged Helga's arm and they pushed their way through the passengers towards her.

'Ah, there you are!' The young woman's face lit up as they approached. She was young, in her mid-twenties perhaps, dark-haired like themselves. With her wide smile and sparkling eyes, she reminded Helga instantly of Miss Ingrid, her beloved teacher.

She folded the name card and slipped it into her handbag and took each of them by the hand. 'I was worried that you wouldn't see me. It's so crowded. Now, come this way. It's not too far to the train station.'

Helga gripped the woman's hand tightly, her legs a little wobbly after spending so long at sea.

'My name is Hannah,' she told them as they detached themselves from the throng of passengers. 'If we go quickly, we'll beat the crowd and I'll be able to find you seats on the train.'

'Aren't you coming on the train with us?' Ruth asked, breathlessly. It was hard to keep up. Hannah wore elegant high-heeled sandals but they didn't slow her pace across the cobbled dockyard.

'No, I'm afraid not, but I'll find you a seat and let the guard know that you're travelling alone. I have some papers in my bag that I will give you. You'll need to show them at the border.'

'The border?' Helga asked and her heart gave a sickening

lurch. An image of leather-coated Nazi officers scrutinising papers swam into her mind, along with one of growling Alsatians straining on chains.

Hannah stopped walking and turned to ruffle Helga's hair. She bent down and looked earnestly into her eyes.

'Please don't worry, little one. There's no need to be anxious here in Belgium. There will be no problem with your papers. The OSE has transported many, many German children into France. And the border you have to cross is only between Belgium and France. So, there will be no problem at all.'

Helga swallowed and nodded, the kindness in Hannah's tone making her want to cry.

'Come on then, we don't want to miss that train.'

'What's the OSE?' Ruth asked as they hurried to keep up with Hannah, carrying their little suitcases in their free hands.

'Didn't Captain Schroder tell you? It's the Oeuvre des Secours aux Enfants. That's French for Children's Rescue Society.'

She walked quickly, picking her way along the dockside, between the ships and the brick warehouses where men were working, lifting crates and boxes under towering cranes. She skilfully avoided workers with sack-barrows and handcarts, speeding ahead of the other *St Louis* passengers making their way to the train station. While they walked, Hannah told them that the OSE had established several children's homes throughout France and that they were looking after many Jewish children who had fled Nazi Germany.

'You will be safe there, there's no need to worry any more. Captain Schroder told us that you've had a terrible time. All the children in the OSE homes have had similar experiences. All have had to leave their families behind in Germany and don't know when they might see them again. So, you see, you won't be alone.'

Soon, they'd left the docks behind and were walking

through the city's unfamiliar streets. Helga looked around her nervously, expecting to see Gestapo or SA officers emerging from every corner, but this place was different. The local people who passed barely gave them a second glance. At last they reached the station, a vast, beautiful building that rose up in front of them, with arches and domed roofs and a huge clock above the entrance. Instinctively, Helga hung back, expecting to have to queue to enter and to see soldiers with guns and dogs, but Hannah's firm hand in hers gave her confidence and they went in through the arched entrance unnoticed by all the people milling about. How strange to be so inconspicuous – it gave Helga a sense of freedom she could barely remember feeling before.

'Come, the train's waiting. Platform Two.'

They hurried across the marble concourse. The train was almost full and Hannah rushed them along towards the front, where the engine was belching out steam. Firemen in blackened overalls were shovelling coal into its bunkers. It reminded Helga sharply of the last train journey they'd taken, from Berlin to Hamburg, when Tate had found them seats and stood at the end of the carriage. She remembered catching his eye and smiling at him, and her heart twisted with pain at the memory.

'Here, there are two seats together.'

Hannah stepped inside the carriage with them and helped them to the empty seats. She put their suitcases up on the rack above. 'Now, here are your train tickets and papers.' She took two brown envelopes out of her handbag and handed them to Helga and Ruth. 'You just need to show the documents you have with you and the ones in these envelopes at the border. They have been prepared by the OSE for you and they're all in order.'

The girls stared at her wordlessly. Helga's stomach was clenching with nerves again. She didn't feel ready to embark on another long journey into the unknown. Ever since the captain had told them what he had arranged, she'd been imagining that someone would look after them when they arrived in Antwerp. She hadn't realised they would have to travel alone. Now, Hannah touched her cheek and looked into her eyes again.

'I can see that you're starting to worry about the journey, Helga. Please, there is no need. When you get to Paris, look out for station signs. It will be called the Gare du Nord. That's the end of your journey and there will be someone to meet you there from OSE. Her name is Beatrice and she will be on the platform waiting for you, holding up a sign, just like I did. Can you remember that? The Gare du Nord.'

'The Gare du Nord,' Helga repeated. 'And the lady is Beatrice.'

'Perfect,' Hannah said.

Helga relaxed a little.

'It should take about three hours to get to Paris. You will be there before suppertime. But there's a restaurant car on this train. Here are some Belgian francs. You can buy drinks and pastries there if you get hungry.'

She handed them each some money. 'Now, I will go and speak to the guard while there's still time. Goodbye, girls. You are very brave and very strong. Take care and good luck.'

Five minutes later, as the train drew out of the station, Hannah stood on the platform, smiling and waving them off. They waved back, Helga's heart heavy at yet another parting from a kind stranger. The train began its journey through the city of Antwerp and out through the suburbs. She settled back against the seat and closed her eyes, exhausted. She'd hardly slept the night before, worrying about what the day might bring. But now she felt Ruth's hand creeping into her own and squeezing it. Ruth rested her head against Helga's shoulder and the swaying and rattling of the train soon lulled them into a deep sleep.

They must have slept for a long time because when they

awoke, the train had stopped in a small village station surrounded by fields where cattle grazed. A wave of shock went through Helga. Two uniformed guards had boarded the train and were making their way along the carriage, checking papers. Helga nudged Ruth, who was blinking awake too. With shaking hands, they found their papers and when the guard reached them and, unsmiling, said something in French, they handed them over nervously. There was a tense few moments as he scrutinised each one carefully. Then he handed them back.

'Merci, mes petites. Bon voyage,' he said with a brief, official smile and moved on to the next passengers. The girls slumped back in their seats, weak with relief. Helga's heartbeat gradually slowed down. Through the window she watched the two guards jump down from the train onto the remote country platform. The whistle blew and the train jerked forward a few times, then began to gather speed. It was soon rattling through the French countryside, dotted with farms and villages, on its way to Paris.

'It will be all right, Helga, you'll see,' Ruth said.

'I hope so,' Helga said uncertainly. 'What if no one's there to meet us?'

'There will be. Hannah promised there would be, didn't she?' Helga felt Ruth slipping her arm round her shoulder and she snuggled up to her sister.

'I suppose so.' Helga wished she shared Ruth's optimistic nature. Once again, there was Ruth's bravery, shining through. How lucky she was to have her.

It was only another couple of hours before they had left the fields and villages of northern France behind and the train was pounding through the suburbs of a big city. Helga stared out. It looked so much like Berlin, with busy roads, tall apartment blocks and factories belching out smoke. The buildings and streets they passed grew more and more dense and then the train was slowing down and finally coming into a big station. PARIS, GARE DU NORD, said the signs.

'We're here,' Ruth said. The train shuddered to a halt and the other passengers in the carriage got up from their seats to haul their luggage down from the racks. 'We'll have to stand on the seat to get our cases down.'

Before Helga had time to feel anxious, another young woman detached herself from the crowd and approached the carriage, shading her eyes to peer through the windows. Relief washed through Helga when she read the words HELGA AND RUTH BEIDER on the card in the young woman's hand.

'Hello, I'm Beatrice,' the young woman said, as they climbed down onto the platform. She looked a little like Hannah, only she was wearing a blue dress and a fashionable blue hat pulled down over light brown hair, 'and you must be Ruth and Helga! Welcome to Paris. Come, there's a car waiting to take us to the villa.'

They followed Beatrice to the end of the platform, carrying their cases, pushing their way through the passengers descending from the train, then across the busy concourse and through a side entrance to the station. A big, shiny black Citroën limousine was waiting on a narrow street, its engine idling. After putting their cases in the boot, Beatrice opened the back door.

'In you get. I will squeeze in with you.'

The uniformed driver turned and nodded briefly towards them as they slid along the leather seat. Then Helga noticed in the front passenger seat an elegant woman in a black feathered hat. She turned round too and gave the girls a warm smile. She wore red lipstick and her face was covered by a black gauze veil.

'Good afternoon, girls. Welcome to Paris. My name is Yvonne de Gunzbourg and I work with the OSE. We're going to take you to a wonderful house in the suburbs that will be your home from now on.'

It felt surreal, being driven in a purring limousine through the streets of this beautiful, alien city, where people walked the pavements under the plane trees, talking and laughing, relaxing, and there were no soldiers or police to be seen anywhere. Helga and Ruth were too overawed to speak for the whole of the journey, but Beatrice and Yvonne kept up a steady stream of conversation in French, with the occasional interjection by the driver.

At last, they drew in through the tall, wrought-iron gates of a big, white-painted mansion. It was surrounded by well-tended lawns and trees in full leaf. The car crunched to a halt on the gravel drive. The driver got out and opened their door and they clambered out of the vehicle. They stood on the driveway, staring up at the beautiful house with its balconies and tall, gracious windows.

'Welcome to Villa Helvetia,' said Yvonne, handing over their suitcases. 'Come on, let's go inside. We will introduce you to the other children.'

She began to walk towards the building, her high heels crunching on the gravel, and Helga and Ruth followed her, Beatrice bringing up the rear. As they got closer to the house, Helga caught sight of the flowering jasmine climbing over the railings of the balconies with its delicate, white flowers. Their scent wafted towards her on the warm early-evening air. The house looked so welcoming that she was suddenly overwhelmed with emotion that their long journey was finally at an end. She put her little battered suitcase down and wept with relief.

TWENTY-FOUR

HELGA

Paris, 1990

Helga finished speaking and took another sip of red wine.
Naomi had brought a bottle of burgundy back with her when
she'd gone out to fetch some food from the pizzeria a couple of
doors down from the apartment. They hadn't wanted to go out
to eat; Helga wouldn't have been able to tell Naomi her story in
a restaurant where others might overhear and with the interrup-
tions from waiters. But even though she was hungry, she hadn't
touched the delicious-smelling pizza Naomi had put in front of
her. Helga's throat was dry. She wasn't used to talking so much
and her chest ached with emotion too. She felt drained from
reliving those traumatic experiences from her childhood while
she described them to Naomi.

When she told Naomi about Ruth, Naomi's face had registered deep shock.

'A sister? An identical twin sister? But why didn't you tell
me about her before, Mum?'

Helga had closed her eyes and fought back the tears. 'I'm sorry. I just shut it all away. I didn't want to talk about any of it. It was all too... too painful.'

'I understand,' Naomi had said slowly. 'But I'm so sorry you felt that way, Mum. You could have talked to me any time. Perhaps it might have helped to share it with me?'

'I know. I know. I just couldn't. But now I know I need to. I owe it to you and to myself. And to poor, dear Ruthie—' Her voice broke as she said her sister's name and she'd had to pause, take deep breaths to recover her composure.

'Do you have any pictures of her?' Naomi asked and Helga reached into her bag and drew out the photograph that she'd taken from the flat in Leipziger Strasse in May 1939 and had kept with her ever since. With trembling hands, she handed it to Naomi.

Naomi gasped when she saw it.

'She's beautiful, Mum. You look exactly alike. How incredible!' She stared at it for a long moment, then handed it back to Helga, who slipped it into her bag again, eager to keep it safe.

When she felt able, she'd carried on and told Naomi everything. As she spoke, the Paris skyline grew dark and the streetlamps came on outside in Avenue Carnot. She told Naomi all about her early life in Berlin, how everything began to change for them and for all the Jews in Berlin as the 1930s drew on, about the horrors of Kristallnacht and how they'd lost Mame that night. Naomi had held her hand then and they had both cried for a while. Then, wiping her eyes, she'd gone on to tell her daughter about hiding in the apartment for months, about the kindness of Frau Moshe and Herr Hollis, and about how Tate's business was confiscated. Then she spoke about how they'd found renewed hope when Tate had found out about the *St Louis* and about how he had been taken from them just as they'd been about to board the ship in Hamburg.

'That's truly terrible, Mum,' Naomi said with tears in her eyes. 'What you've been carrying all these years...'

'It's the last time I ever saw him,' Helga said. 'If I close my eyes, even to this day, I can still see the expression on his face as those brutes dragged him away. To the end, he was fighting for his family. He handed Ruth and me our papers and urged us to get on that ship.'

'Do you know what happened to him?' Naomi asked, tentatively. It was the inevitable question. Helga hung her head and swallowed hard. She'd told no one except her husband and the people who had helped her discover the truth. That truth was so painful to utter out loud, but Naomi's father had understood; he had lost his own family in the same way. Now she reached out and took Naomi's hand and looked into her eyes. All she could see there was love and sympathy and an earnest and natural desire to find out the truth about her family history. Why had Helga held it back from her daughter for so long, she wondered? As well as wanting to guard her secrets, she'd been trying to protect Naomi, of course. But now Naomi was a young woman, embarking on a new chapter of her life, striking out on her own. It struck Helga forcefully then that Naomi needed to know about the past in order to move forward into her own future. She took a deep breath.

'I discovered what happened to him after years and years of searching. In the end, I managed to find out with help from a friend in America – Eleanor, her name was, I first met her on board the *St Louis*. I will come to that soon, but poor Eleanor passed away very young too. Her own father had been taken away to a concentration camp in the late thirties. She commissioned some research in the archives in Bad Arolsen in Germany, just after the war. On my behalf she also asked the researcher to look into Tate's records. He discovered that Tate was taken to Neuengamme concentration camp near Hamburg. His records showed that he must have been taken there the day we boarded the *St Louis*. They also showed that he died in a cholera outbreak in the camp a year or so later...'

She gripped Naomi's hand. 'I looked into what happened at Neuengamme and discovered that prisoners there were used as slaves to work the brickworks nearby. It was brutal work in terrible conditions and many of them died of starvation and of overwork too. Not a day goes by that I don't think of what he must have gone through during those terrible months. While Ruth and I were travelling to Cuba on the *St Louis*, swimming in the pool, eating in the first-class restaurant, he was suffering in that hellhole. There's no getting away from what happened to him. It never gets any easier to bear.'

'How dreadful, Mum. How much you've had to carry all on your own.'

Helga smiled wistfully and looked into Naomi's eyes. 'Not quite alone. I shared it with your father. He understood. But since he went too...'

There was silence between them for a while, as they both thought of Naomi's father. Kind, loving, practical and generous. Then Naomi asked, 'What happened on the *St Louis*, Mum? Did you get to Cuba?'

'Oh yes, we got to Cuba, but we never managed to step onto Cuban soil.'

She went on to tell Naomi all about the ill-fated voyage of the *St Louis*, about the kindness of Herr and Frau Weiss and Eleanor, and how the ship was rejected by every state it appealed to. She described the frustration and impotence of the passengers and the kindness of the captain and how the *St Louis* was eventually forced to return to Europe with all its passengers except those who'd had US passports and were able to disembark at Havana. Then she told Naomi how Captain Schroder had found them a place in a children's home in Paris and how they'd made the train journey from Antwerp docks to the Villa Helvetia.

Helga took a long glug of wine and put her glass down. 'So that's how we ended up in that orphanage on the outskirts of Paris.'

She said that with an air of finality, admitting at last that she had stayed at the Villa Helvetia, that she knew all about the place and that it held a special place in her heart.

'What was it like there?' Naomi asked after a pause. 'From the photographs, it looks as though it must have been a beautiful place to stay.'

'It was wonderful there. From the moment we arrived, we were made to feel welcome. On that first evening Ruth and I were given two little beds right next to each other in the girls' dormitory on the first floor. We were introduced to all the other children. Some were very young and others were in their mid-teens. I don't know how many were there altogether, about fifty perhaps. Many of them had come from Berlin or other parts of Germany, just like us, only they had been brought straight to Paris by train, not gone halfway round the world and back on a ship first.'

She smiled ruefully, thinking back over that incredible journey.

'All the staff were kind and loving at the Villa Helvetia and we instantly felt safe. The place quickly became home to us and we gradually began to recover from the traumas of the past few years and to settle down. All the children, except the tiny ones, had lessons every day from wonderful teachers – Beatrice, the young woman who met us from the train, was one of them. I don't remember the names of all of them, but they were mostly young, Jewish and incredibly kind. We'd lost a lot of schooling and we were glad to be able to learn again. We absorbed the lessons like blotting paper. We made some good friends there too. I can barely remember their names now... Rebecca, I think, from Munich, Ada from Hamburg. I often wonder what became of them.

'We would often take our lessons out in the garden under the trees, during that long, hot summer of 1939. We would sometimes be taken out too, especially in those early months. Sometimes the teachers would take us to the nearby lake at... I don't remember its name, but it was a sort of spa town. We used to swim there on really hot days. We had fun, splashing about in the water. At times like that we managed to put aside what we'd been through and allow ourselves to be children again.'

'Enghien-les-Bains?' Naomi put in quietly.

'Yes! That's it. How did you know?'

'I went there, Mum. Remember? I told you...'

Helga looked down at her hands, a prickle of shame passing through her. 'Oh yes, of course. And I denied knowing anything about the place, more than once. I'm so sorry, Naomi. I wasn't thinking straight. I just wanted to protect my secrets at any cost. It was just so painful to even think about it. I hope you'll forgive me.'

'Of course. There's nothing to forgive, I understand.'

'Enghien-les-Bains was where the nearest train station was, as you must know,' Helga went on. 'Once or twice the teachers took us down to Paris on that train to see the sights. The Eiffel Tower, Notre-Dame Cathedral, the Louvre. Paris was such a beautiful city and I've always remembered those outings.'

She looked out at the twinkling street lights of Avenue Carnot. 'It still is, of course. Even the Nazis couldn't destroy its beauty.'

Then she remembered that Naomi wanted to know all about her time in Villa Helvetia.

'Of course, Ruth and I were recovering from losing our parents and what had happened to us in Berlin, but, just as Hannah had told us before we boarded the train, we were not alone. All the children had left their parents behind, but not all had lost them as we had. Some of the parents wrote to them and it made us sad that we didn't receive any letters. But there were some others whose parents had disappeared like ours, arrested and taken away suddenly by the SS or the Gestapo. Rebecca and Ada had lost theirs, if I remember correctly. We were all in the same situation. So, although we were carrying a lot of sadness, Ruth and I settled down quite quickly. We were so grateful to be there...'

'Where is she now, Mum?' Naomi asked, her voice gentle. 'Your sister, Ruth. What happened to her?'

Helga shook her head, unable to say the words. She screwed up her eyes and tried to prevent the inevitable, but still the tears came.

'I'm sorry,' Naomi said then, leaning forward and taking Helga's hand once more. 'You don't have to tell me if you don't want to. Why don't you tell me when— or if you're ever ready.'

'All right, I will do that.' She blew her nose, took another sip of wine and glanced at her watch. 'Goodness me, look at the time! Kitty will be starting to worry about me. It's after ten o'clock. I need to get back to the hotel.'

'Why don't you stay here?' Naomi asked. 'I could sleep on the settee and you could have my bed.'

Helga looked around her at the tiny apartment. 'I don't have any of my things with me.'

'I could lend you a nightie. It's late to be travelling now.'

'I suppose I could stay, but I must phone the hotel and let Kitty know.'

After Helga had called Kitty, Naomi poured more wine and they carried on talking until they were both too tired to form words. Naomi had endless questions about Helga's life in Berlin, about her family, about her friends and her childhood, and now she'd started, Helga wanted Naomi to know everything. Talking about it brought home to her what a wonderful childhood she'd had, until the hatred of the Nazis had destroyed everything they had.

Before they went to bed, Naomi said, 'Would you like to go

to Montmorency, Mum? See the villa, what it looks like now? We could go on the train tomorrow.'

'I'm not sure...' Nerves washed through Helga at the very thought. 'I'm not sure what Kitty would say.'

'I'm sure she would want to go there with you. She's come with you to Paris to help you face the past, hasn't she?'

Helga nodded. 'You've both been so kind. And so patient.'

When she finally sank into bed in Naomi's bedroom, after midnight, she lay back on the pillows and listened to the sounds of the city through the shutters. It was a city she'd vowed never to come back to, but she realised now that she was glad she'd allowed Kitty to persuade her to come. It had brought her and Naomi closer than ever and having told Naomi some of her story made it feel as though a huge burden she'd carried alone for years was now beginning to lift from her shoulders. But she knew she hadn't yet told the whole story, that it would take so much more courage to do that. Perhaps she would tomorrow. Perhaps she would go and see the villa. Perhaps that was the right thing to do now that she was finally here.

TWENTY-FIVE
HELGA

Paris, 1990

In the morning they met Kitty for breakfast in a café in the Champs-Élysées. Kitty was immaculately coiffed and dressed in a chic summer suit. She greeted them warmly.

'Thank you so much for coming to Paris,' Naomi said as they kissed her good morning. Helga realised that Naomi was thanking Kitty for persuading Helga to come to Paris and for helping her to get to the point where she felt able to share her story. They sat down and ate croissants and pains aux raisin and sipped their coffee, on the sunlit pavement, watching chic Parisians going about their business.

Kitty said, 'Do you two have any plans for today?'

Helga looked up and made her announcement. 'Naomi suggested we go out to Montmorency to see the villa. I've been thinking about it and I've decided that I would like to go. If you'd both like to come with me?'

Helga noticed that Naomi and Kitty exchanged a quick look.

'Are you sure, Mum?' Naomi asked, looking a little anxious. It was only natural, Helga supposed, since so much emotional capital was at stake.

'I'm very sure. And please don't worry. I want to go there, I've made up my mind now.'

'You and Naomi should go,' Kitty said. 'It's a family thing. You don't want me tagging along, I can keep myself busy for a few hours.'

'Nonsense, Kitty! You must come too. After all, if it hadn't been for you I wouldn't even be here. Please, I want you to be there with me when I go back.'

It felt like a huge step forward and, as soon as they'd agreed to go there, Helga wanted to get straight on with the journey. She drained her coffee and waited impatiently for Naomi and Kitty to do the same.

They eventually left the café and took the metro from Charles de Gaulle–Étoile to Gare du Nord. When they came up into the main train station Helga looked around her nervously. Even with this distance of time she was half expecting to see Nazis in uniforms and red banners bearing swastikas adorning every pillar. It was a relief that the station was filled with ordinary people, but she was shocked at how the cavernous building had deteriorated over the years. It looked dingy now, its grand structures peeling and dirty, people sleeping rough in bundles of rags in the passages and beggars wandering about amongst the milling passengers. She felt Naomi's arm slipping through hers and realised she was being guided gently towards the platforms.

'Come on, Mum, the train for Enghien-les-Bains is this way.'

It felt strange making that train journey again through the northern suburbs of Paris that she and Ruth had first made with the staff and children from Villa Helvetia more than fifty years before. The place looked so different now, so built up. Modern apartment blocks lined the railway track, their walls covered in graffiti, but as the buildings thinned out they passed through the more prosperous suburbs, where neat houses stood in gardens; and, nearing their destination, the surroundings began to look a little more familiar.

At Enghien-les-Bains they got into a waiting taxi, which took them through streets lined with the luxury apartment blocks and villas of the wealthy.

Kitty looked around her in awe. 'This is magnificent,' she murmured, staring out at the beautiful buildings. But Helga could tell she was keeping the lid on her enthusiasm: this wasn't a sightseeing tour. When they reached the tree-lined lake and began to skirt its edge, Helga caught her breath. It was a sunny day and boats with white sails were skimming the mirror-like surface. Day-trippers were bobbing about in pedalos. People were swimming in the lake too, jumping and diving from a jetty. If she half-closed her eyes, she could almost see her younger self there, splashing and playing with the other children from Villa Helvetia in the dazzling sunlight. And there was Ruth beside her, squealing with joy and excitement, throwing herself off the jetty and splashing in the water.

Helga couldn't bear to watch; she turned away from the lake and stared in front of her, focusing on the road ahead. She was suddenly besieged with doubts. Was this the right thing to do? Would she be able to cope with the powerful emotions she was already experiencing and which might overwhelm her when they reached the villa itself? But it was too late to ask herself those questions now; they were driving through Mont-morency itself, rumbling over the cobbles of the neat town square. Helga stared out of the window, disorientated. This was so different from what she'd expected. The little town that she'd preserved in her memory for fifty years as a dull, unassuming pre-war suburb was filled with Saturday-morning shoppers, some relaxing at tables outside cafés, enjoying the sun, others going in and out of the fashionable-looking shops. She'd imagined it would always be the same, completely unprepared that the place would be modern and vibrant now.

What would the villa be like?, she wondered, nerves coursing through her again. It was too late to have regrets. The taxi turned in to a narrow road and drove slowly past some large villas set in their own grounds. Then she saw the familiar street-sign, rue de Valmy, and the taxi pulled up in front of some tall wrought-iron gates. She peered through them, but all she could see was a half-empty car park.

'Are we in the right place?' she asked.

'Yes, this is it. Are you OK, Mum?'

'I think so.'

Naomi came round and opened her door and asked the taxi driver to wait for them by the gates. Helga eased herself out of the car and stood on the road.

Now she was standing up, she could see the huge house behind the few cars and vans in the car park. She gripped the railings and looked through the fence. The outline of the building was exactly as she remembered it: those three elegant roofs and the front porch were almost the same, but the building in her memory and in the photograph in her bedroom was elegant and well maintained, surrounded by tranquil lawns and orchards. This building looked neglected. The paint was peeling from its walls; the balcony above the front porch had been boxed in and ugly modern extensions added. The lawns had been covered in asphalt to make the car park. A sign beside the front gate announcing that it was the police headquarters gave it a slightly forbidding air. The whole place had an unloved, institutional feel to it.

Helga stood there, stock-still, staring; then she walked forward, through the open gates and towards the front steps. In

her mind she was that little girl again, overwhelmed with gratitude that she and Ruth had reached the end of their journey,
carrying her battered leather suitcase towards the house that
would be their refuge and their sanctuary. She walked as if in a
reverie. She could even feel Ruth's arm brushing against her
own as she moved forward.

She felt a hand on her shoulder.

'I'm not sure if it's open today, Mum.'

'Open?' she repeated, confused. Then Kitty was beside her
too, her arm round her friend's shoulder.

'Are you all right, Helga? You've gone very pale.'

Of course she'd gone pale. It was a shock to be here again,
walking the very ground where she and Ruth had regained
some of their childhood, had even been happy and made
friends. Seeing it looking so very different had brought home to
her cruelly the passage of time. She realised how many years
had passed since she'd played under the trees during those few
months of sun-filled days. Time had moved on and left her
behind. That beautiful house and the children who'd lived
there and all those who'd shown them such kindness were long
gone.

'Are you all right, darling?' Kitty repeated and her voice
sounded a long way away. She looked into Kitty's eyes and
realised that, like her, her friend was getting on in years.

'I'm all right. It's a bit of a shock, that's all,' she managed
to say.

'Let's go then, shall we?' Naomi's voice sounded anxious.

Helga allowed them to guide her back to the taxi and help
her get into the back seat. The driver reversed into the drive to
turn round and she had her last glimpse of the villa through the
railings as they drove off back towards the town centre and the
railway station.

She felt Naomi's hand slide into hers as the taxi drew out of
rue de Valmy.

'Are you OK, Mum?'

She nodded, barely able to speak, buffeted by conflicting emotions. She felt paralysed by them, unsure what to think or to feel. She had been completely unprepared for how much the villa would have changed and the sight of that shabby, unloved building had brought so many things home to her. She stared out at the affluent suburb, its well-heeled inhabitants going about their business, at the lake, glittering in the noonday sunlight as the taxi retraced its route to the station at Enghien-les-Bains. None of these people had been here when she had. They were probably completely unaware of what had happened here during the war. Time had moved on and left her behind.

'We're at the station now, Helga.' It was Kitty's voice breaking into her thoughts. She looked around her, disoriented.

'Shall we get out and get the train back to Paris?'

Go back to Paris? Leave all the memories behind here? 'I'm not sure...'

'Is there somewhere else you'd like to go, Mum? If you don't feel like going on the train, we could always ask the driver to take us all the way back into town.'

Helga's heart began to beat a little faster. Of course there was somewhere else. It was the place she hadn't had the courage to mention yet to either Kitty or Naomi. It was the place even she only returned to in her mind in the darkest of times. But she knew it was the place she needed to visit, to come to terms with what had happened back then and to let Kitty and Naomi know the final, dreadful truth about what had happened.

'There is somewhere,' she said in a cracked voice. 'I don't think it's too far away from here, although my memory is a bit hazy.'

Then she leaned forward and addressed the driver. 'Do you know the Convent of Sainte Claire?' she asked.

'Oui, oui, madame, bien sûr.'

'Could you take us there, please?' Helga asked. He nodded, started the car again and pulled back out of the station fore-court. Helga closed her eyes and said a small prayer. Neither Naomi nor Kitty said anything but she felt Naomi's grip on her hand tighten. She was glad of that, because this step really did feel like stepping off a cliff into the abyss.

She'd never thought that she would ever have the courage to go back to the convent, even though the place had barely been out of her thoughts for more than forty years.

TWENTY-SIX

HELGA

Paris, 1939

During those heady summer months in 1939, Helga, in common with all the Jewish children and young people being cared for at the Villa Helvetia, was largely unaware of what was happening in the outside world. The staff did their best to shield them from unpleasantness. They seemed to see it as their mission to make the children's lives as normal as they could, trying to repair the damage they had all suffered living in Nazi Germany and the trauma of losing their families or having to leave their loved ones behind. And sometimes Helga managed to forget, for a moment, about everything she had lost.

There were around ten teachers in all. All were in their twenties and most were Jewish; some were German and some Austrian. Only a couple of them were French. They all had their own reasons for having left Germany. The domestic and catering staff who looked after the villa were mainly French and came from the local community. Despite the initial language

barriers, they were all unfailingly kind and sympathetic to the
children too.

Helga and Ruth passed the summer settling into Villa
Helvetia, making friends with the other children, enjoying the
routine of daily lessons and being taken out and about on visits
to Paris and to swim in the lake at Enghien-les-Bains on sunny
days. They quickly learned French, so they could make themselves understood on these outings and with the villa staff, but
the teachers were careful to ensure that the children did not
lose their native language too, so lessons were always in
German. There were often celebrations – any birthday or
anniversary or important event was marked by singing and
dancing and feasting with cakes and candles. Helga and Ruth
had their thirteenth birthday there at the villa. The sadness of
spending it without their beloved parents was tempered by the
kindness and love of those around them.

During those early days, Helga tried not to think of what
the future might bring, although of course she could never
forget that Tate was suffering back in Germany. One day, when
the days were shortening and there were the beginnings of an
autumnal nip in the air, Helga came down to breakfast in the
dining room and noticed all the teachers conferring anxiously in
hushed tones at their table. She'd never seen them look like that
before; normally they were smiling and positive, at pains to
create and maintain a happy atmosphere for the children at the
villa. Helga felt the stirrings of anxiety in her own stomach,
wondering what this could mean. She didn't say anything to
Ruth – her sister had seemed so settled lately and she didn't
want to see that old anxious look on her face again. But later
that morning, when she passed the staffroom on her way to
collect a book from the dormitory, she overheard a muffled
conversation.

'It won't be long now before Britain declares war. You can
count on it. Hitler's aggression against Poland can't go unpun-

ished. Not after their disastrous appeasement over Austria and the Sudetenland. The British government has guaranteed Poland's borders. They can't fail to act this time.'

'I know, it's terrifying. That means France will have to declare war too. You know that, don't you?'

'I can hardly bear to think about it. We need to get in touch with Yvonne and make plans for the children.'

Helga sidled past the door, her heart beating fast, trying to work out what this impending war might mean for the children at the villa.

That afternoon, while they were sitting under the cherry trees listening to Alfred, one of the young male teachers, giving a reading of *Faust*, Yvonne's sleek black Citroën drew up on the drive. The children were always excited by a visit from Yvonne. She often brought them little presents from Paris, chocolates or books, and was interested in all of them. She knew all of them by name and she knew all their tragic stories too. A ripple of excitement went through the group as she got out of the car, glamorous as ever in her summer hat and a dress of blue silk that seemed to float around her, waved to the children and tripped up the steps to the villa.

Alfred put down his book abruptly, stood up and made an announcement: 'Lessons are over for today, children. You can play in the garden until teatime. Madame de Gunzbourg has just arrived for an urgent meeting, so I need to join her straight away.'

A murmur rippled through the group in excitement at being let off lessons early, but Helga bit her finger nail anxiously, knowing what Yvonne had come to discuss and dreading what might happen next. But to her relief, nothing dramatic did happen that afternoon; Yvonne just called the children together and told them that Germany and France were at war, but that they were not to be alarmed, she would make sure they were safe. Yvonne was such a reassuring presence, her words comforted Helga. But then she thought about Tate. What would this mean for him? Would he be in even more danger than before? She didn't want to upset Ruth by mentioning it to her, but she could tell from her sister's expression that she was thinking about it too.

It was several months before anything really changed for the children at the Villa Helvetia; life went on as normally as possible, despite news sometimes filtering through to the children of developments in the war. Gradually new lessons were introduced to reflect the fact that they were now at war. In handiwork classes they made crude gas masks and were taught how to use them. One of the teachers brought in yards of black cotton and one afternoon they all made blackout curtains for the dormitory windows and fixed them up with drawing pins.

The months wore on and there were increasing signs of the war around them. One day, there was an announcement that Erik and Alfred, two of their beloved young teachers, would no longer be coming to teach them. The children were bemused. What could have happened to them? There had been no sign that either of them was sick. Then the news gradually leaked out that the two young men had been interned by the French government. As German citizens, and because they were Jewish too they were regarded by the French government as enemy aliens.

'It's so unfair,' Ruth muttered when she heard what had happened to them. They were sitting side by side on her bed in the dormitory. 'Why is it that everyone who is kind to us has to leave or is taken away from us?'

'You're thinking about Tate, aren't you? I am too.'

Ruth nodded. 'I never stop thinking about him, really.'

'Me neither,' Helga said, gripping her hand. Moments like these brought the pain of their separation back to them afresh.

The rest of the teachers struggled on, taking bigger classes and working longer hours, and soon the days were shortening and getting colder and winter was upon them. There were no more trips to the lake or into Paris and no more lessons in the garden for several months either. With fewer staff, the teachers were struggling to manage.

That winter was mainly spent huddled round a huge log fire in the schoolroom, being taught by Beatrice or Nicole. At night they had shuddered under blankets in the dormitory, while the windows iced up even on the inside. At break times they played out in the frosty garden bundled up in coats, anxiously listening out for any news of the war that they knew was going on all around them. Sometimes they would see locals hurry past, averting their faces, where before they had smiled at the children inside. Helga could sense how much things were changing for them, even there in Paris where they'd thought they were safe.

Winter gradually passed into spring and once again lessons could take place in the garden, but the atmosphere was tense now and there were no more outings to the lake or into Paris. One day Yvonne appeared, ashen-faced, and went straight to the staffroom to confer with the teachers. After a short meeting, she came into the schoolroom and made an announcement to the children.

'I'm very sorry to say that France is now falling to the German army. It will not be long before the French surrender and Paris falls to them too. Then we will no longer be safe here in the villa, we are sure of that. But you must not be alarmed. We have been making plans for this for several months now and we are well prepared. We have found temporary places for all of you, but for a short time you will no longer all be together, I'm afraid. We are working on opening replacement children's homes in the South of France, but for the time being, you will be sent separately to stay with sympathetic French people who are our friends. They have bravely agreed to look after you until we are able to take you south.'

The next morning, everyone gathered in the front hall of the villa, clutching their luggage, white-faced and anxious. All had had to flee their homes once before and all had bad memories of what had happened on the first occasion. Helga looked around at the faces of the children she'd got to know well over the past few happy months at the villa. Some were with their brothers and sisters, but others were alone and she felt especially sad for them, particularly the young ones. Holding Ruth's hand, she gave her sister a reassuring smile. She counted herself lucky that they were still together and that they would always have each other.

Yvonne had roped in friends and others sympathetic to the OSE cause to help transport the children to their new temporary homes. Helga watched from the porch as the first ones were squeezed into cars and vans and driven out through the gates. All of them turned and waved as they left and those left behind waved too, with tears in their eyes. A gaggle of curious locals stood on the pavement watching the children leave. Helga's arm ached from waving and she kept having to blink away the tears. She was acutely aware that this all-too-brief interlude in their lives was drawing to a close, even though it was possible that some of them would meet again in these other homes in the South of France.

When it was Helga and Ruth's turn to go, they were put in the back of Yvonne's limousine and Yvonne gave the driver instructions.

'Take them to the Convent of Sainte-Maria in Méry sur Oise,' she said. 'The nuns know they are coming. Drive quickly, keep to the backroads if possible and don't go anywhere near the centre of the city. It is already occupied by German soldiers.'

TWENTY-SEVEN

HELGA

Paris, 1940–41

The journey took longer than Helga had expected. The driver
took them through backstreets under darkening skies and she
lost all sense of where they were. Even those backstreets were
crammed with vehicles: cars and vans, their roofs piled with
suitcases; even horse-drawn carts laden with possessions. Often
the traffic ground to a halt and the driver would swear in
French.

'Everyone is leaving Paris. Fleeing south,' he told them.
'People are terrified of the Nazis.'

It was almost dark by the time they were travelling through
the narrow streets of a little town a few miles outside the city.
The car turned in through wrought-iron gates and drew up in a
courtyard. Helga looked out nervously. They were in front of a
forbidding stone building with narrow shuttered windows. An
unsmiling woman with an anxious, lined face, her hair hidden
under a veil, opened the back door of the car and motioned for

them to get out. She didn't even greet the girls as they climbed out with their cases. She spoke to the driver in French in hushed tones, slammed the back door and the car drew away immediately. Helga swallowed hard and looked at Ruth. Ruth shrugged her shoulders.

'I am Mother Joan, the mother superior here at the convent,' the woman informed them in broken German. 'We are Franciscan nuns here. I don't speak your language well, but Madame de Gunzbourg has asked for our help with her Jewish orphans and we are happy to give it. We will look after you here until arrangements can be made for you to go south.'

Helga and Ruth muttered their thanks and followed the nun inside the building, through a huge, vaulted dining hall, up a narrow stone staircase and along an equally narrow corridor. At the end, Mother Joan pushed back a studded oak door to reveal a cell-like room. It was sparsely furnished with one little bed on either side, a chest with a jug and bowl and a wooden cross on the whitewashed wall above them.

'The nuns are all at prayer at the moment, but you can join them later on for your evening meal. Please make yourselves at home, but you must put these clothes on before you come downstairs. Now that Paris has fallen to the Nazis, we expect the convent to be searched without notice. We will say you are young novices. I understand you speak some French. It would be better if you were fluent of course, but there's nothing to be done about that. There is water in the jug for drinking and washing. I will come and fetch you before supper.'

When she had gone, her footsteps echoing away down the stone corridor, Helga and Ruth sat down on one of the beds, silently taking in the new situation they found themselves in.

'I don't like it here,' said Ruth after a pause, voicing the very same thought that Helga herself was having.

'We'll get used to it,' Helga replied, wondering why she sometimes felt the need to jolly her sister along.

'Mother Joan seems such a cold person,' Ruth said. 'Why couldn't Yvonne look after us, or one of the teachers?'

'We probably wouldn't be safe with them. They are Jewish, after all. They might need to hide too.'

'How long do you think we will have to stay here?'

It was Helga's turn to shrug. 'I don't know, Ruth. Yvonne said just until they can take us to a new home.' She put her arm round her sister's shoulders. 'It's not that bad. We've been through worse, after all.'

'I know...' Ruth fell silent then and Helga knew that her mind was running over everything that had happened to them over the past two years. It was like a terrifying nightmare from which there seemed to be no escape. And the more they moved around, the less likely it was that Tate would ever find them – if he survived. 'When will it ever end, Helga?' Ruth turned to her with pleading eyes. Helga had no answers for her sister. She felt just as Ruth did, but she knew she must stay strong. One of them had to.

'I don't know,' she said. 'One day it will. Look, why don't we put these clothes on and get ready, like Mother Joan said? It all feels strange now, but we'll get used to it here. We always do.'

Half an hour later, Mother Joan knocked on their door and took them down to the huge refectory, where the long tables were filled with young women dressed just as they were, in long, shapeless black dresses. It had felt strange putting the costumes on, fastening the headdresses over their hair, almost like getting ready for a fancy-dress party when they were little. They had stood together and looked into a blemished mirror on the bedroom wall and laughed at each other. That had lightened their mood a little. The young novice nuns smiled kindly and passed them food and water at the meal, but none of them spoke any German, so they had to get by with their French. The food was simple and basic – bread, steamed fish and green vegetables – but there was plenty of it and the girls were hungry. When it was over the nuns filed silently away to their dormitories. Mother Joan approached.

'It is bedtime now, girls,' she said briskly. 'Early to bed and early to rise here. The novices wake before dawn for early-morning prayers. We don't expect you to join us for prayers, but breakfast is always at six thirty. I will wake you at six o'clock so you have time to get ready.'

On the very first day a strict routine was established. They were up before dawn, shivering as they washed in the cold water from a jug in their bedroom, then they dressed in those shapeless, anonymous costumes. Breakfast of plain bread or unsweetened porridge was taken in the vaulted refectory, followed by daily chores. They were kept busy – helping the nuns out in the convent kitchen garden, weeding between the rows of vegetables or picking fruit and vegetables for meals, feeding or mucking out the animals that the nuns kept – chickens for their eggs, goats for milk. Sometimes they worked in the huge but simple convent kitchen, peeling and chopping vegetables, stoking the fire with wood, plucking chickens. They quickly got to know the names of most of the novice nuns. All of them were earnest, kind young women, devoted to God and to helping others. They took Helga and Ruth under their wing and, although this place had its failings and could never replace the warmth and love they'd experienced at the Villa Helvetia, they at least felt safe and cared for.

The weeks wore on. The two sisters gradually made friends with some of the younger novices, who took a particular interest in them. Their French improved in leaps and bounds because there was no other way to make themselves understood. Mother Joan brought them some books to read, but they were prayer-books and pious texts in French and the girls quickly gave up trying to understand them. The hours dragged by and they would lie on their beds and talk about the old days, about school and Berlin and about Mame and Tate, trying to keep their memories alive. They often spoke about the Villa Helvetia too, wondering where all the other children had gone and when they would get to see some of them again.

'It's so boring here,' Ruth would say repeatedly, looking longingly out of the slit-like window in their room. 'When will Yvonne come back?'

'I don't know, but she *will* come back for us, I'm sure of that,' Helga replied, but she shared Ruth's frustration. How long would they be there for?

After a few months, though, life became a little more interesting. Two new faces joined them at suppertime, two women in their early twenties; but these two looked different. Helga could see instantly by the expression in their eyes that these two newcomers weren't normal novices. She could tell from the way their hair fell out from beneath their wimples that they had long hair, like hers and Ruth's, not the neat, short hair-cuts of the novice nuns. One of the new young women had red hair and freckles and the other one was blonde with blue eyes. They were introduced as Sister Françoise and Sister Genevieve but no one explained why they were there.

Although the two newcomers lived in the convent and were there at most mealtimes, they didn't attend prayers with the other nuns and often left the convent for hours at a time. Helga and Ruth speculated as to who they might be.

'Perhaps they're in hiding like us?' Ruth suggested, but Helga wasn't sure.

'They don't look Jewish. Why would they be in hiding?'

One day, shortly after the two newcomers had arrived, as Helga and Ruth were dressing for breakfast they noticed a little van parked outside in the courtyard. That was unusual at this time of day. A dark-haired man dressed in a blue boiler suit got out of the driver's seat and came round and opened the back doors. Two women climbed out, dressed in baggy workmen's clothes.

'Look, that's them. That's Genevieve and Françoise,' Ruth said. Helga stared, gradually recognising them by their hair colour and realising that Ruth was right.

The man slammed the doors of the van, the three conferred briefly and then the man got into the van and drove away.

The two young women were late for breakfast that morning, sliding in at the end of the table near to where Ruth and Helga were sitting. They both looked tired, with dark shadows under their eyes, but they ate voraciously. Helga was itching to ask Genevieve and Françoise what they'd been doing, but it was Ruth who had the courage to speak up first.

'We saw you this morning,' she said in a low voice, leaning towards Genevieve, who had moved their way to offer them the bread basket. 'We saw you getting out of a van. Where did you go last night?'

Genevieve's hazel eyes widened in shock then she looked around nervously and held a finger up to her lips.

'Be careful who you speak to about that. All the nuns here are trustworthy, but be sure not to tell anyone else.'

'We don't ever see anyone else,' Ruth said. 'You can trust us. You might have been told, we are in hiding here, so we wouldn't tell anyone any secrets. But what were you doing?'

Again, Genevieve looked around, then she leaned forward and spoke in a whisper.

'We are members of a new organisation that's springing up all over France since the German occupation. People are calling it the Résistance. Many French people are very angry at what is happening in this country. People are being made to pay for the occupation and those who protest are being arrested. We're working against the Nazis, doing our bit to make things difficult for them. We had to leave our homes in Paris last week because things got dangerous for us. Mother Joan offered to take us in here. She is a strong, brave woman.'

Helga and Ruth both fell silent, contemplating this momentous revelation.

'So, were you out with this organisation last night?'

Françoise nodded and spoke in a whisper. 'We were. But you mustn't talk about this to anyone. You promise?'

Helga and Ruth nodded solemnly. 'Of course we won't. But won't you tell us where you went? What were you doing?'

'We can't tell you that, it would be dangerous for you to know. Now, please eat your breakfast and don't ask any more questions.'

The arrival of these two members of the Résistance gave an instant source of interest to life in the convent for Helga and Ruth. If the two young women failed to turn up for meals, they would spend hours speculating about where had gone to and would sit at the bedroom window looking for the little grey Peugeot van that always brought them back from their missions. At mealtimes they would try to sit near Genevieve and Françoise so they could engage them in conversation and try to find out what they had been doing.

At first the two women were reluctant to divulge any details of their missions, but gradually, as they learned what Helga and Ruth had been through themselves, they became more willing to let the girls into their confidence. One day after Genevieve and Françoise had been at the convent a few weeks, Ruth pressed them for details of what they had been doing the previous night and this time Genevieve put down her knife and fork, leaned forward and whispered, 'All right, this time I will tell you but keep it to yourself. Last night we went to sabotage a railway line, to disrupt German troop movements.'

Helga's eyes widened and she regarded the two with even more respect than before.

'Sabotage?' she repeated, wondering what that meant.

'We cut the signals on the line to cause delays and confusion to the rail routes. We know the Nazis are planning to move troops to the front line, so this is one way of delaying that and helping the Allied war effort.'

'Can't we join your organisation?' Ruth asked, her voice eager. 'We've told you what the Nazis did to us. They killed our mother. They arrested our father and took him away. They stole his business from him. We would do anything to stop them.'

Genevieve gave Ruth a sympathetic look. 'That's terrible. I understand how you must feel,' she said, 'but you are far too young to join, I'm afraid.'

Ruth drew herself up. 'We're not young, we are almost fourteen.' That wasn't quite true, but Helga did nothing to correct her sister's white lie.

Françoise patted Ruth's hand consolingly. 'It's very brave of you to offer, but we wouldn't want to put you in danger.'

Every day Helga and Ruth asked the same question and every day Genevieve and Françoise gently rebuffed them. Helga and Ruth became fascinated by the two young women, their bravery and the cause they were working for. Ruth in particular barely talked of anything else when she and Helga were alone. Helga understood her sister's feelings. She knew she felt that way because these women and their comrades were risking their lives to fight against the very regime that had robbed them of everything they held dear.

One day after the evening meal, when the nuns were trooping up to their dormitories and Genevieve and Françoise had gone to the room they shared, no doubt to change into the clothes they wore on their missions, Ruth said to Helga, 'Why don't we slip out and follow them tonight? See where they go to?'

Helga's heart started beating faster. 'It could be dangerous, Ruth.'

'We've been in plenty of danger before, haven't we? What does it matter? I'm not afraid.'

'We're not allowed to leave the convent.'

'I know that!' Ruth snapped, rolling her eyes. 'Let's break the rules for once, do something worthwhile! Come on,' she pulled Helga by the arm, 'let's get changed.'

TWENTY-EIGHT

HELGA

Paris, 1941

Reluctantly, Helga agreed and followed Ruth to their bedroom, where they changed into old pairs of trousers they had in their suitcases. As Helga pulled hers on, she realised how short they were on her now and how difficult it was to do up the buttons. She'd grown so much since she'd worn them last. Sadness washed through her as she realised how long ago it was since they'd left their home in Berlin. How long ago since they'd been with Mame and Tate, living as a normal family.

'This is a crazy idea,' she said to Ruth. 'Françoise and Genevieve will go out in that van and we won't be able to follow them anyway.'

'They don't always go in the van,' Ruth countered. 'Sometimes they walk. They walked last night, remember?'

Helga couldn't find a ready excuse not to go, but her stomach was tightening with nerves as they crept downstairs, let themselves out onto the drive by the front door and waited in the shadow of the convent walls. After a few minutes, Françoise and Genevieve came out through the front door and crossed the drive. To unsuspecting eyes they could have just been out for an evening stroll.

'Come on,' Ruth hissed and they set off after the two young women, walking arm in arm. They followed them down the quiet road, keeping their distance, waiting behind bushes or lampposts if they got too close. They were nearing the centre of the little town when the two women stopped suddenly and Françoise turned round. Helga and Ruth darted into an alleyway.

'We know you're following us,' Françoise said. 'Go back to the convent. You're putting yourselves in danger.'

Shamefacedly, Helga and Ruth stepped out from the little alley.

'We want to help,' Ruth pleaded. 'Won't you let us come with you? Just this once?'

The two young women hesitated, but only for a second.

'No.' Genevieve's voice was fierce. 'You need to go back. Right away, or I will tell the mother superior that you've been out of the convent. Who knows what the punishment would be for that? She might refuse to let you stay there.'

'Please! We want to help you,' Ruth persisted.

'No! You're endangering all of us. Go back. You're holding us up too, we shouldn't be hanging about on the street like this.'

Françoise stepped in. 'Look,' she said more gently. 'Genevieve is right. We can't take you with us. Not tonight, it's too dangerous. But if you go back now, without a fuss, we might let you come another time.'

'Françoise! You have no authority...' Genevieve protested.

'They want to help. And they could be useful. Think about it.' Then she turned back to the girls. 'Look, go back now and we'll talk in the morning.'

Ruth stood facing the two Frenchwomen, her eyes blazing,

and for a few moments Helga thought she was going to carry on protesting. She put her hand on her sister's arm.

'Come on, Ruth. Let's go back now. They've said we can go with them another time.'

Helga sensed her sister's reluctance, but eventually Ruth gave in and turned round and they retraced their steps to the convent. There, they let themselves in quietly through the front door and slipped through the corridors and up to their room unnoticed.

Genevieve and Françoise kept their word. Two nights later, at supper, Françoise leaned forward and whispered to Helga and Ruth: 'We've talked it over and decided that you can come with us tonight. It should be quite straightforward. You can keep a lookout for us while we cut some wires. Meet us outside the front door at nine o'clock and we'll explain more then.'

Helga's nerves started tingling again at the thought of the danger they would be putting themselves in. She wished she was brave like Ruth; as she glanced at her sister's face, she could see from the way Ruth's eyes shone that she was already relishing the prospect of the mission whatever the dangers. *How different we are underneath everything*, she thought.

But she knew there was no getting out of this, so she followed Ruth meekly up to their room and got changed, her stomach fizzing with nerves and her hands shaking so much she could hardly fasten her buttons. Then they hurried downstairs and were already waiting outside the front door, dressed in their trousers and sweaters, when Genevieve and Françoise emerged from the building into the moonlit courtyard at nine o'clock sharp.

Genevieve spoke first.

'I'm still not sure this is a good idea,' she said, looking at the girls, her face deadly serious, 'but Françoise has persuaded me that you could be useful to us and I'm going along with her wishes. It means you must do exactly as we say and if you put a foot out of line this will be the last time we ever let you come out with us.'

'You can trust us,' Ruth replied staunchly.

'This is what we're going to do,' Françoise said. 'Genevieve and I are going to climb onto the roof of the town hall, which is where the Nazis have their local headquarters, and we're going to cut the telephone wires to the building. There are two points at which the lines enter the building and if we cut both at the same time we will be quicker. We need you to keep a lookout. The building is empty in the evenings but there are guards who patrol outside. They take eleven minutes to go round the perimeter of the building, but we need you to let us know if they come back sooner than expected, or if anyone else approaches. Do you think you can do that?'

'Of course,' said Ruth, pride in her voice.

Helga's heart was hammering against her ribs as she and Ruth followed the two Frenchwomen through the quiet, moonlit streets of the little town. A couple of vehicles crawled past and in one she recognised Nazi officers, with swastikas on their epaulets. Shock washed through her and she dropped her gaze to the ground, terrified that the officers would stop and question them. What would she and Ruth do then? They had no papers on them and away from the convent and dressed as they were no one would believe they were novice nuns. With their dark hair and eyes, she and Ruth would surely be recognised as Jewish. But to her relief the van drove past without stopping and Helga realised that four young women walking together might pass for sisters or friends walking home from an innocent family gathering.

They reached the entrance to the square and Helga was shocked to see draped over the fronts of the buildings red banners bearing the ominous swastika. For a second she was back in Berlin, hurrying through the streets, fearing the SS and the Gestapo could be waiting round every corner for them.

'We don't need to go into the square,' Françoise hissed, 'we will go round the back of the building. There's a way we can climb up to cut the wires. Look, the guards have come out to do their round of the square. We need to hurry.'

Helga followed the others down a narrow side street that ran behind the town hall. There were some tall metal gates behind it that led into a cobbled service yard. The gates stood open.

'Come on, this way.' Françoise beckoned them on and in through the gates, keeping to the shadows.

A single-storey outhouse ran the length of the back of the town hall building.

'We're going to climb up onto the roof here.' Genevieve waved towards some dustbins. 'You two wait here in the court-yard. Crouch down behind the bins but keep a lookout. If the guards come back, or anyone else comes, make the hoot of an owl. Can you do that?'

'Of course,' Ruth said. Helga just nodded. She was sure she wouldn't be able to speak even if she tried, let alone make an owl noise. Obediently, they huddled down beside the large metal bins and watched as Françoise and Genevieve climbed up onto them and hoisted themselves up onto the roof of the one-storey building. Then they disappeared from view. The minutes ticked past. All Helga was aware of was the sound of her own heartbeat, Ruth's breathing and the foul smell of the dustbins. Every second seemed to drag and, although her ears were primed for the sound of Françoise and Genevieve's foot-steps on the roof, many minutes seemed to pass and still they didn't appear. Helga kept her eyes glued to the open gateway, hoping against hope that the guards wouldn't come back.

Suddenly the sound of an engine in the street outside broke the silence and within seconds, headlights appeared in the gate-way. Helga and Ruth made desperate hooting sounds but their voices were drowned out by the engine noise. The next second

Françoise and Genevieve appeared above them and were scrambling down from the bins.

'This way!'

The two Frenchwomen darted away from the bins and towards the side of the building, where a concrete path ran around the town hall, hemmed in by a fence on one side. Genevieve stopped halfway along the side of the town hall and looked around. Then came the sound of the doors of the vehicle slamming in the courtyard.

'We have to climb over this fence,' she said urgently, her face strained and white. 'You girls go first. We will help you over.'

'I don't need help,' Ruth said, her foot already on the lower rail of the fence. Helga watched helplessly as in one swift motion Ruth pulled herself up and over the fence; but, as she tried to jump free, her trouser leg caught in one of the spikes on top of the railings and, with a ripping sound and a muffled squeal, she fell awkwardly onto the road beneath.

'Ruth!'

'Quick now, be careful.' It was Genevieve's voice. The next second Helga felt Genevieve's hands under her armpits, lifting her up and helping her scramble over the fence, while Françoise climbed over beside her. Then all three of them had landed on the ground on the other side and were kneeling briefly beside Ruth, whose face was pale in the moonlight, wet with tears. She was biting her lip to stop herself crying out in pain.

'We need to get away before they find us,' Françoise said and even as she spoke they could hear gruff German voices in the courtyard behind them.

'I heard something!' barked a male voice. 'Round the side of the building. We need to check.'

'Come on!'

Françoise and Genevieve hoisted Ruth onto their shoulders between them and half walked, half ran away from the town hall, staggering between the buildings and lurching towards one of the side streets. Helga followed. Everything happened in a blur as they struggled along, trying to find shelter in the dark streets. There were shouts from the courtyard behind them, then came the choking sound of the engine starting up again.

'This way!' Halfway down a side street, Genevieve opened a solid gate in a wall and led them through it. They found themselves in the dark back yard of a house and crouched against a wall, listening breathlessly. The engine sound came closer and from the flash of headlights against the buildings opposite they knew that the vehicle had turned in to their street. Had they been seen? Helga wondered with dread in her heart, crouching there beside Ruth. She was shaking from head to toe. She held her breath as the vehicle drew closer, then for an endless moment it seemed to be lingering beside the gate they were hiding behind. Helga held her breath, but the vehicle eventually crawled past on the road. The light from the headlights finally disappeared and they heard the crunch of gears as it turned into the next street.

The sound of the engine faded away and, as her heartbeat slowed down, Helga became aware that Ruth was whimpering beside her.

'Are you all right?' Françoise asked.

'No,' Ruth gasped. 'My leg is killing me, I really feel sick.'

'It's the shock. Genevieve and I will carry you back to the convent. Mother Joan will help you, she has medical training.'

They left the darkened yard behind and, checking to make sure they weren't being watched, they crept back out onto the road. Then, cautiously and tentatively, listening out for the sound of an engine or voices, they began to make their slow and painful way back to the convent.

They took the backstreets and kept to the shadows all the way. Helga followed behind the others as Ruth hopped along between the two Frenchwomen. She couldn't even put her left foot on the ground. It was slow progress because each time a vehicle approached, they stopped and pressed themselves against a wall or hid in a nearby alleyway.

At last the dim lights of the convent came into sight and Helga breathed a sigh of relief that safety was only a few steps away. But the relief was tinged with anxiety. What would Mother Joan's reaction be when she found out what they'd been doing?

Once inside, Genevieve and Françoise laid Ruth down on a bench in the refectory and fetched Mother Joan. She came down, still wearing her habit despite the hour, holding a lamp in one hand. She was frowning deeply and shaking her head in disapproval, but she said nothing at first. Instead, she got down on her knees and ripped Ruth's bloody trouser leg away up to the knee. Ruth yelled out in pain and Helga gasped when she saw her sister's shinbone protruding from a ragged wound in her skin.

'This is serious,' Mother Joan said. 'I should fetch the doctor.'

'Don't do that, Holy Mother, please,' Genevieve implored. 'Nobody can be trusted.'

Mother Joan gave her a withering look. 'You shouldn't have taken these children out with you – you know that, I'm sure. I can only hope it was worth it.'

'It was,' Françoise said. 'We managed to cut the telephone wires to the town hall. But someone came along and we had to make a hasty escape.'

'I hope and pray that nobody saw you,' Mother Joan said. 'I agreed to give you two shelter but I don't want trouble from the Nazis here. Now, will one of you go and fetch some warm water and some muslin cloths from the kitchen.'

'I'll go,' Helga volunteered and hurried away. She'd begun to feel faint at the sight of Ruth's leg and needed some air. She went down the passage to the convent kitchen, found some muslin rags in the storeroom and filled a large mixing bowl with water. Then she began to make her way back along the passage towards the refectory. But as she neared it, she froze; the door-bell was ringing and fists hammering on the front door. She stopped in her tracks, shrinking back into a doorway.

'I'll go,' she heard Mother Joan mutter. 'Take Ruth upstairs and put on your habits. Lock the bedroom door.'

The frantic banging and ringing of the bell continued. Helga heard Genevieve and Françoise grunting with effort as they heaved Ruth across the refectory and up the narrow stair-case. Then came the sound of Mother Joan's footsteps approaching the door, drawing back the bolts and unlocking it.

'Good evening,' Helga heard her say.

'Good evening, Holy Mother.' The unmistakeable German accent: it was a Nazi officer! Helga's blood froze in her veins and she felt sick with terror.

'We are looking for a group of young women who have been causing problems for us. We need to search your premises.'

'You will do no such thing, officer,' barked Mother Joan. 'I have been promised by your commanding officer that he will respect the sanctity of my convent.'

'That may be the case, but tonight is an exception.'

'There *are* no exceptions, I was given a cast-iron guarantee.'

'I really must insist on searching your premises, Holy Mother. I have reason to believe the women are hiding here.'

Helga couldn't stop shaking. She was holding the bowl of water and the surface was trembling. It was all she could do not to drop it.

'Don't be ridiculous, Captain. The only women here are my novice nuns and they are all asleep. Their privacy must be respected. Your commanding officer gave me his word about that. You need to go back and speak to him right now.'

There was a long pause, then the German clicked his heels together and said, 'If you insist, I will do that, Holy Mother.

And don't worry, I will be back again soon. If we find those women here, you will soon come to understand that we don't take lies and disobedience lightly.'

Helga heard the door slam and the vehicle leave the court-yard with a squeal of tyres. She walked forward into the refectory and caught sight of Mother Joan's haggard face. She was leaning against the doorframe breathing heavily. Her whole frame seemed to droop. But when she saw Helga, she straightened up.

'Take that water upstairs, Helga. I will follow and attend to your sister's broken leg.'

After giving a trembling and sobbing Ruth some painkillers and a sleeping draught, Mother Joan bathed her leg and bandaged it up to a piece of flat wood. A few minutes later and Ruth was sleeping soundly.

'Now, you two go back to your room,' she addressed Genevieve and Françoise, who had been waiting with Ruth in the bedroom. 'In the future you must be more careful. I've already had to lie for you this evening. This must not happen again.'

Then she left them alone. Françoise and Genevieve left too and Helga got into bed, her nerves jangling. She knew she wouldn't be able to sleep after everything that had happened that night. She was also terrified that the Nazi officers would come back and discover them there. In those moments she longed for Tate's arms to be wrapped round her and for Mame's soothing voice to say to her, 'Everything will be all right, little one. There's no need to worry.'

In the morning, she awoke from a fitful sleep to the sound of car tyres on the gravel outside the window. She glanced over at Ruth, who was still asleep. Helga crawled out of bed and looked out, thinking it would be the officer back again. But her heart lifted when she saw Yvonne's black Citroën drawn up on the drive and Yvonne herself, dressed stylishly in a black coat and wide-brimmed hat, approaching the front door. Helga dressed quickly in her habit, left Ruth sleeping and went downstairs.

Yvonne and Mother Joan were sitting at the end of one of the long tables, conferring with their heads bent together. The kitchen staff were moving about preparing the room for breakfast. Helga approached tentatively and Yvonne looked up, her face breaking into a smile.

'Helga, my dear,' she said brightly. 'I have some good news for you. I've come to take you away from here.'

TWENTY-NINE

HELGA

Paris, 1941

Helga didn't want to offend Mother Joan by letting the relief she felt at the announcement that she was to leave the convent be too obvious, so she remained silent. Yvonne held out her hand. 'Come, Helga. Come and sit down. Let me tell you all about it.'

Helga sat down beside Yvonne at the table. She was all too aware of Mother Joan's disapproving eyes on her face.

'There is a ship leaving for America in a few days. I have booked a passage for you and your sister on that ship, the SS *Mouzinho*. This is your opportunity to get away from Europe and start a new life.'

'Oh,' Helga whispered, biting her lip, her spirits plummeting like a stone. Hadn't they tried this before? Hadn't the American president himself turned them away from Florida only last year? She recalled the twinkling lights of Miami and their excitement as they spotted them from their cabin window.

Why would it be any different this time? What was the guarantee that they wouldn't be turned away yet again?

'The downside is that you must leave today,' Yvonne was saying now. 'There is no time to waste. The ship is leaving from Lisbon in Portugal – it can't dock in France, for obvious reasons – and I need to put you on a train to Marseille to start your journey south without delay.'

Helga had no words; she hung her head, avoiding Yvonne's eyes. Her thoughts were a turmoil of confused emotions. She was thinking about Ruth and her broken leg. But then Yvonne gave voice to her fears. She took Helga's hand and squeezed it.

'Mother Joan has told me all about what happened last night,' she went on in a gentle voice. 'She tells me that Ruth has broken her leg very badly.' Yvonne paused and leaned forward, looking into Helga's eyes, her own dark ones deadly serious. 'You do know what that means, don't you?'

Helga shook her head quickly, not wanting to face what Yvonne was about to tell her.

'I'm afraid that Ruth won't be able to make the journey with you, Helga darling,' Yvonne said softly. 'It's clear that neither of you can stay here in the convent in case the officers come back, but I will take Ruth away from here and shelter her until the next ship sails to America. She can stay with Beatrice and her family. She will be safe there. Many more transports are being planned by Jewish charities across the world so there will be another ship very soon. She can join you then.'

Helga felt tears spring instantly to her eyes and she shook her head. 'I can't go without Ruth,' she said vehemently. She felt Yvonne's arms round her shoulders. Yvonne pulled her close and she caught the scent of the woman's expensive perfume. It was the same perfume Mame used to wear. She tried to pull away.

'Now, I know this is difficult, but you need to be brave, Helga. I have paid for that passage to America for you. Some of the others from the Villa Helvetia will be going with you, so you won't be alone. All of you children need to get out of France as soon as you possibly can. I can assure you that Ruth will be able to follow you once she is better.'

'But we want to be together. I need to look after her, I need to help her to get better.'

'*We* can do that, Helga. Ruth will be in the best of hands.'

'But why do I have to go without her? Why can't I stay and wait for the next ship too?'

She noticed a quick look pass between Mother Joan and Yvonne.

'I'm sorry, Helga,' Yvonne said, her voice firm now, 'but we have been working very hard to secure you and Ruth passages on that ship. I have made sure you have all the right papers and at such short notice I won't be able to get papers for another child to fill Ruth's place. That means we are wasting one place already. I don't want to waste your place on the ship too, my dear. People have been working hard and making many sacrifices to enable each child to escape Europe. Many kind people have donated money they can't afford so that you can go. You wouldn't want those sacrifices to be in vain, would you?'

Guilt washed through Helga, but still she resisted. A crazy thought flashed through her mind that it might even be better to stay here and be arrested by the Nazis than to be separated from Ruth.

'If you hadn't gone on that escapade last night, your sister would be going to America with you this morning. The pair of you have only yourselves to blame,' Mother Joan cut in.

'Holy Mother, please,' Yvonne protested. 'There is no need to remind her of that.'

'We were only trying to do what we thought was right.' Helga finally found her voice. 'We wanted to help.'

'And look where helping has got your sister, child,' Mother Joan said bitterly.

'Please, Holy Mother,' Yvonne repeated. She pushed her chair back. 'I am going to speak to Ruth now. She will understand that this will only be a temporary separation, Helga, I'm sure. Wait here.'

Yvonne got up from the table. Helga watched her walk away towards the stairs. Mother Joan got up too and looked down at Helga, her face softening a little.

'I'm sorry for my harsh words, Helga my child. Forgive me. They were said in haste and I know you had the best of motives. But you need to take this opportunity to leave France. If you don't go now, who knows, the charities might not be prepared to pay for a second passage for you.'

By now the other nuns were filing into the refectory for breakfast and Mother Joan and Yvonne's places were taken by novices. They passed Helga bread and porridge and urged her to eat. Nobody asked where her sister was, or why Genevieve and Françoise hadn't appeared for breakfast. Nobody mentioned the visit from the Nazi officer in the middle of the night either, but Helga knew that some of them must have heard the banging on the door. She toyed with her bread miserably, unable to eat, thinking about the decision she must make that either way would have momentous consequences.

She didn't have to sit there for long. Soon there was a tap on her shoulder and Yvonne's voice in her ear.

'I've spoken to your sister. As I predicted, she is being very sensible about this. She is keen for you to go on ahead of her to New York. Come and talk to her yourself.'

Upstairs in their cell-like room, Ruth was sitting up in bed, her face as white as the wall behind her. As soon as Helga entered, she held out her arms. Helga ran to her and flung her arms round her.

'I can't go without you, Ruthie. We need to stay together. Mame and Tate would have wanted us to.'

Ruth shook her head. 'They wouldn't have wanted that,

they would have wanted us to do what is right for both of us in the long run. If you don't go now, there might not be another chance for you to go in the future, then we would both have to stay. Mame and Tate wouldn't have wanted that, would they?'

Helga shrugged, looking deeply into her sister's eyes. All she saw there were optimism and bravery, and she looked away in shame. She felt neither of those things herself.

'Pack your suitcase, Helga,' said Ruth. 'Yvonne and Beatrice will look after me and when I'm better, I will join you on the next transport. It won't be for long.'

'But I don't want to leave you,' Ruth protested. 'What if... what if...?'

'Don't think like that, Helga. Be positive. Yvonne always keeps her word. She will make sure I can come and join you later on.'

Helga looked from Yvonne to Ruth and back again. Both were urging her to go, neither of them thinking that their plan could fail.

'Ruth is right,' Yvonne said briskly. 'Pack your bag, Helga. We need to leave right away to get you on that train.'

Hardly able to see what she was doing through the blur of tears, Helga pulled her little leather suitcase out from under her bed and began to fold and pack the few clothes she had first packed from her bedroom drawer in Leipziger Strasse. She kept back her trousers and sweater, shrugged out of her shapeless habit and pulled the old clothes on, even though the knees of the trousers were grubby from kneeling down behind the bins of the town hall. All too soon she was ready. Yvonne was standing in the doorway, waiting for her. Helga fastened the suitcase.

'Say your goodbyes for now. I'll meet you downstairs.'

The door closed and Helga flung herself into Ruth's arms again.

'I'm so sorry, Ruthie,' she said through the sobs.

'There's nothing to be sorry about. Don't cry, we'll be

together again soon.' Ruth's eyes were filled with tears too. 'Go on, Helga. Don't worry about me.'

Like a sleepwalker, Helga tore herself away from Ruth and, with one last agonising glance, left the room and made her way downstairs to where Mother Joan, Françoise and Genevieve were waiting. The two Frenchwomen embraced her tearfully, but Mother Joan said briskly, 'Good luck, Helga. You are a brave girl and God is watching over you.'

'Merci, Mother Joan,' she managed to say.

She walked slowly, reluctantly out of the convent door and onto the drive. Yvonne was already sitting in the passenger seat. The driver was holding the back door of the limousine open for her and, with an aching heart, she slid onto the back seat alone. The front door slammed, the engine started and the car began to move. Helga turned and looked up at the narrow window of the little bedroom she and Ruth had shared for the past few months, not expecting her sister to be there. To her surprise Ruth's face was pressed against the glass and she was waving frantically. Behind Ruth, supporting her, stood Françoise, who was waving too. The car swung out onto the street and accelerated away, towards the city centre and the Gare de Lyon, where Helga would board the train that would take her south to Marseille and then on to Lisbon. As they drove towards the city, Helga sank back into the leather seat. She didn't want to see the streets of Paris for the last time. All she could think of was Ruth's tearful face pressed against the window and how leaving her behind was like leaving a part of her own heart back there in that convent.

THIRTY

HELGA

Paris, 1990

'She was standing just there. In that window, when we drove away,' Helga said, her voice choked with emotion. 'It was the last time I ever saw my sister.' She was pointing up to the narrow window that was now blackened with the accumulated dirt of decades. Several of its small panes were broken and the frame was rotting too.

She, Kitty and Naomi were standing in front of the forbidding Gothic building that had once been the Convent of Sainte-Maria. They stood behind the makeshift metal fence constructed by developers. There were PRIVATE, DANGER and NO ENTRY signs at regular intervals all along the fence, which made it impossible to get anywhere near the building. The convent building itself was crumbling and derelict. A chimney and part of the roof had fallen in, many of the windows were smashed and vegetation was sprouting from the gutters.

It had been a shock to Helga when they had first driven up in the taxi and she'd seen the state of the once-pristine building.

'Did you know it had closed down, Mum?' Naomi had asked when Helga took a sharp intake of breath at the sight of it.

'No, I didn't know it had finally closed but I did know that it was on its last legs. I came here, you see, after the war. I was trying to find Ruth.'

'You came to Paris?' Kitty exclaimed.

Helga nodded. 'I'm sorry I lied to you both,' she said. 'I just couldn't face telling you the truth. I hope you'll forgive me. I'm ready to tell you everything now.'

'We've told you before, darling,' said Kitty gently, 'there's nothing to forgive.'

The taxi had dropped them there half an hour before. They'd stood there, staring at the forlorn building, while Helga had gradually unravelled the truth of what had happened to her and Ruth there.

Now Naomi said, 'So, did you find out what happened what to Ruth after you left, Mum?'

Helga took a deep breath and swallowed her tears.

'This is so hard for me to say, but I know she died. During the war. I don't know the full story, but I did manage to find out some of what happened when I came back here after the war.'

It had been spotting with rain and at that moment it started to pour down in earnest. Kitty, ever practical, said, 'Why don't we find a café or somewhere else to sit down, Helga darling? Then you'll be able to talk properly.'

'All right. I expect there will be one on the square in front of the town hall,' Helga said. 'I'll probably be able to tell you where that is.'

They hurried through the streets of the little town, their heads bowed against the light summer drizzle. None of them had brought an umbrella. Traffic sped past, splashing through the puddles, and they all had wet legs by the time they approached the rear of the town hall from the backstreets.

'There it is... there's the courtyard,' Helga said, pointing to an unremarkable car park full of cars.

The place was quite recognisable to her still. There was that one-storey extension that ran the length of the building where Françoise and Genevieve had clambered up to sever the telephone wires that fateful night. She shivered, not just because of the rain soaking through to her skin. She was remembering crouching there behind the bins, the sound of the German army vehicle coming into the courtyard.

'Let's go into the square,' she said hurriedly, not wanting to linger in that place any longer than necessary, remembering the trauma of what had happened that evening in 1941.

She led them round the side of the town hall into a large, cobbled square. As they emerged into the square, Helga realised that she'd never actually seen the front of the town hall before, but she did remember glimpsing the other buildings in the square, festooned with red banners bearing the swastika. They crossed the square and found a café on the other side with some tables under a canopy. They sat down and ordered coffee.

'I remember crossing Paris in Yvonne's limousine that day,' Helga continued. 'She kept telling me to keep my head down. Every time I lifted it up and peeped out my blood froze. There were Nazis everywhere. Strutting about in their jackboots and grey uniforms, proudly bearing their swastikas. There were huge banners with swastikas draped from the buildings too; buildings I'd seen before and admired for their beauty. The Louvre, the Arc de Triomphe, the Eiffel Tower. In the Place de la Concorde, there were army vehicles drawn up outside the Hôtel de Crillon and a Nazi guard outside, saluting some high-ranking official going in. I'll never forget it, the sight was terrifying.'

'So that's why you went white when I mentioned the Hôtel de Crillon a few weeks back,' Kitty murmured.

'Yes, it brought it all back. I wish I'd been able to tell you why at the time.'

Kitty rubbed her arm soothingly. 'You're not to worry about that.'

'Yvonne and the driver took me to the Gare de Lyon and put me on a train to Marseille. Then another to Lisbon, and finally eleven days on the ship to New York. And all I could think about on the journey, in every line I waited in, on every platform, was my sister. I was pining for her and everything I'd left behind. I was saying goodbye to the war but I was leaving everyone I loved behind.

'The OSE had arranged for me to stay with foster parents on the outskirts of the city and they came to fetch me from the ship and take me home on the train. They were very kind, but no matter what they tried to do to make me happy, my heart ached for Ruth from the first day I was there in 1941 to the last in 1946.

'Every day I ran downstairs, hoping for a letter to come. I had great faith in the network of charities and was sure that Ruth would be able to contact me through them, but in reality, France was in chaos at that time and Germany was at war with the United States, so there was no chance of any post between the two countries. Even so, I fully expected her to be in touch. I wrote her many letters, care of the OSE in Paris. I took them to the post office and posted them off, but I don't know if any of them ever reached her.

'The Goldmans reminded me of Herr and Frau Weiss on the St Louis. They tried everything they could to help me feel at home. I spoke no English when I arrived, but they both spoke Yiddish and we were able to communicate that way. Mr Goldman contacted the Jewish charities in New York to find out about ships bringing Jewish children to New York. He discovered to my horror that there were no more ships arriving from Europe – it had become impossible with the German occupation of France. I was devastated when I heard that news. Mr Goldman told me I'd been lucky to get out when I did. But I didn't see it like that. I could never be happy without Ruth. I was safe now. I had a bedroom of my own, enough food to eat... But my heart was back in Europe with Ruth and every day that passed without her was another day of loneliness.

'I watched the events of the war unfold through the *New York Times*. Mr Goldman used to get it delivered to the house daily. I would pore over the war reports with almost obsessional fascination. I was so scared for Ruth.

'On 8 May 1945 I marked the German surrender with work friends in central New York. I wanted to celebrate like everyone else, but all the time we were dancing in Times Square I was thinking of Ruth. Would this mean she and I would be reunited soon?

'By the time the war ended I was seventeen. I'd left school the year before and had a job as a secretary in New York, commuting by train from my home with the Goldmans in the suburbs every day. When I started work and had a bit more independence and was spending more time in the city, I'd managed to track down Eleanor, the older girl who'd befriended us on the *St Louis*. I can't remember precisely how I did it. It was made all the more difficult because Eleanor had married and changed her name. She had become rather grand and, when I finally found her, she told me that she wanted to leave the war and all the hardships she'd suffered behind. She didn't seem thrilled that I'd turned up out of the blue, reminding her of the *St Louis* and everything we'd suffered on that ship.

'She lived in a huge apartment near Central Park. She was married to a financier and already had a child – a beautiful little girl. She was amazed to see me. She invited me to her apartment and told me that she was looking into what had happened to her father with the help of some people she knew in Germany. That was when I asked her to help look for Tate. I think it was because she felt a little guilty that she wasn't keen to renew our friendship that she agreed to help. It only took a few months to get the information back from Bad Arolsen, where they were building archives from the concentration camps.'

Helga had to pause there and compose herself. She took a sip of coffee and dabbed her eyes with her handkerchief.

'Take your time,' Kitty patted her hand. Helga took a deep breath and carried on.

'When I found out what had happened to Tate in that concentration camp near Hamburg it broke me. It was then that I vowed to get back to Europe and find Ruth. I became even more determined to put the plan I'd been hatching since I'd arrived in America into action. I was aiming to get the first ship I could over the Atlantic back to France and to find Ruth.

'It took me a few months to put enough money aside and to make preparations for my journey. When I was ready, I packed my bags and said goodbye to my friends and foster parents. I knew that I was leaving for good. I would never live there again.

'My foster parents were sad to see me go but they didn't attempt to stand in my way. They were both elderly. Very sadly, they both died within a few years of the war ending. When they came to wave me off from New York Harbour early in 1946, I think we all knew I'd never come back. I was sad to say goodbye to them. I hugged them both and thanked them for what they'd done for me. I often think of them and how I owed them a great debt of gratitude for what they did for me. I feel guilty to this day that I couldn't return the love they showed me, or even give them my appreciation properly, during those years that I lived with them but I think they understood the depth of my unhappiness.

'I had tried writing to the OSE from America as soon as the war was over, but my letters hadn't been answered. When I finally tracked down their offices in Paris I understood why. They were overwhelmed with requests for help from children and young people who had been displaced during the war and who wanted to be reunited with loved ones. They were trying to repatriate as many children as they could and were drowning in paperwork.

'I asked them about what had happened to Ruth and eventually they found her record card in a dusty filing cabinet. The serious young woman in the office told me that she'd been evacuated from Paris to an orphanage in the South of France when it was under the Vichy regime. She told me that it was relatively safe to go there at that time and the OSE sent many of their children south to escape the German occupied zone. The young woman looked harassed and overworked but was still doing her best to help me. I asked where Ruth was now, whether she was still at the home in the south, but the young woman said she had no up-to-date records. She said that most of the orphanages had been evacuated again once the Vichy regime fell. Some Jewish children were smuggled out to Switzerland, others were given shelter within monasteries or with French families. She couldn't tell me what had happened to Ruth, but she did tell me the name of the orphanage she'd been sent to. It was in Izieu in the Rhône Valley, south-east of Lyon.

'The next morning, I was on another train south. This time to Lyon. When I reached the city, I checked into another little hotel and left my luggage. Then I got a local train to a nearby town and a bus to the little village of Izieu. It was a hamlet really, no more than a few farms and cottages in a quiet, green valley. I had to ask some locals where the orphanage was. It was a little way away from the village, up a wooded track, completely isolated. By the time I reached it, it was getting dark. The big, white-painted building was closed and shuttered up. There was no sign that it had once been a children's home. I hadn't really been expecting anything else, but at least I'd located the house where Ruth had been sent.'

Helga stopped then and swallowed hard. What she had to say next would be so difficult to say out loud. She'd never told anyone but her husband this in the last forty-five years. Even as she opened her mouth to say the words, she wondered if she'd actually be able to speak them. Naomi and Kitty were waiting, their eyes focused on her face. Helga knew she needed to tell them.

'I was told by the local shopkeeper that the Germans had tracked the children down on the orders of Klaus Barbie, the head of the Gestapo in Lyon. They'd come in trucks one day in 1944 and taken them all away. The villagers heard a lot of screaming and shouting and when they went to the house later that day they found signs of a violent struggle – the furniture overturned, windows broken. There were forty-four children living in that house. They were all taken away. They took all the staff too and the place was left empty. I asked her what had happened to them. She said that rumours had filtered out in the last few months that they had been taken to Auschwitz. She said she was very sorry, but she understood that the children had been murdered there.'

Naomi and Kitty gasped and the next second Helga felt Naomi's arms round her. She was drained and empty, but she had to finish her story.

'I was stunned. I couldn't accept it at first. The next day, I went back to the OSE in Paris and asked if they could tell me any more about Izieu. A man was there that day. He was more senior than the girl I'd first spoken to and he confirmed that the story I'd heard from the shopkeeper was true. He was as devastated as I was. I remember us both crying. He said that all the children and their teachers had been taken away and transported to a camp at Drancy. From there they were transported to Auschwitz in Poland and murdered. No one who'd been taken that day had survived.

'I was numb. Ruth had died a pointless, terrifying death at the hands of those monsters. I would never see her again, hear her laughter, share our little secrets, stories and memories. We'd been inseparable from when we were born until I left the convent. The fact that she was no longer in the world was impossible to bear.

'I wanted a new start. I couldn't bear to stay in Paris a moment longer, the memories were too painful.' She looked at Naomi for reassurance. 'I couldn't go back to Germany, the memories lingered there too, and by that time so much of Berlin had been reduced to rubble and it was divided into East and West. I'd often thought about visiting London and now I could speak English perfectly, I realised there was nothing to stop me going there on my American passport, getting a job and starting a new life. So that's what I did.'

She stopped and smiled through her tears at Naomi and Kitty. The two people she loved most in the world. She reached out and took their hands. 'And within a couple of years I'd met your father, Naomi. He'd been through so much too and there was an instant meeting of minds. Without needing to say much about it, we understood each other's pain. But even though I moved on, I never forgot my sister. She's been with me every day since we parted. In fact, I can feel her with me now.'

THIRTY-ONE

NAOMI

Paris, 1990

It was late afternoon by the time Naomi got back to the apartment in Avenue Carnot. The taxi had taken Kitty and Helga back to their hotel to rest. Naomi too felt physically and emotionally drained by her mother's story. The shock of finding out that Helga had had an identical twin sister who had died in Auschwitz had affected her like a physical blow.

She decided to walk from the hotel in one of the streets behind the Champs-Élysées back to Avenue Carnot. She wanted that time to be alone and to think over what she'd just heard. She walked slowly, oblivious to the crowds of tourists and shoppers that thronged around her. She was going over and over in her mind her mother's incredible story of survival, the sadness Helga had been carrying for decades at the loss of her mother and father and her beloved twin sister. Naomi had been most affected though by the photograph of the two twelve-year-olds, their dark heads tipped together, their bright, optimistic smiles leaping out of the faded print. What a cruel stroke of fate to have been born when and where they had been, to have been torn apart by world events as they had, and for one of them to have died so tragically, barely out of childhood. Naomi was touched though that Helga had finally found the courage to let her into the secret sadness of her past. She now understood her mother's steely will, her strength and discipline while Naomi had been growing up, her refusal to let standards drop. Hearing her story had brought them closer than ever, Naomi knew that too. She'd tried to apologise to her mother for dredging up the past, for making her relive the pain of losing her sister, but Helga had brushed her apologies away. 'It had to come out in the end,' she'd said. 'Please don't blame yourself.'

She reached the top of the Champs-Élysées and looked up at the majestic Arc de Triomphe that loomed above the confluence of avenues. It was illuminated by floodlights in the early-evening sky. She shuddered suddenly, imagining red banners bearing swastikas covering its wide columns, Nazi troops goose-stepping under its great arches beside a convoy of tanks. No wonder Helga had been reluctant to come back to the city.

She carried on and was soon walking down Avenue Carnot and approaching the apartment. At the building she tapped her security code into the keypad and the door buzzed open. Then someone stepped out of the shadows.

'Naomi?'

She looked round. To her surprise Oliver was standing there, cradling a huge bunch of flowers in his arms. Extravagant white lilies mixed with purple irises. He handed the bouquet to her. 'This is for you,' he said. She swallowed and took the flowers, feeling perplexed.

'What are these for?'

'I'll explain. Could I come in? Or maybe we could go somewhere for a drink, if you'd prefer?'

'No, come on in,' she said, bemused. He followed her up the

stairs to the apartment. As they passed the concierge's apartment, the door clicked shut ominously.

Naomi held the apartment door open for him. 'It's not very tidy, I'm afraid. My mother stayed last night and I didn't have time to clear up this morning.'

'No need to apologise. I'm sorry for surprising you like this.'

'Sit down, please.' She waved him towards the settee, and went into the kitchenette to put the flowers into water. 'Would you like a drink? Tea? Coffee?'

'Tea would be great. Thanks. I don't want to put you to any trouble, though.'

When she'd made two cups she brought them through to the living room.

'Were you waiting outside for me to come back?'

'I was, I'm afraid.'

'How did you know what time I'd be home?'

'I didn't. I waited the best part of the afternoon in the pizza house below here. I was just about to give up and go home actually. The concierge said you'd gone out with your mother this morning, so I guessed you wouldn't be too late back.'

'Really? Honestly! That woman is so nosey.'

Oliver laughed. 'She would see that as part of her job. But seriously, the flowers are a very small token of my appreciation to thank you for all your hard work on the case so far. I also wanted to let you know some developments. Late yesterday, I found out that the court has accepted our submission to postpone the hearing for two months to give us more time to review the new evidence that we were sent recently.'

'That's great news, Oliver,' Naomi said, sitting down in the armchair opposite him. 'It will give us some breathing space.'

'Yes, it is. So things won't be quite so frenetic for the coming weeks. I was wondering if you'd like to take some time off? You've been working incredibly hard these past few weeks.'

'That might actually be a good idea,' she said, thinking of her mother's impromptu visit.

'Good,' he said, 'and... well, there's something else.'

'Something else?'

He hesitated, twisted his hands. 'Well, this is a bit awkward, but I suppose I should just come right out with it.' He cleared his throat, clearly embarrassed. 'I think I've been a little unfair on you, Naomi. I really enjoy your company and I realise now that I'd started to rely on it rather. Looking into my heart, I suppose it's because you remind me a bit of Evelyn when she was young. It's not just in looks, but in your spirit, your determination, your work ethic. You really are quite similar. I began to get a bit too fond of you, I'm ashamed to say. When you said you couldn't come out for a meal with me on Friday, it made me think and reflect on what was happening.'

Naomi didn't know what to say. She couldn't meet his gaze and felt colour creeping into her cheeks. She couldn't say that she hadn't reciprocated the admiration, or even that it had been unwelcome.

'I realise now that I was being stupid,' Oliver went on, 'losing my head, and that it was very unprofessional of me. It won't happen again, I can promise you. But the fact is, I really admire your intelligence and your legal skills and would love you to come and work in the Paris office permanently, if we can get beyond this hurdle, which was entirely of my making. Is that something you think you could consider?'

'Gosh! That's an awful lot to take in,' she replied. 'I'll think about it. Maybe I *should* take a few days off. It might be good to spend some time with my mother and think about the future. As you probably found out from the concierge, my mother turned up out of the blue yesterday. We've had an incredible day looking into her past. She finally told me and Kitty, her best friend, who is here with her, why she'd been so reluctant to speak about it before.'

'Oh?' Oliver leaned forward, his eyes full of interest.

'It's really sad. She had a twin sister who died in Auschwitz.'

Oliver gasped. 'Oh, no! That's so tragic to hear.'

'I know. Poor Mum. Even all these years later she can hardly talk about it. She told me that they both stayed in the Villa Helvetia in the late thirties when it was an orphanage. We went there together this morning and she told us her whole story. What she went through was incredible.'

'That's amazing, Naomi. You must be glad she finally told you. Are you able to share it with me?'

So, Naomi told him what her mother had told her, about Kristallnacht, about having to leave Berlin, about the journey on the ill-fated *St Louis*, about the Villa Helvetia and the convent, about their attempt to help the Resistance that led to Helga and Ruth being separated, how Ruth was transported south to Izieu and how her orphanage was raided by the Nazis.

'What an incredible story,' Oliver said when she'd finished. 'You know,' he went on slowly, 'Thinking back, from the research I did to help Evelyn I made some contacts who might have more information about the orphanage at Izieu. I know a bit about the Polish lady who set up the orphanage there, Sabine Zlatin. She was away from the home by chance when it was raided that day. Her husband was taken by the Gestapo and murdered too. She gave evidence at Klaus Barbie's trial in 1987. I've followed her story. Since then, she has been trying to persuade the authorities to open a museum on the site to commemorate the victims. We met a woman when I was helping Evelyn, who has been archiving photographs and documents for the museum.'

'Really?' Naomi sat forward. 'I'm sure Mum would be really interested in finding out more about it. Might you be able to put me in touch with this person?'

'Of course. We've kept in touch on and off since Evelyn died. I'll try calling her tomorrow.'

'It would be amazing if she has more information about it. When Mum went there after the war, the place was deserted. She heard the story from the local shopkeeper.'

'Your mother sounds an incredible woman. I'd really love to meet her.'

'She is,' agreed Naomi proudly. She was still reeling from what she'd heard that day. 'And I'm sure she'd love to meet you too.'

'I was thinking, why don't you bring her for lunch at my place tomorrow? I haven't entertained for a long time, but I can still cook a mean Sunday roast.'

'All right,' Naomi said. 'If you're quite sure. Oh... but she has her friend Kitty with her, remember.'

'Well, why not bring her too? The more the merrier.'

The next morning, just before twelve, Naomi, Helga and Kitty arrived by taxi in the Place des Vosges. They got out and admired the beautiful square, lined with cloistered buildings and with a neat garden with ornamental trees and a fountain surrounded by railings in the middle.

'I say, this is rather chic,' Kitty exclaimed, widening her eyes. 'Your boss clearly has taste.'

'And money, by the looks of it,' Helga muttered, appraising the surroundings.

They left the street, walked under the cloisters and rang the bell to Oliver's apartment. It was on the top floor of one of the seventeenth-century buildings and they climbed a majestic staircase. Helga and Kitty took their time but every time Naomi asked if they'd like some help, they both waved her away.

Oliver greeted them wearing an apron and holding a bottle of champagne. 'Hello! You made it! Sorry about the stairs, there's no lift here, I'm afraid. Wonderful to meet you.' He shook hands with Helga and Kitty. 'Come inside. My other guests have already arrived.'

'Other guests?' Naomi asked, puzzled, but when she went into the apartment with its vaulted roof and oak floors, there were Martine and her grandmother, sitting on a settee with drinks in their hands.

'I've been meaning to ask Madame Clément over for a long time,' Oliver said, 'and she has a soft spot for you, Naomi, so I thought it would be perfect to combine my invitation.'

Introductions were made. Oliver poured champagne and everyone started chatting. Naomi sat down beside Martine.

'I hope you're not annoyed with me for what I said the other day,' Martine said in a hushed tone.

'What you said?' Naomi asked, stumped for a second.

'You know, about you and Oliver.'

'Ah... I'd forgotten about that. So much has happened. But there's nothing to worry about. Oliver and I have had a chat about it. He came to see me yesterday and apologised. He actually offered me a job, too!'

'That's fantastic. Are you going to take it up?'

'I'm tempted. I'm going to have a few days off to think about it.'

'I suppose there's your boyfriend to consider...' Martine said.

Naomi reflected. It was days since Liam had even crossed her mind. 'He hasn't been in touch since our argument when I went home. I've been waiting for him to call me but he hasn't. And you know, I've hardly thought about it. And when I do think about it, I'm coming to realise that the relationship had been grinding to a halt long before I came to Paris. Coming here has given me a fresh perspective on it, to be honest. It's made me realise that we probably don't have a future together, that it's run its course.'

'Oh, I'm so sorry, Naomi. That must be tough for you.'

'In some ways, yes. We had a wonderful time together, but we've grown apart recently and it might be time for us both to face up to it.'

They were interrupted by Oliver calling them to the table, a huge oak dining table under the vaulted roof, overlooking the Place des Vosges. Kitty, Helga and Madeleine Clément were already deep in conversation and carried on as they moved to the table, Madeleine helped by Martine.

Oliver served up roast beef, perfectly cooked roast potatoes and cauliflower cheese. Everyone exclaimed at what a fine spread it was. Oliver filled their glasses with Côtes du Rhône and they all began to eat. Soon the conversation turned to the war and the research Oliver had done into his late wife's family.

'Did you say your wife came from Berlin originally, Oliver?' Helga asked.

'Well, she was born in England but both her parents came from Berlin. Both families were well-established Jewish families in the city. They'd lived there for centuries. The Heinrichs and the Rosenthals. We managed to discover that her mother's parents and her father's mother died in Auschwitz, but sadly we never found out what happened to her father's father.'

'The Heinrichs?' Helga asked. 'My father knew a Professor Heinrich. They lived across the street. He and my father were good friends.'

'Incredible!' Oliver put his knife and fork down and stared at Helga. 'Perhaps it was the same person. He would have been my wife's grandfather. He was a professor of economics. He lost his job at the university when the Nazis decreed that Jews couldn't hold university posts.'

'Professor of economics at Berlin University?'

'Yes.'

'I know what happened to him,' Helga said, shaking her head.

'Really? That's amazing. Can you tell me?'

'It's a very sad story, I'm afraid. The mob broke into his apartment block on Kristallnacht and took him away. We saw it happen from our apartment window. Later, someone told my father that he'd been taken to Sachsenhausen that night and that he died there. I'm so sorry, Oliver.'

Oliver's face fell. 'That's terrible news...' He paused for a moment. 'But thank you for telling me,' he finally said, sadly. 'All the pieces are finally coming together. It's such a shame that poor Evelyn never found out but I can relate it to the rest of her family. They will be glad to have closure.'

'At least they will know the truth finally. Even if the truth isn't palatable, it is better to know than not to know,' Helga said. 'You know, I've only been able to speak about what happened to me in the last couple of days. I've been keeping it bottled up all these years, but since Naomi came to Paris I've begun to realise I needed to speak about it. And I'm so glad now that I did.'

She held out her hand and took Naomi's over the table. Naomi held it tight and smiled into her mother's eyes. 'It's a comfort that my dear Naomi and Kitty now know what I went through. That Ruth is no longer hidden away.'

'Naomi tells me that your sister was sent south,' Oliver said gently, 'To the home at Izieu. Did she tell you that I know someone who is archiving material for the museum there?'

'Yes, Naomi mentioned it. That's very interesting to know.'

'I called her this morning and mentioned you. She said she'd be happy to show you some of the documents and photographs she's turned up, if you'd like to go down there. You'd just need to call her in advance. Give her a few hours' notice.'

'Why don't we go down there, Mum?' Naomi asked. 'While you're here, I was thinking of taking a few days off work. We could go tomorrow.'

'I'm not sure,' Helga said, that old, guarded expression

entering her eyes. Was it too soon, Naomi wondered? She didn't want to rush her but this did look to be a perfect opportunity.

'No need to decide now,' she said hastily. 'Let's talk about it later.'

Everyone had finished their first course now and Oliver cleared away the plates amid general congratulations about his cooking. Then he brought out another dish. A meringue-covered pie, perfectly risen.

'Can anyone guess what this is?'

'Queen of puddings!' Kitty exclaimed. 'Traditional English pudding. It looks like perfection.'

He served it up. Madeleine took a bite and said, 'I've never tasted anything like this before but it's delicious.'

'I told you Oliver was a good cook, Grand-maman,' Martine said. 'I'm so pleased we came.'

'Me too,' Madeleine said. 'I have hardly been out of the flat for months. But I'm very glad I did. I'm particularly glad to have met you both, Helga and Kitty.'

Naomi recalled what Madeleine had told her about the Villa Helvetia and about being in Paris at the outbreak of war.

'I'm glad to have met you too,' Helga said. 'I understand it was you who told Naomi about the orphanage so I have to thank you for that. If you hadn't told her, I might never have been prompted to tell her my story.'

Madeleine Clément put her spoon and fork down and dabbed her eyes with her napkin.

'There is no need to thank me. You have nothing to thank me for.' Then her eyes filled with tears.

'It is me who owes you an apology for what happened during the war. I often think that if we locals had done something, had acknowledged what was happening to the Jews in France, things might have turned out differently. We could have come forward and offered your children shelter when the Nazis invaded, but we did not. We all looked the other way. For that I am deeply and profoundly sorry, Helga my dear.'

There was a silence. Naomi looked at her mother, wondering if she still felt bitter about the way the children at the orphanage had been shunned by the locals. But Helga turned towards Madeleine, her face open and forgiving.

'Everyone has their burden to carry, Madame Clément,' she said. 'And none of us should sit in judgement. I have my own burden of guilt from those years, so you are not alone.'

THIRTY-TWO

NAOMI

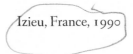
Izieu, France, 1990

When the taxi dropped them in front of the old house in Izieu, Naomi and Helga stood in front of the building, staring up at the shuttered windows, the neglected white façade stained with mould and bird droppings. It stood quite alone, up a tree-lined track, beside a large barn. It was just as Helga had described.

'It hasn't changed much in forty-five years,' Helga said with a note of sadness. Naomi shuddered, knowing what had taken place there. The house itself looked forlorn. Perhaps its walls could remember that dreadful day back in April 1944.

They had caught a train from Paris down to Lyon the day before. When they emerged from the Part-Dieu station, the air in the city felt different to Paris. It was noticeably warmer, the atmosphere more relaxed. It had a definite feel of the south. They spent the night in a modern hotel near the station. Although the cathedral and other sights beckoned to them, they decided to wait until after their visit to Izieu to explore the city.

'We've got a few days, there's no rush,' Helga said, and Naomi agreed. Neither of them would have been able to concentrate on sightseeing with the Izieu visit looming over them so that evening they'd eaten in the hotel. In the morning they got up early and caught a train out to a remote little station called Gare de la Tour du Pin.

The journey south from Lyon took about two hours and from time to time Helga would stare out of the window and exclaim, 'This is the way I came in 1946, the countryside looks exactly the same.'

The researcher Oliver had put them in touch with had organised a taxi to pick them up from the station. It took them through evergreen forests and farmland dotted with sheep, through the occasional small villages straddling the road. They crossed the Rhône on a wide bridge, then turned off onto a country road which wound through woodland into the hills. The road grew narrower and the countryside wilder with rocky hills on either side. At last, they turned off onto a track and in front of them was a square farmhouse beside a large barn.

They waited outside the building for a few minutes then a small, dark-haired Frenchwoman appeared from round the building, waving to them.

'I'm so sorry to keep you. Welcome...' They shook hands. 'I'm Ginette Gilles. I got waylaid on the telephone for a few minutes. Please, come this way.'

They followed her round the side of the building and into a yard, where a little red Renault was parked.

'Come – my office is in here.' She took them inside one of the outbuildings, where there was a makeshift office set up. On a big trestle table, documents and photographs were laid out.

'I put these out for you when I knew you were coming. Please, take a look through them. You will see from these photographs that the children who were staying here spent a lot of time out and about together. There are many group photographs of them on outings and picnics.'

Naomi watched as her mother walked slowly along the table, peering at the photos and documents on display. At one point she gasped. 'May I?' she asked, indicating that she wanted to pick up one of the photos.

'Of course,' said Ginette. 'Go ahead. But they are quite old and fragile, so please do handle them carefully.'

Helga picked up one of the photographs. Naomi could see that her hands were trembling. The photograph itself was shaking. Helga stared at it for a long moment, then turned to Naomi.

'I've found Ruth,' she said, 'my dear sister is here.' Naomi rushed over to her mother, tears welling in her own eyes. She put her arms round her and held her tight. She had no words to convey her emotions.

Helga passed Naomi the photo. It was of a group of about ten children of varying ages, some sitting, some kneeling, around a picnic blanket. There was a wicker hamper in the foreground, in front of it plates and cups and bottles. They were in countryside and behind them were some rocky cliffs. Naomi recognised them as features of the landscape they had driven through as they had come down the valley towards Izieu. There, in the middle of the group, sat Ruth, a wide smile on her face, her eyes brimming with mischief and pleasure. On one side was a girl about her own age, her arm slung casually round Ruth's shoulder, and on the other side a boy, a little older, had his arm round her from the other side.

'She looks so happy,' Helga murmured, her voice choked with tears. 'She looks so at home. She was amongst friends.'

'She does, Mum. She was happy here.'

'There are more photos from that trip. You might want to look at these,' Ginette prompted from the other end of the table.

They moved along the long table. There was photograph

after photograph from the same reel. All taken on the same trip. First the picnic, then walking beside a river – was it the Rhône, Naomi wondered? Ruth was in all of these photos, always smiling and having fun, her arms around the other children. In one, they were in bathing costumes paddling by a pebble beach on the river; in another, a couple of the children were flailing about in a canoe, the others laughing uproariously on the bank.

'This is so wonderful to see. I can barely believe my eyes,' Helga said, leaning on the table. Naomi saw that tears were streaming from her eyes, running down her cheeks unchecked.

'Would you like to sit down a moment? It must be a shock for you.' Ginette hurried forward with a folding chair and Helga sat down, burying her face in her hands, her shoulders shuddering. Naomi put her arms round her and held her tight. Helga cried for a long time. When the sobs had subsided, Naomi said, 'Are you all right, Mum?'

Helga looked up at her, her face blotchy, tears still trickling down her cheeks. 'I can't thank you enough, Naomi my dear. It's only because of you that I'm here. I would never have seen these photos otherwise. Would never have known how happy Ruth was in her last years here. That's such a great comfort for me, I can't tell you how much it means to me.'

'It means a lot to me too, Mum. I'm so pleased we've made this trip together.'

'I'm so glad I've told you everything. Kitty, too. Thank you for persuading me to talk about it. I'm so pleased that you know. I'm only sorry it took so long for me to tell you.'

'I understand, Mum.'

Ginette had left them for a moment. Now she came hurrying back with a jug of water and some glasses.

'I thought you might need a drink,' she said.

'Thank you.' Naomi poured water for all three of them. Then she had an idea.

'Do you think you might be able to make copies of these photographs for my mother? The ones her sister is in?'

'Of course. That would be no problem at all. If you leave me your address, I can send them on to you. It will only take a couple of days.'

'Thank you so much, Ginette. It would mean so much to my mother to have some mementos of her sister's last days.'

'There's something else that I need to show you,' Ginette said. 'I'm not sure if it belonged to your sister, Helga, but I thought I would ask you. It was found in the attic along with some other things left behind when the children left.'

She went to a cupboard in the corner and lifted out a small brown leather suitcase. It was old and battered, its corners scuffed with use. She handed it to Helga.

'Did this belong to your sister, by any chance?'

Helga took it and looked up into Ginette's eyes, her own eyes welling with tears once again. Her fingers traced the initials on the suitcase: RB. 'Yes,' she muttered. 'This did belong to Ruth. I have an identical one at home.'

'Then please, take it with you. There's something inside that might interest you too.'

Naomi watched her mother lift the lid and look inside. She gasped as she drew something out from inside.

'Mame and Tate,' she said, 'Your grandparents, Naomi,' and she handed a small, sliver-framed photograph to her daughter. Naomi took it and stared at the cracked, fading image of two young people standing arm in arm in winter coats in front of a shop. Above them, a sign in flowing writing said BEIDER. In their eyes, Naomi saw their pride, love and hope for the future. As she looked at it, a surge of conflicting emotions passed through her. She felt a deep, visceral connection to the couple in the photograph. At last here was the answer to her questions about her mother's past. Her grandmother even looked a little like Naomi herself. But as she studied it, she realised that she felt anger too. A surge of deep, bitter anger on behalf of them and her mother and all those whose lives had been destroyed or cut short during that murderous regime, all the injustices they had suffered. As she stared at it, she felt Helga's hand on her arm.

'They were happy then too, Naomi,' she said. 'And I'd like to remember them like that.'

'There's something else in the lining of the lid too,' Ginette prompted.

Helga turned back to the little suitcase, opened it again and felt inside the lid. At first she frowned and then, as she drew out what she'd found, her expression cleared and she smiled and shook her head.

'I can hardly believe it. My letters!' She held up a bundle of dusty envelopes held together with string. 'She got them after all!' And once again, Helga sat down in the chair and buried her face in her hands, overwhelmed by emotion.

Later, Ginette drove them back to the station. Helga sat in front and talked away to Ginette in perfect French and Naomi stared out at the rolling scenery, the beautiful, remote valley. She had a decision to make and she'd been mulling it over ever since Oliver's surprise job offer on Saturday evening. And although she hadn't quite acknowledged her decision, she'd known what it would be in her bones ever since he'd asked. Her future was in Paris, working on cases that mattered. And despite Oliver's apology and promise that things would be different between them, she felt in her bones that the spark between them would never be extinguished. It was there inside her whenever she thought of him. It gave her a warm feeling inside. There was no future for her in London.

She knew what she had to do. She would call Liam in the morning and have the conversation that both of them had been avoiding for months. Then she would be able to focus on her new life here in France, doing work she loved and in the city she'd already made her home. And now that Helga had made the journey to Paris and had told her story, Naomi knew that her mother would come to see her often and they would travel across Europe together, retracing the past and making up for all those lost years of disconnection.

That evening when they arrived back at their hotel in Lyon, exhausted from the day's emotional and physical journey, Helga switched on the television in their room. She sat down on the bed to watch the news. A reporter was speaking from the ruins of part of the Berlin Wall, piles of rubble behind her.

Travel restrictions are being lifted at last after the recent tumultuous events in East Germany and the fall of the Berlin Wall on 9 November last year. Foreign visitors are now being welcomed to East Berlin for the first time.

'How about going to Berlin sometime, Mum?' Naomi asked tentatively, wondering if this was a step too far, if her mother was ready for that yet. But to her surprise, Helga said, 'Yes, I'd very much like to go back now. I think it's time.'

'Are you sure?'

Helga smiled, her eyes faraway. 'I'd like to see Leipziger Strasse again and find out if our apartment building is still standing. I've always wondered if it survived the bombing at the end of the war, not to mention the Cold War. I'd like to know whether Tate's shop is still standing too. Would you come with me, Naomi?'

'Of course. I'd love to see where you spent your childhood.'

'I don't mean right now, but some point in the not-too-distant future? After all, if you're going to be making your home in Paris, there will be plenty of opportunities for me to come over and for us to travel in Europe together from now on, won't there?'

'Yes, I suppose there will. That's exactly what I've been hoping,' Naomi said, slipping her arms round her mother and holding her tight.

EPILOGUE

HELGA

Berlin, 1990

The stairs to the apartment in the old block in Leipziger Strasse were no longer bare concrete. Now they were covered in heavy-duty black carpet and the stairwell had been freshly painted. Gone were the greasy marks from years of occupants trailing their fingers along the walls.

Walking up to the fifth floor was not as easy as it had once been for Helga and she had to stop a few times to catch her breath. She paused outside the Abramsons' apartment and again outside Herr Hollis's on the fourth floor. The front doors looked new and were painted gleaming white. Helga wondered who lived in those apartments now.

Though the building looked different, the dimensions and feel of the stairwell were exactly as they had been in her childhood. Helga couldn't help remembering the last time she'd come down those stairs, clutching her leather suitcase in one hand, bringing up the rear behind Tate and Ruth, that fateful day back in May 1939. She'd been a child then. How much had happened to her since and how much she had changed.

'Take your time, Mum,' Naomi had said as she paused on each landing to wait for her. 'There's no hurry.'

They had walked from their hotel near the Hauptbahnhof that morning and Helga had been astonished at how much the district had changed since she'd left Berlin in 1939. So many streets had been razed to the ground, whole streets had disappeared; it was virtually unrecognisable. There had been so much new building too, a lot of it utilitarian, communist architecture.

'I hadn't quite realised before that Leipziger Strasse must have been in East Berlin. Behind the wall,' she said, looking around her at the drab, shabby buildings, the potholed streets and broken pavements. 'No wonder it looks as it does.'

'There must have been a lot of bombing here during the war,' Naomi said. 'Most of the buildings look quite modern.'

'The place is transformed,' Helga had said. 'It's unbelievable.'

They'd emerged onto Leipziger Strasse and walked along the wide pavements. It was no longer a shopping street, but a wide boulevard with fast-moving traffic streaming in either direction. Helga stared about her, exclaiming at the difference. As they neared the far end, close to Potsdamer Platz, she stopped in her tracks.

'It's gone!' she said, stunned. 'The Wertheim department store. It must have been destroyed in the war, or demolished by the communists. What a travesty! It was such a wonderful building.'

And she stood there for a moment, remembering the huge store with its floor-to-ceiling windows and ornate pillars and entrances, its welcoming lights glittering during winter evenings, customers thronging through every door. It had been replaced with some square, anonymous-looking apartment blocks.

They moved on down the road towards Potsdamer Platz and within a few steps she stopped again and put her hand on Naomi's arm. To her astonishment, her old apartment block was still standing. It was one of the few old buildings to have survived.

'That's it, Naomi. That's where we lived!'

She walked forward with purpose in her stride then, approaching the building with a mixture of nerves and excitement. The glass entrance doors were firmly shut but there was an electronic entrance system with a buzzer for each apartment.

'Shall we try the fifth floor?' Helga asked with trepidation.

'All right,' Naomi said. 'You do it.'

Helga took a deep breath, then pushed the buzzer firmly. There was a long pause before a disembodied female voice said, 'Yes? Who's there?' The woman sounded suspicious.

'You won't know me,' Helga began, in her best German, her heartbeat in her mouth. 'My name is Helga Rosen. I lived in your apartment during the 1930s. I've come back to Berlin with my daughter for the first time since I was forced to leave. I know this is unexpected, but I was wondering if I might come up and take a look at the apartment?'

There was a further pause, then the woman said, 'All right, I will buzz you in. Come straight up.'

Now they were on the final flight of steps to the fifth floor and at last they arrived on the top landing. After Helga had caught her breath, she knocked on the door. It opened almost immediately and a young woman stood in the doorway.

'You are welcome to look around, but I need to go out soon, I'm afraid,' she said, holding the door aside.

'Thank you. Thank you so much,' Helga said, walking past her into the hallway. There she stopped and looked about her. The layout of the apartment hadn't changed at all, but the decor and furniture were very different now. Lino floors, utilitarian furniture and white-painted walls replaced Mame and Tate's ornate antiques, plush carpets and floral wallpaper. Fleetingly, Helga wondered what had happened to all their furniture when they left. She recalled too that Tate had owned the apartment, but guessed that it would have been confiscated by the communists after the war.

'Come, look round, please.' The young woman was shy but seemed keen to show off her home. She showed them into the kitchen, now fitted out with wooden cream-painted cabinets, the living room, with plain sofa and chairs, and the sparely furnished dining room. The fireplaces had gone, boarded up and painted over long ago. Helga half closed her eyes and could almost see Mame kneeling there in front of the fire, laying kindling on scrunched-up newspaper to get it started on those chilly winter evenings.

'The bedrooms are across the passage.'

Helga followed, her heart in her mouth. They stood in the doorway of her parents' old room. It was tidy and sparse, with a narrow double bed exactly where Mame and Tate's huge old bed had been. Helga recalled Tate lying there, sick with fever, the night Mame had disappeared.

'This is the children's room.' The woman opened the door into a sunlit bedroom with two little beds side by side and more memories came flooding back. This was where she and Ruth had slept, played, sung songs and shared secrets.

'May I?'

'Of course.' The woman beckoned her forward. She stepped inside while Naomi hovered in the doorway. Unlike the rest of the drab apartment, this room was colourful, with cartoon posters and children's paintings decorating the walls and soft toys on the beds.

'How old are your children?' Helga asked.

'Four and six. I have two daughters. They are at school at the moment, I have to go and collect them soon.'

'Two daughters! Oh, how marvellous. I hope they like the room. This is where I slept with my sister.'

'They love to sit in the window and look out.'

'May we look? Come, Naomi.'

'Of course, go ahead,' the owner said.

Helga crossed to the window and leaned on the sill. Naomi joined her and they looked down at the street together. How many times had she done this as a child? The street below was transformed: apartment blocks replaced the shops opposite, the trams and cables gone. Her eyes strayed to the spot where Tate's shop had been: she knew its exact position from this window.

She'd known the shop wouldn't be there any more and had expected an apartment block in its place. Instead there was a patch of green where Tate's racks of clothes had once been, swings and slides and climbing frames on what had once been his shop floor. There were a couple of benches at the edge of the garden where parents could sit. Helga felt a lump in her throat and moisture in her eyes and turned back to the woman.

'There's a playground across the street. I didn't notice that before.'

The woman's eyes lit up. 'My girls love it, it's their favourite place. It's why they love living in this apartment. They never want to leave,' she said.

Helga smiled back at her. 'I completely understand how they must feel. This is such a wonderful home. A lovely place to be a child.'

She felt Naomi's arm round her shoulder. She didn't say a word, but no words were needed.

Helga felt a lightness in her heart she hadn't felt for so long, perhaps all the way back to the times she had sat at the sill with Ruth, watching the street below.

'Thank you, Naomi,' she said, 'thank you for everything.'

A LETTER FROM ANN

I want to say a huge thank you for choosing to read *The Forgotten Children*. If you did enjoy it, and want to keep up to date with all my latest releases, just sign up at the following link. Your email address will never be shared and you can unsubscribe at any time.

www.bookouture.com/Ann-Bennett

I hope you loved reading *The Forgotten Children* and if you did, I would be very grateful if you could write a review. I'd love to hear what you think and it makes such a difference helping new readers to discover one of my books for the first time.

I love hearing from my readers – you can get in touch on my Facebook page, through Twitter, Goodreads or my website.

Thanks,

Ann

facebook.com/annbennettauthor

twitter.com/annbennett71